A CARTOON NETWORK ORIGINAL

PUNCHING UP

**ROSS RICHIE** CEO & Founder
**MATT GAGNON** Editor-in-Chief
**FILIP SABLIK** President of Publishing & Marketing
**STEPHEN CHRISTY** President of Development
**LANCE KREITER** VP of Licensing & Merchandising
**PHIL BARBARO** VP of Finance
**ARUNE SINGH** VP of Marketing
**BRYCE CARLSON** Managing Editor
**MEL CAYLO** Marketing Manager
**SCOTT NEWMAN** Production Design Manager
**KATE HENNING** Operations Manager
**SIERRA HAHN** Senior Editor
**DAFNA PLEBAN** Editor, Talent Development
**SHANNON WATTERS** Editor
**ERIC HARBURN** Editor

**WHITNEY LEOPARD** Editor
**CAMERON CHITTOCK** Editor
**CHRIS ROSA** Associate Editor
**MATTHEW LEVINE** Associate Editor
**SOPHIE PHILIPS-ROBERTS** Assistant Editor
**AMANDA LaFRANCO** Executive Assistant
**KATALINA HOLLAND** Editorial Administrative Assistant
**JILLIAN CRAB** Production Designer
**MICHELLE ANKLEY** Production Designer
**KARA LEOPARD** Production Designer
**MARIE KRUPINA** Production Designer
**GRACE PARK** Production Design Assistant
**CHELSEA ROBERTS** Production Design Assistant

**ELIZABETH LOUGHRIDGE** Accounting Coordinator
**STEPHANIE HOCUTT** Social Media Coordinator
**JOSÉ MEZA** Event Coordinator
**HOLLY AITCHISON** Operations Coordinator
**MEGAN CHRISTOPHER** Operations Assistant
**RODRIGO HERNANDEZ** Mailroom Assistant
**MORGAN PERRY** Direct Market Representative
**CAT O'GRADY** Marketing Assistant
**LIZ ALMENDAREZ** Accounting Administrative Assistant
**CORNELIA TZANA** Administrative Assistant

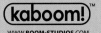

WWW.BOOM-STUDIOS.COM

# STEVEN ✦ UNIVERSE

## A CARTOON NETWORK ORIGINAL

created by
**REBECCA SUGAR**

written by
**GRACE KRAFT**

chapters five and seven
illustrated by
**MEG OMAC**

chapter six
illustrated by
**RII ABREGO**

chapter eight
written by
**MELANIE GILLMAN**
illustrated by
**KATY FARINA**

colors by
**WHITNEY COGAR**

letters by
**MIKE FIORENTINO**

cover by
**MISSY PEÑA**

designer
**GRACE PARK**

assistant editors
**MICHAEL MOCCIO &
KATALINA HOLLAND**

editor
**WHITNEY LEOPARD**

Special Thanks to
Marisa Marionakis, Janet No, Curtis Lelash, Conrad
Montgomery, Jackie Buscarino, Alan Pasman
and the wonderful folks at Cartoon Network.

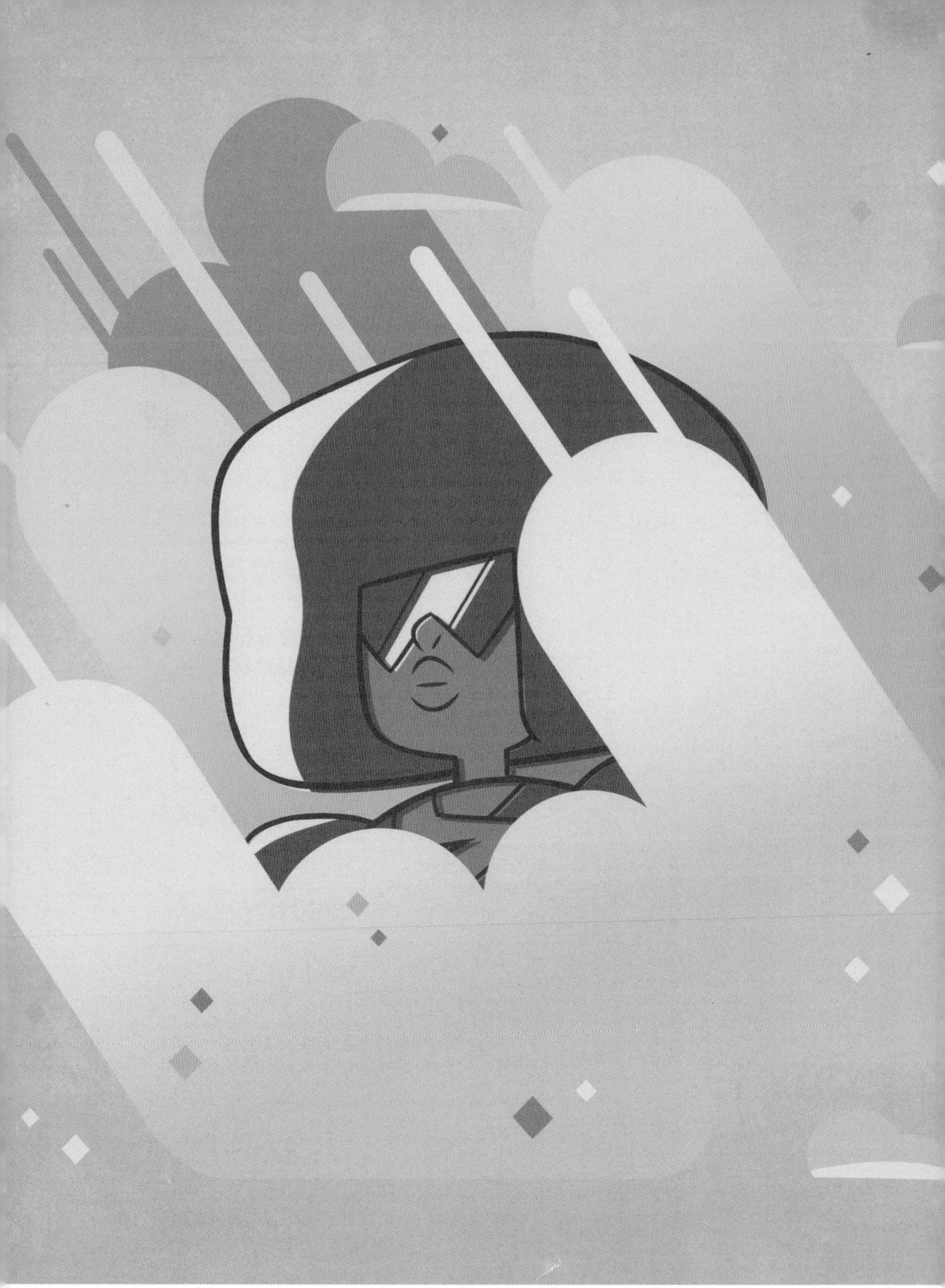

# CHAPTER FIVE

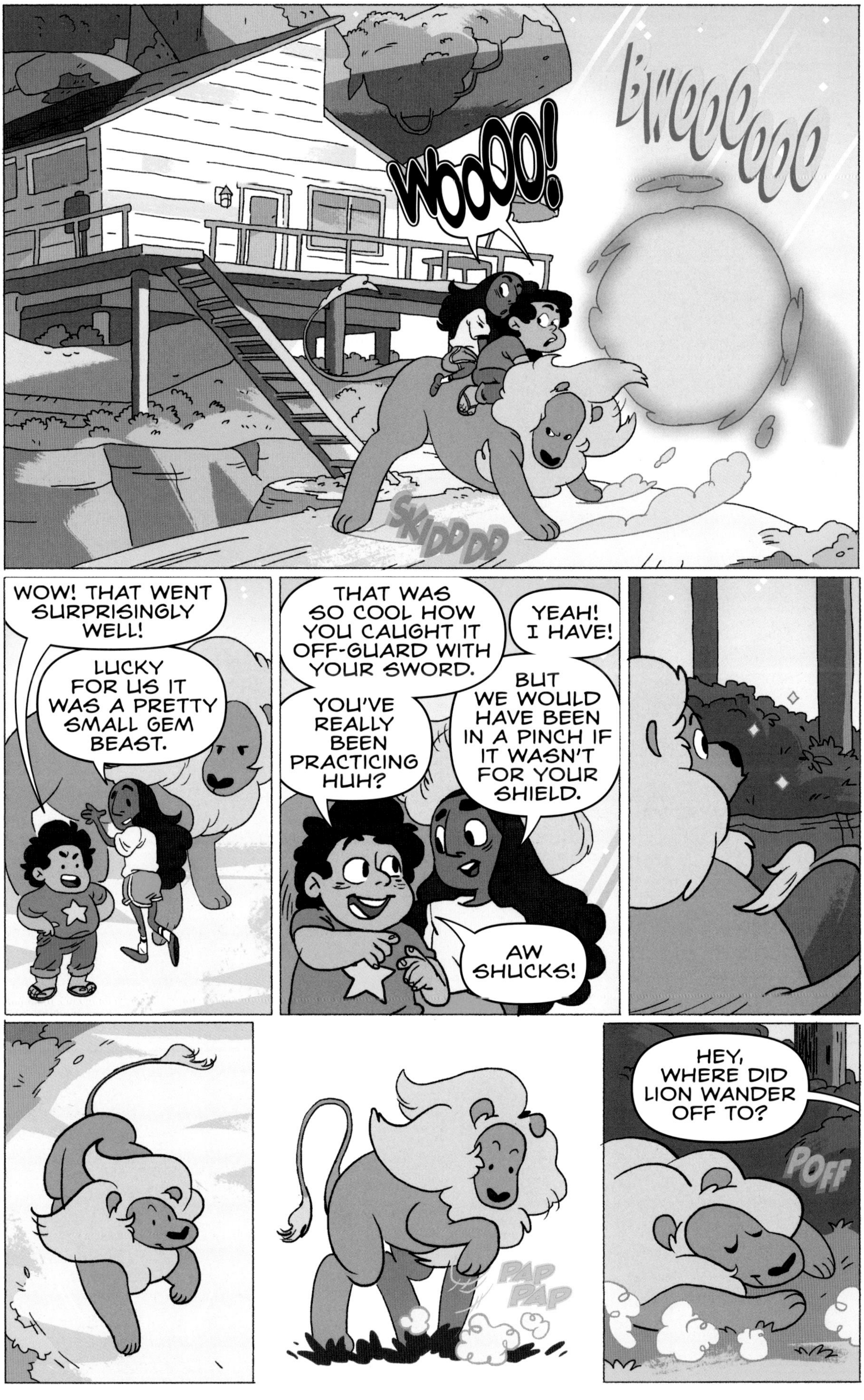

WOOOO!
L'WOOOOOO
SKIDDDD
WOW! THAT WENT SURPRISINGLY WELL!
LUCKY FOR US IT WAS A PRETTY SMALL GEM BEAST.
THAT WAS SO COOL HOW YOU CAUGHT IT OFF-GUARD WITH YOUR SWORD.
YOU'VE REALLY BEEN PRACTICING HUH?
YEAH! I HAVE!
BUT WE WOULD HAVE BEEN IN A PINCH IF IT WASN'T FOR YOUR SHIELD.
AW SHUCKS!
PAP PAP
HEY, WHERE DID LION WANDER OFF TO?
POFF

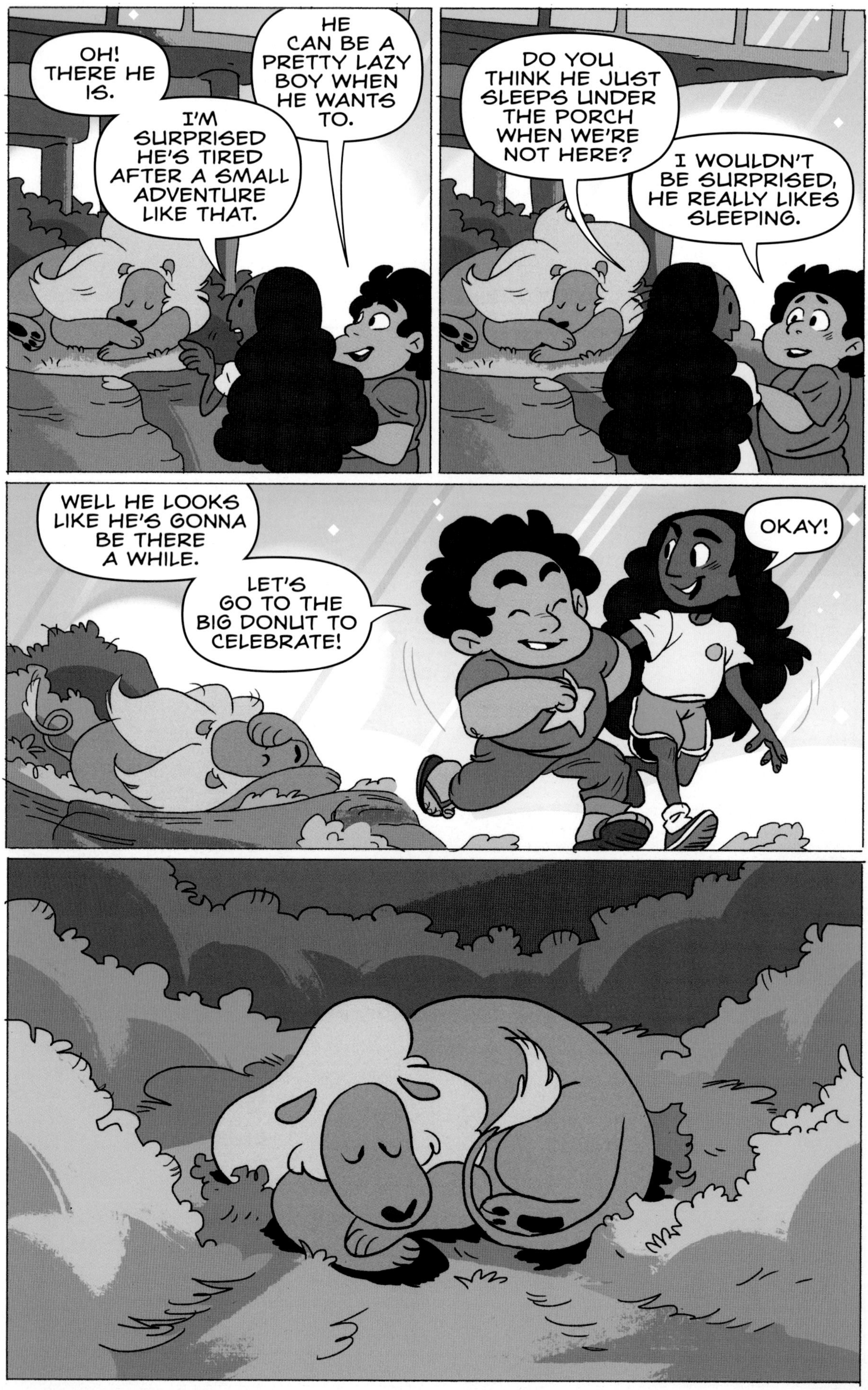

OH! THERE HE IS.
HE CAN BE A PRETTY LAZY BOY WHEN HE WANTS TO.
I'M SURPRISED HE'S TIRED AFTER A SMALL ADVENTURE LIKE THAT.
DO YOU THINK HE JUST SLEEPS UNDER THE PORCH WHEN WE'RE NOT HERE?
I WOULDN'T BE SURPRISED, HE REALLY LIKES SLEEPING.
WELL HE LOOKS LIKE HE'S GONNA BE THERE A WHILE.
LET'S GO TO THE BIG DONUT TO CELEBRATE!
OKAY!

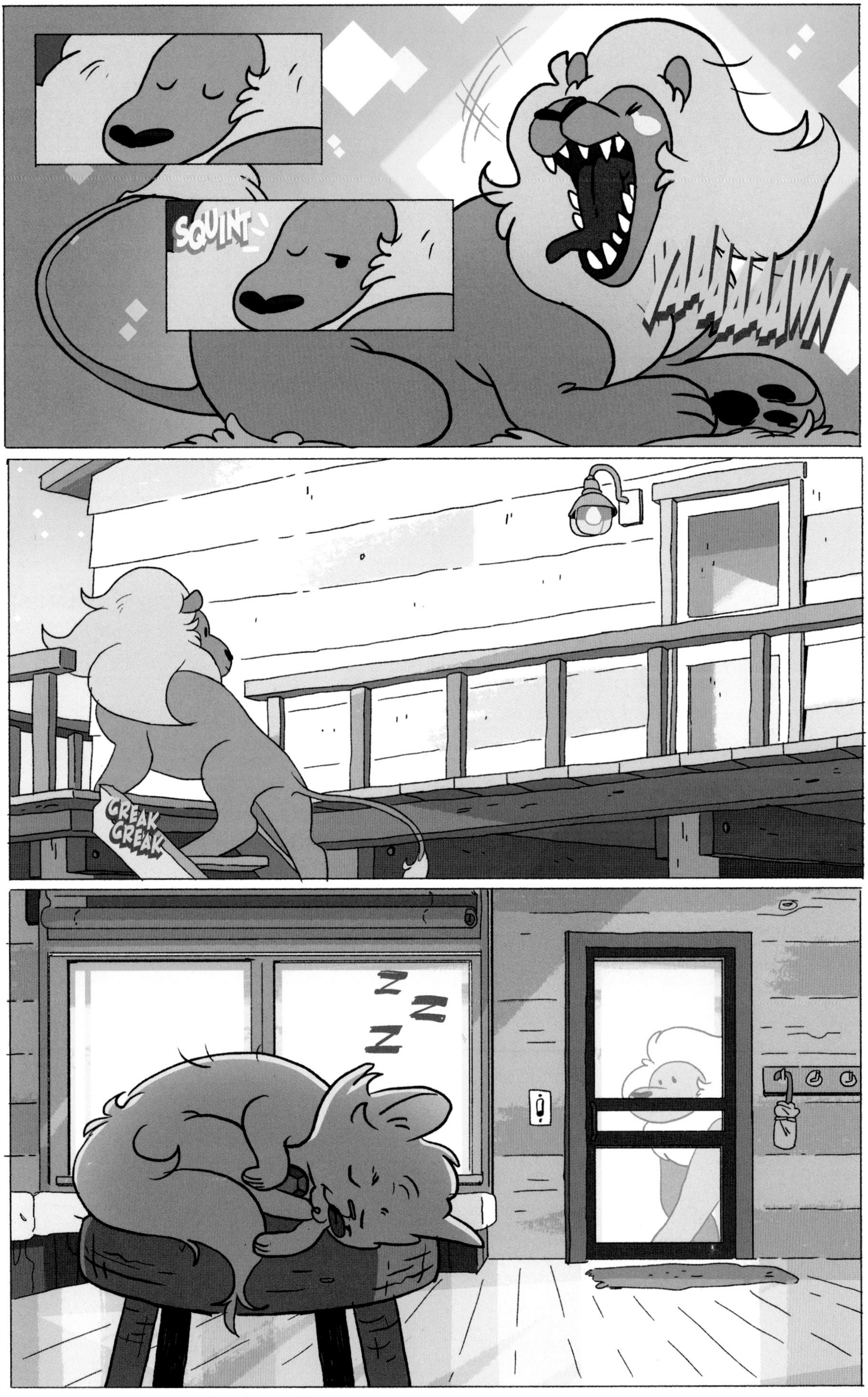
SQUINT
YAAAAAWN
CREAK CREAK
Z Z Z

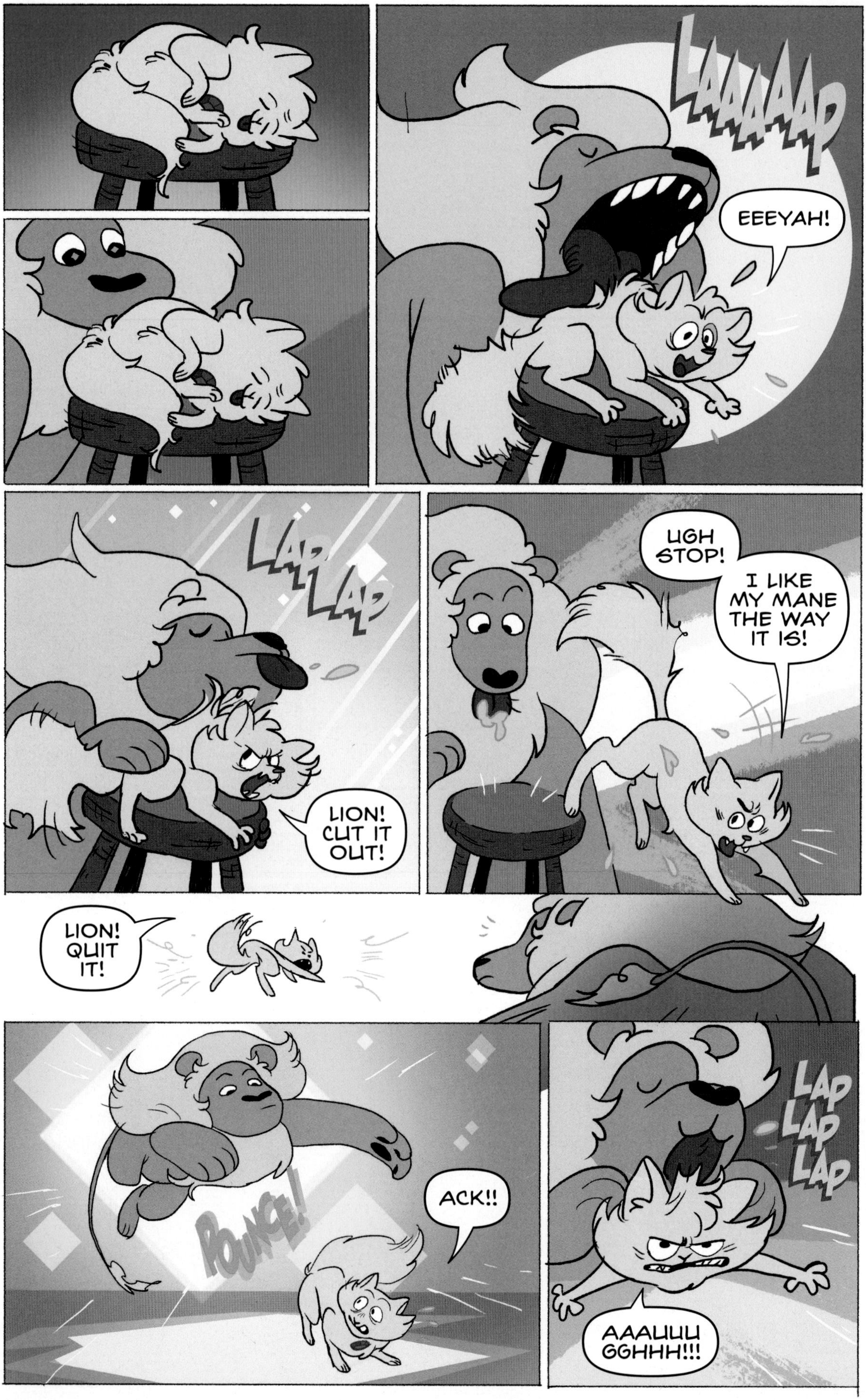
LAAAAAP
EEEYAH!
LAP LAP
LION! CUT IT OUT!
UGH STOP!
I LIKE MY MANE THE WAY IT IS!
LION! QUIT IT!
POUNCE!
ACK!!
LAP LAP LAP
AAAUUU GGHHH!!!

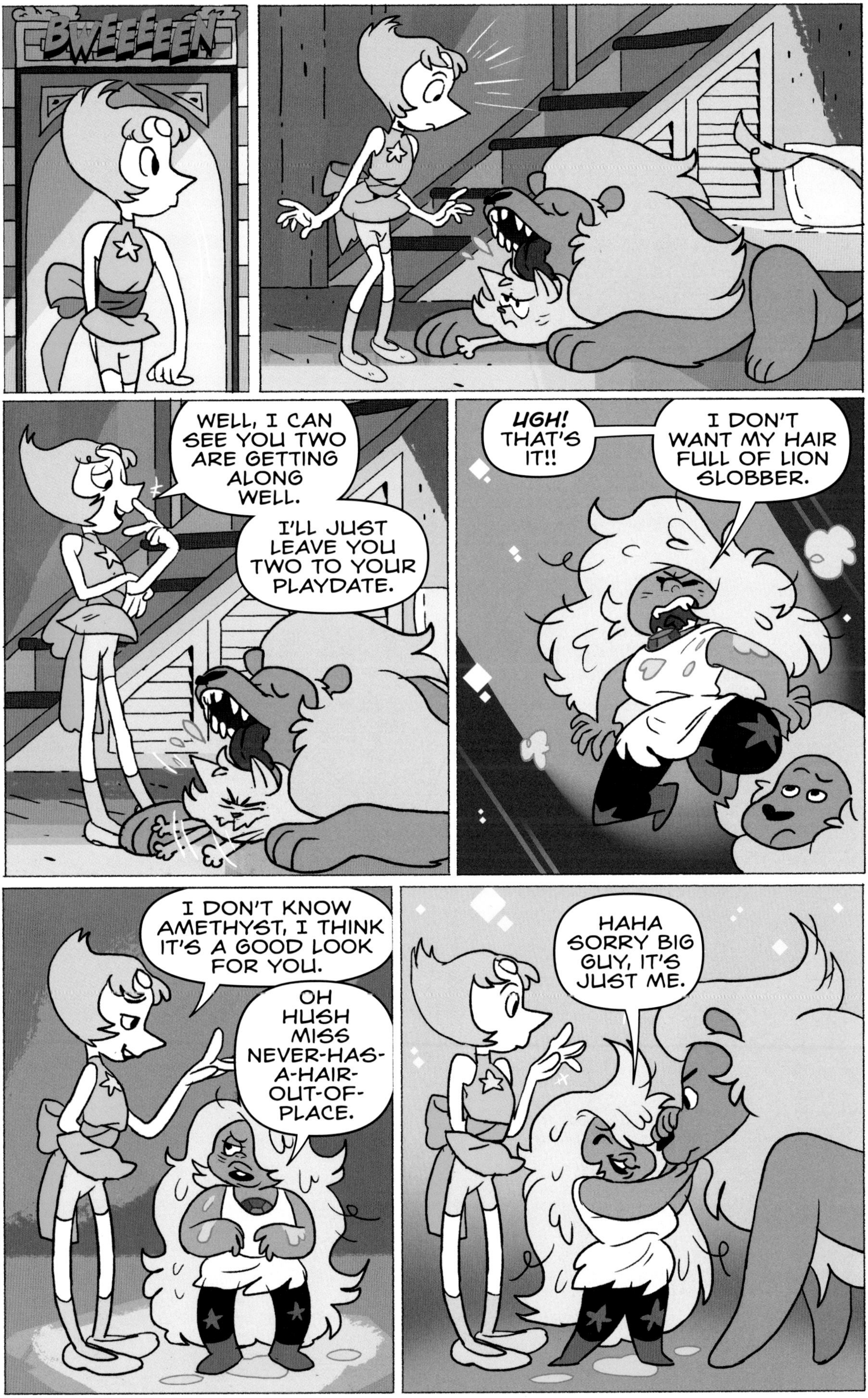
BWEEEEEN
WELL, I CAN SEE YOU TWO ARE GETTING ALONG WELL.
I'LL JUST LEAVE YOU TWO TO YOUR PLAYDATE.
UGH! THAT'S IT!!
I DON'T WANT MY HAIR FULL OF LION SLOBBER.
I DON'T KNOW AMETHYST, I THINK IT'S A GOOD LOOK FOR YOU.
OH HUSH MISS NEVER-HAS-A-HAIR-OUT-OF-PLACE.
HAHA SORRY BIG GUY, IT'S JUST ME.

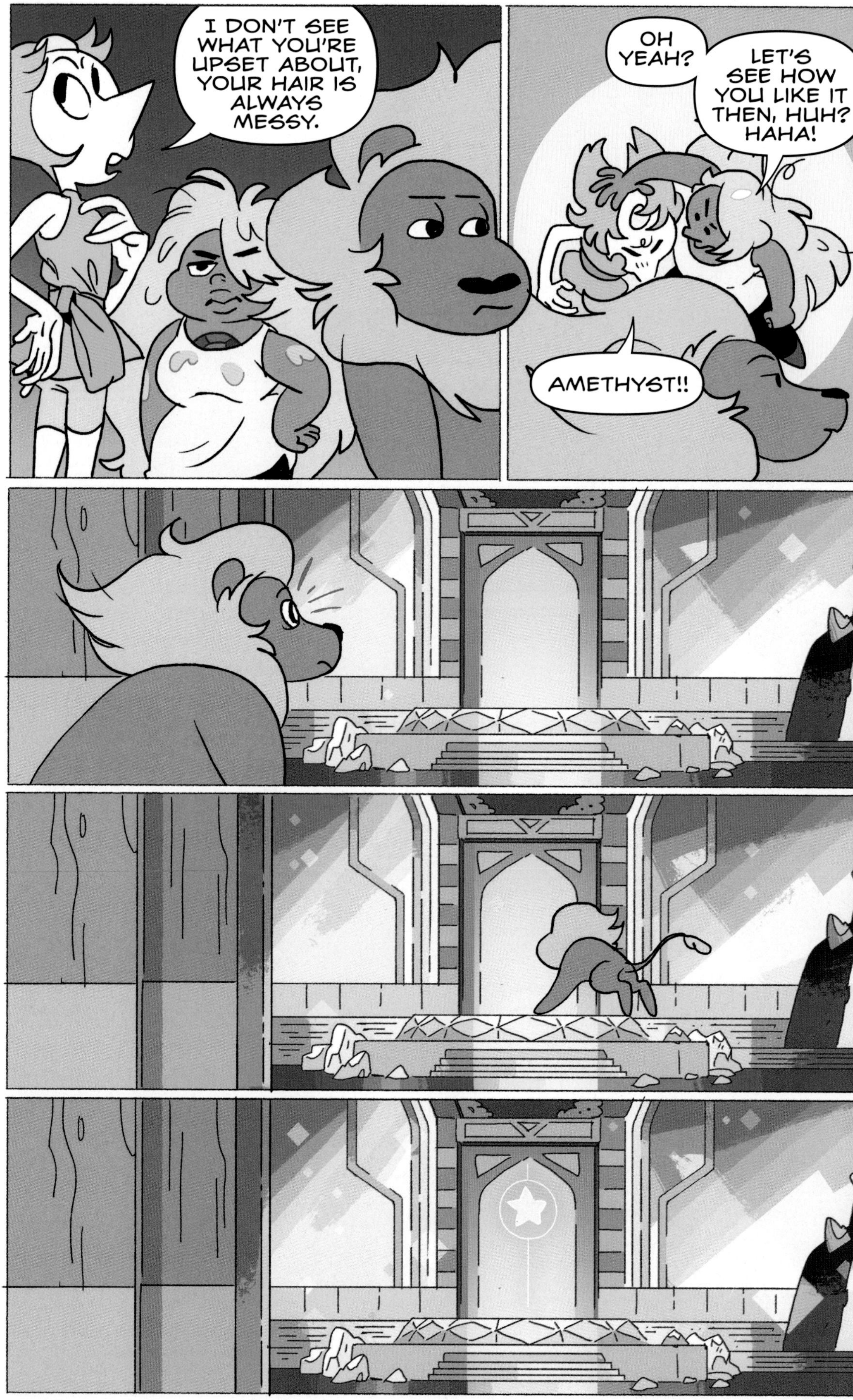
I DON'T SEE WHAT YOU'RE UPSET ABOUT, YOUR HAIR IS ALWAYS MESSY.
OH YEAH?
LET'S SEE HOW YOU LIKE IT THEN, HUH? HAHA!
AMETHYST!!

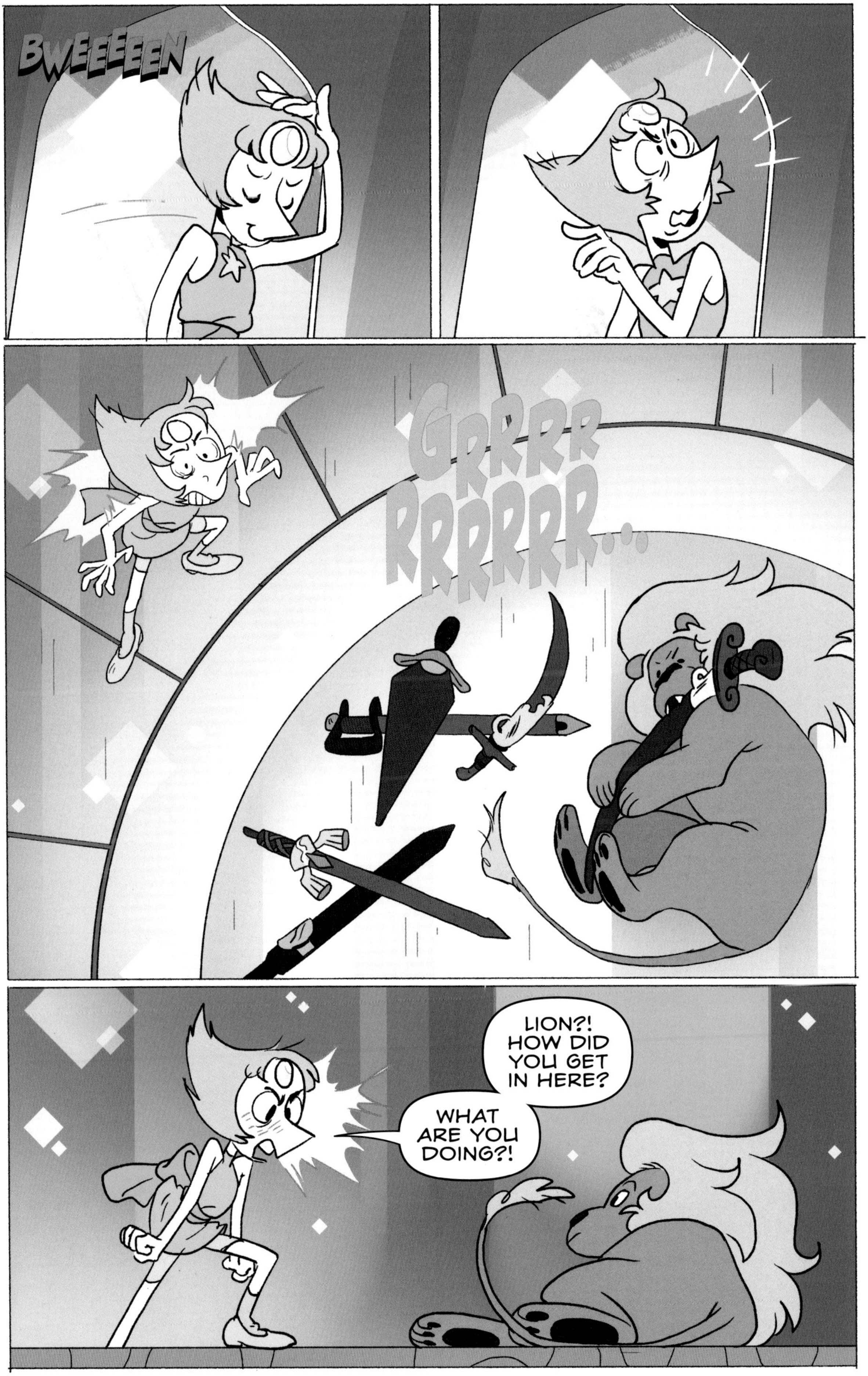
BWEEEEEN
GRRRR RRRRRR...
LION?! HOW DID YOU GET IN HERE?
WHAT ARE YOU DOING?!

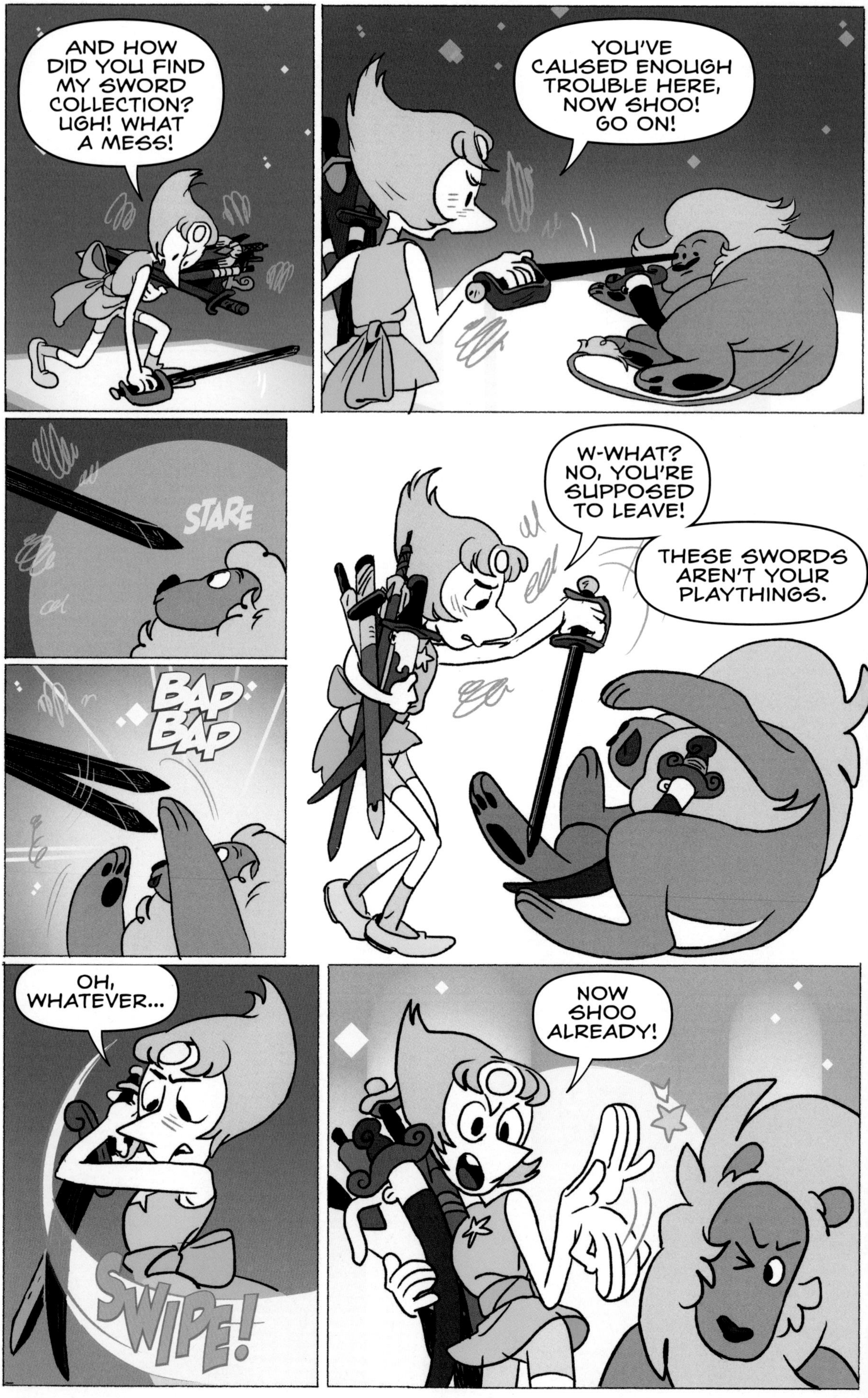
AND HOW DID YOU FIND MY SWORD COLLECTION? UGH! WHAT A MESS!
YOU'VE CAUSED ENOUGH TROUBLE HERE, NOW SHOO! GO ON!
STARE
BAP BAP
W-WHAT? NO, YOU'RE SUPPOSED TO LEAVE!
THESE SWORDS AREN'T YOUR PLAYTHINGS.
OH, WHATEVER...
SWIPE!
NOW SHOO ALREADY!

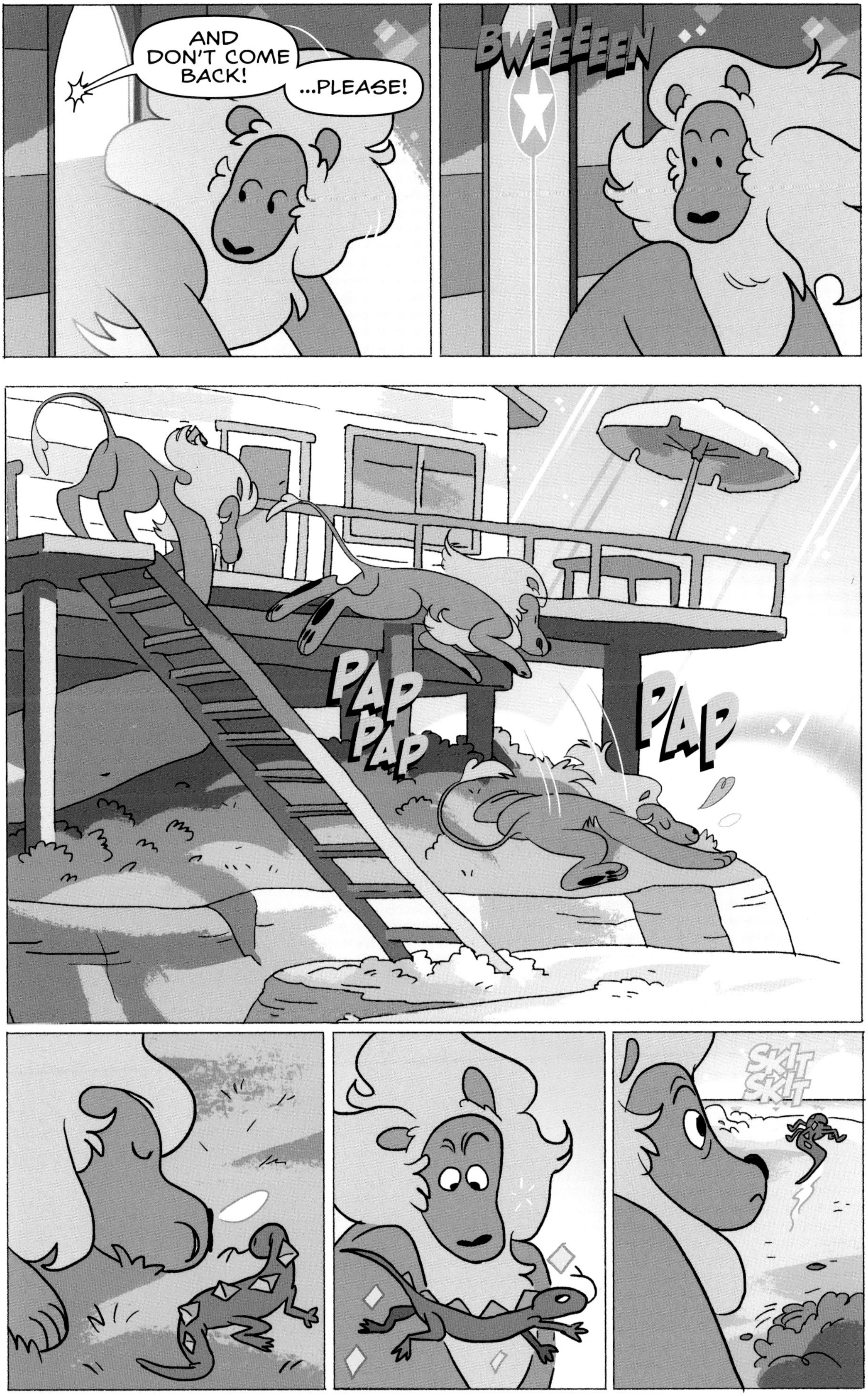
AND DON'T COME BACK!
...PLEASE!
BWEEEEEN
PAP PAP
PAP
SKIT SKIT

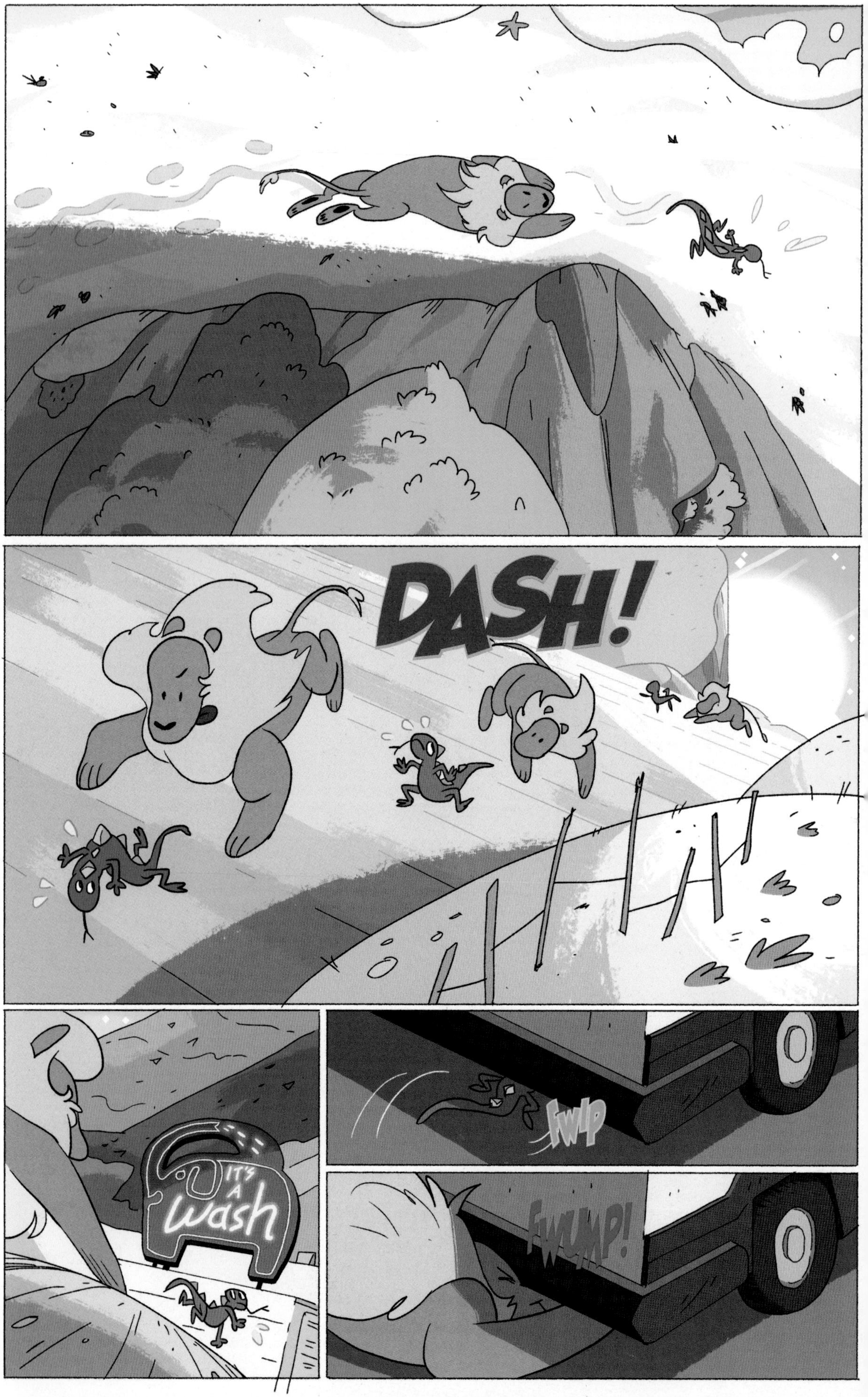
DASH!
IT'S A
wash
FWIP
FWUMP!

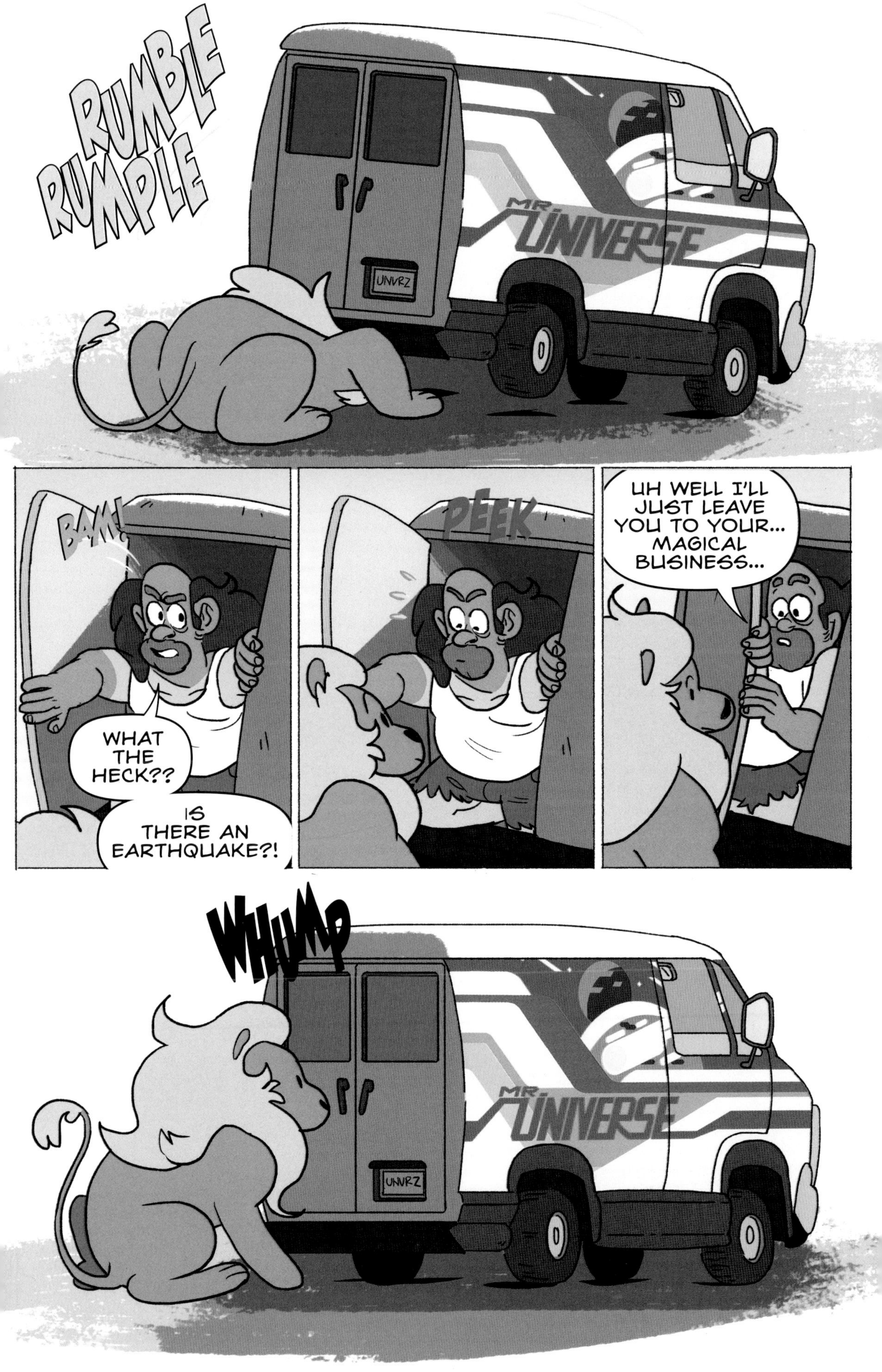
RUMBLE
RUMPLE
UNVRZ
MR UNIVERSE
BAM!
WHAT THE HECK??
IS THERE AN EARTHQUAKE?!
PEEK
UH WELL I'LL JUST LEAVE YOU TO YOUR... MAGICAL BUSINESS...
WHUMP
MR UNIVERSE
UNVRZ

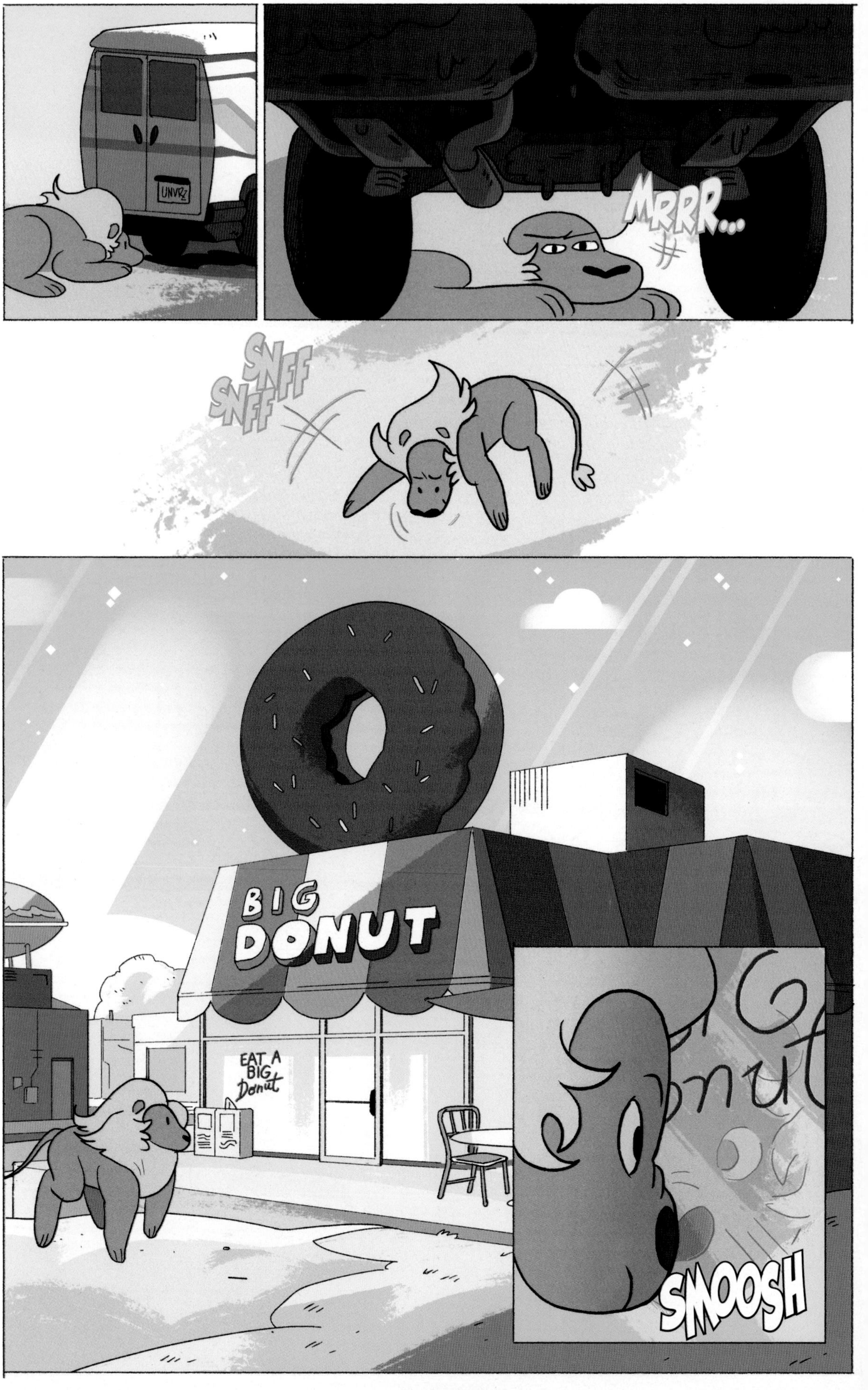
UNVRZ
MRRR...
SNFF SNFF
BIG DONUT
EAT A BIG Donut
SMOOSH

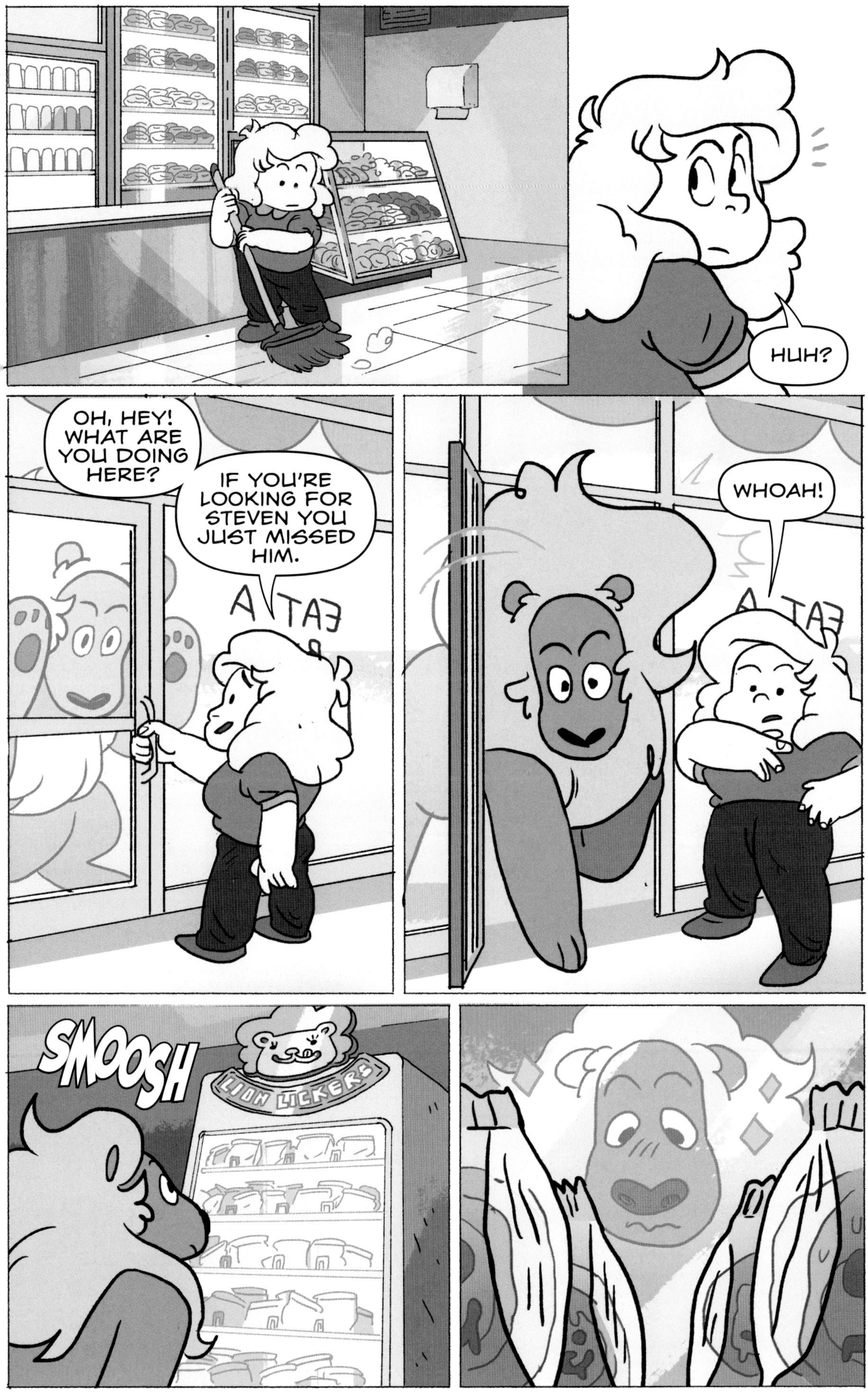
HUH?
OH, HEY! WHAT ARE YOU DOING HERE?
IF YOU'RE LOOKING FOR STEVEN YOU JUST MISSED HIM.
WHOAH!
SMOOSH
LION LICKERS

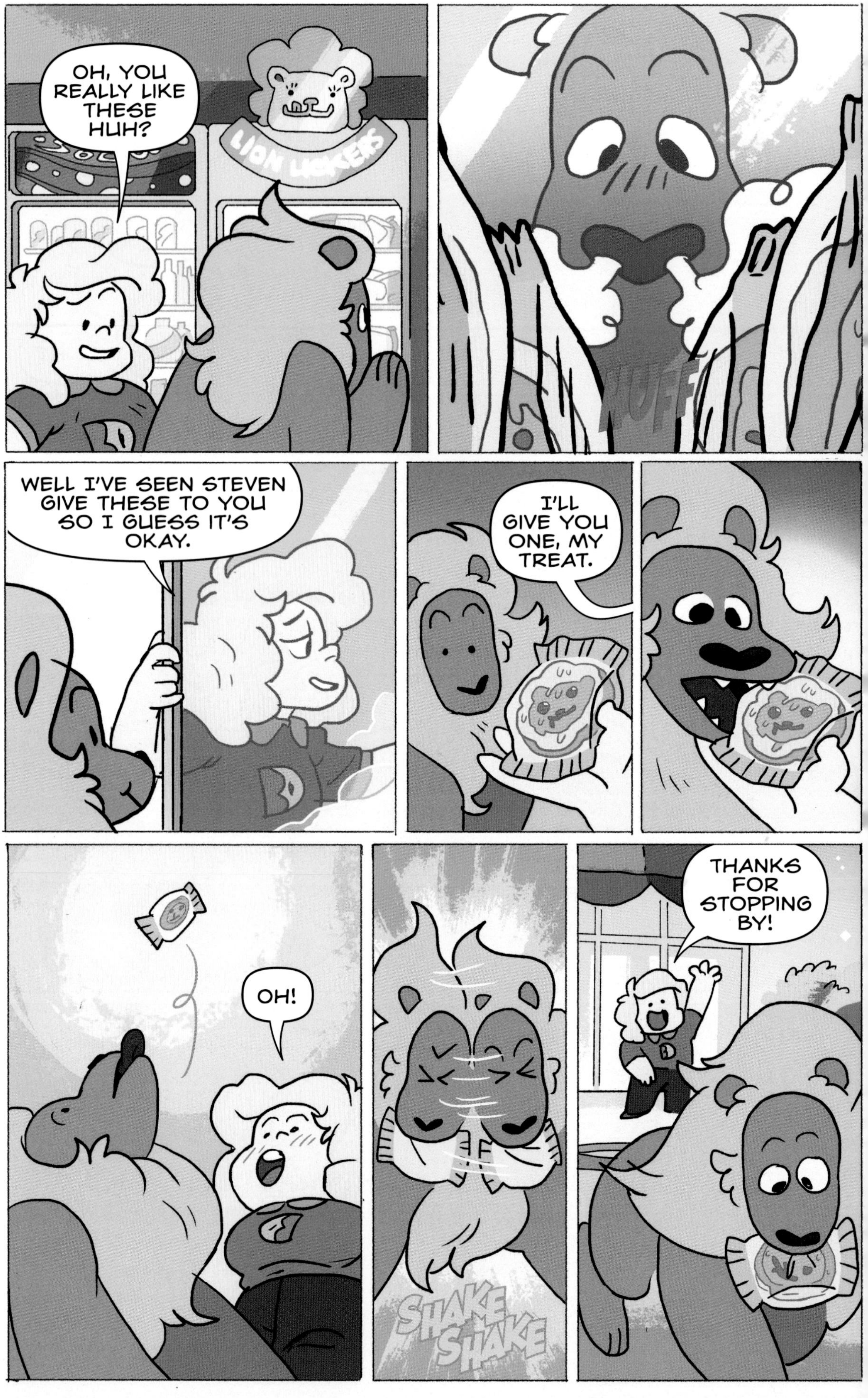
OH, YOU REALLY LIKE THESE HUH?
LION LICKERS
HUFF
WELL I'VE SEEN STEVEN GIVE THESE TO YOU SO I GUESS IT'S OKAY.
I'LL GIVE YOU ONE, MY TREAT.
OH!
SHAKE SHAKE
THANKS FOR STOPPING BY!

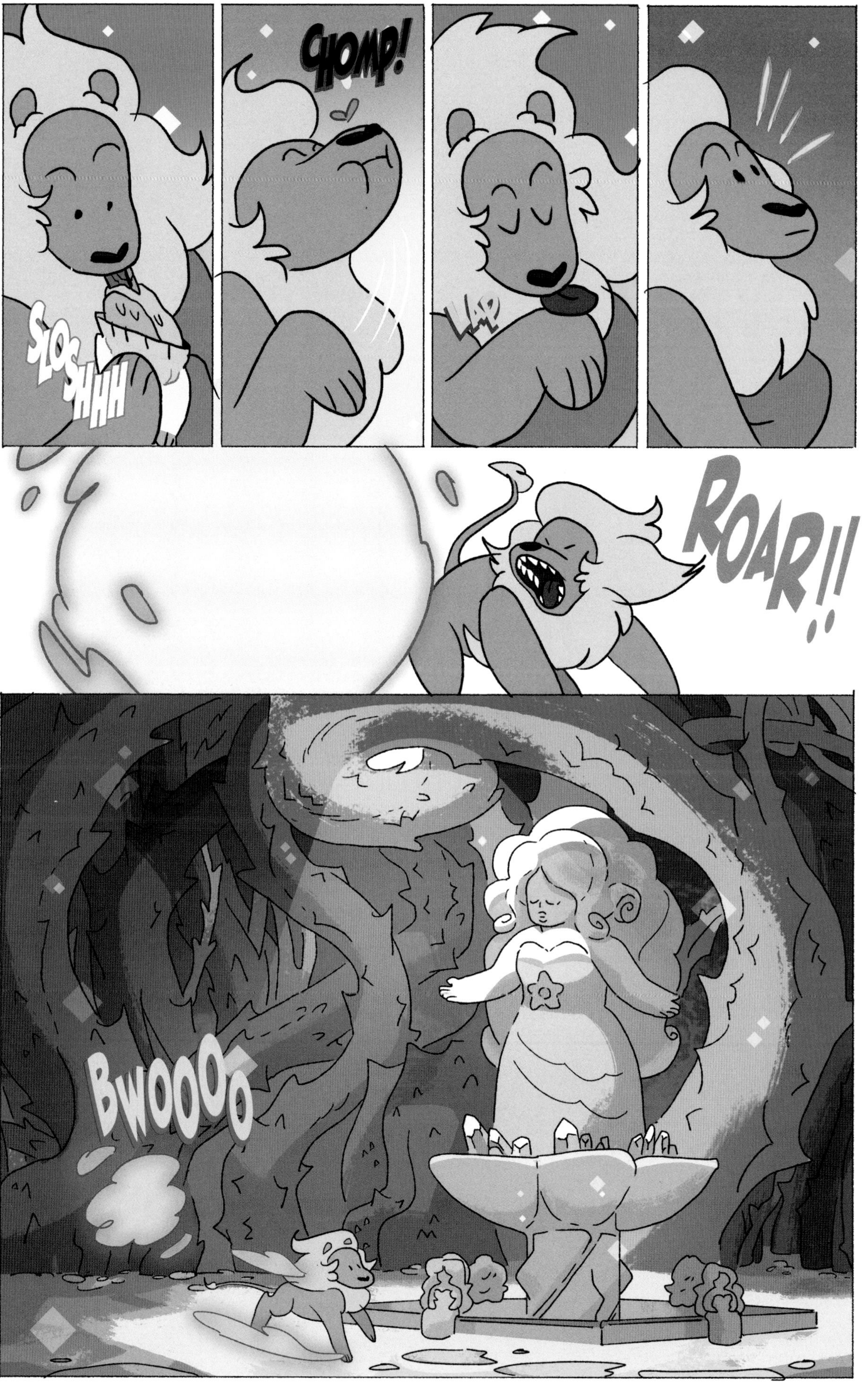
SLOSHHH
CHOMP!
LAP
ROAR!!
BWOOOO

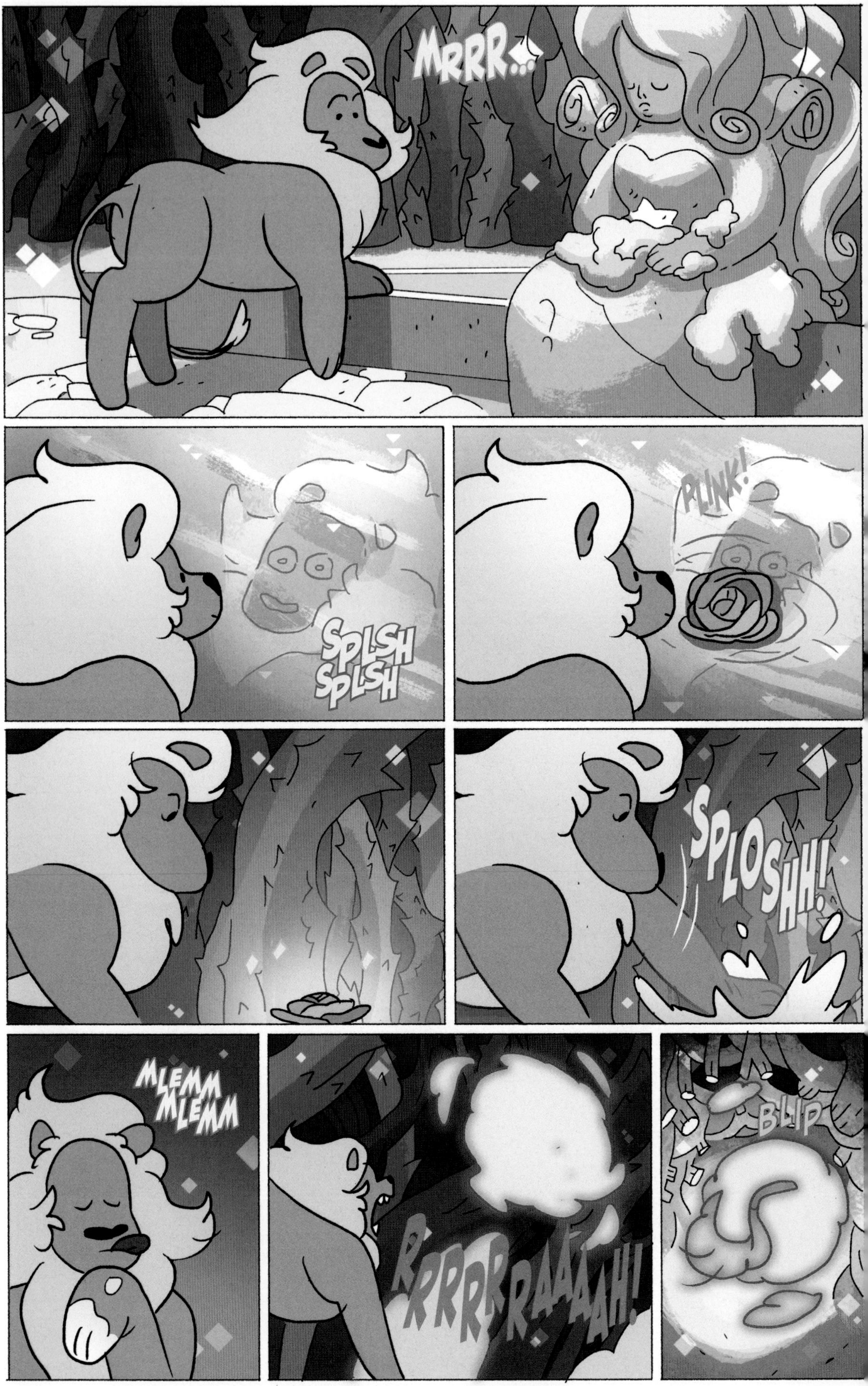
MRRR...
SPLSH SPLSH
PLINK!
SPLOSHH!
MLEMM MLEMM
RRRRRRAAAAH!
BLIP

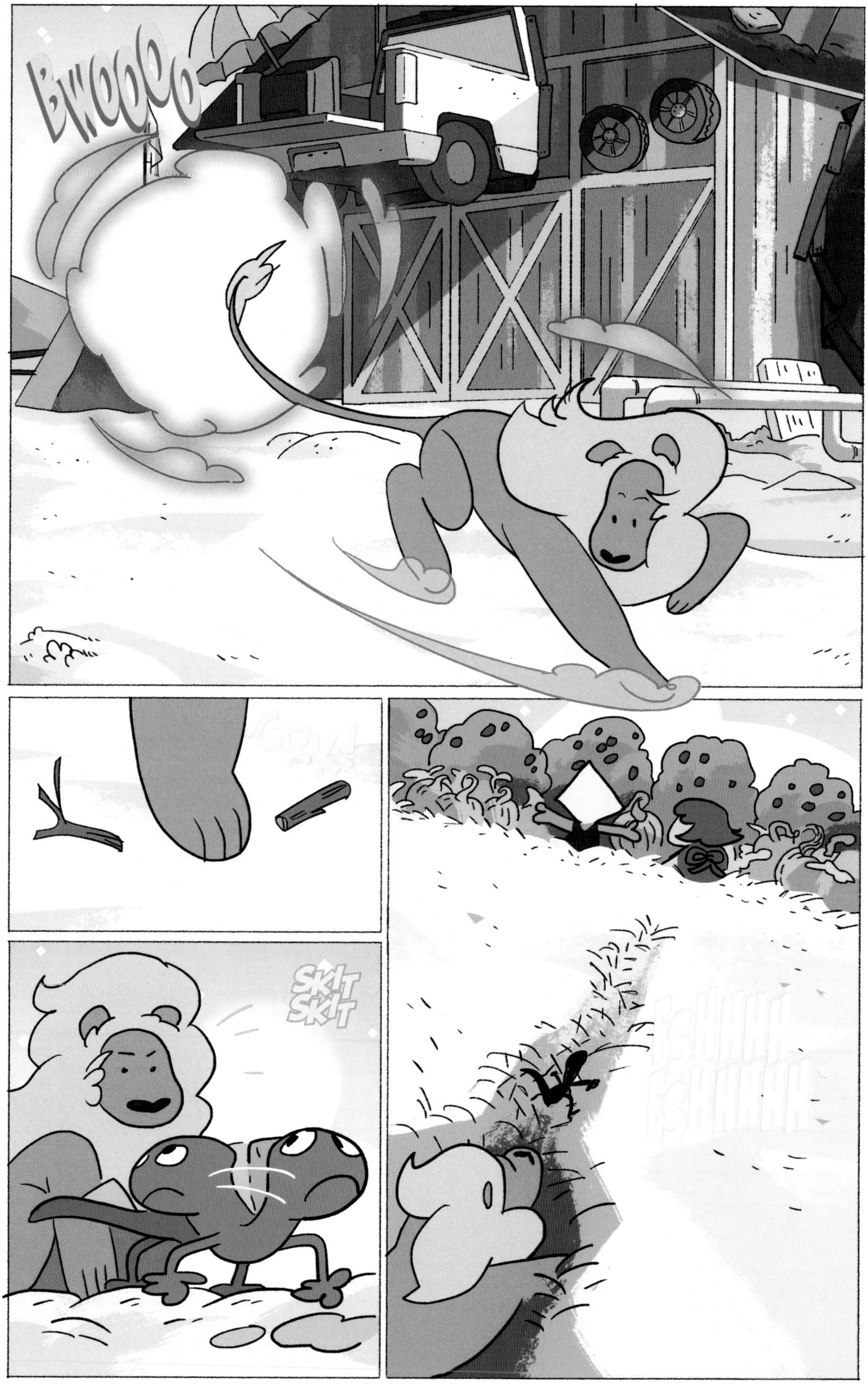
BWOOOO
CRK!
SKIT SKIT

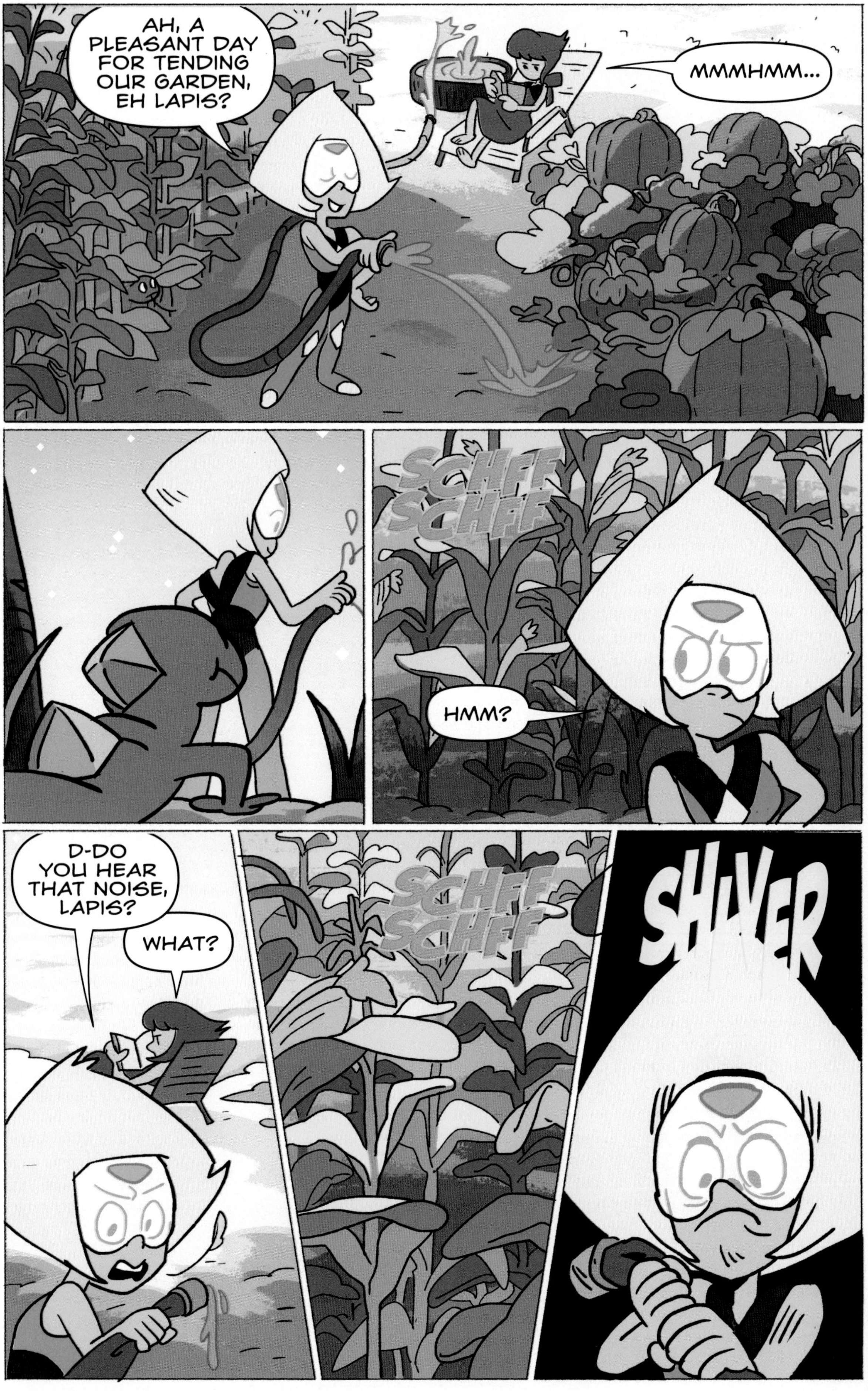
AH, A PLEASANT DAY FOR TENDING OUR GARDEN, EH LAPIS?
MMMHMM...
SCHFF SCHFF
HMM?
D-DO YOU HEAR THAT NOISE, LAPIS?
WHAT?
SCHFF SCHFF
SHIVER

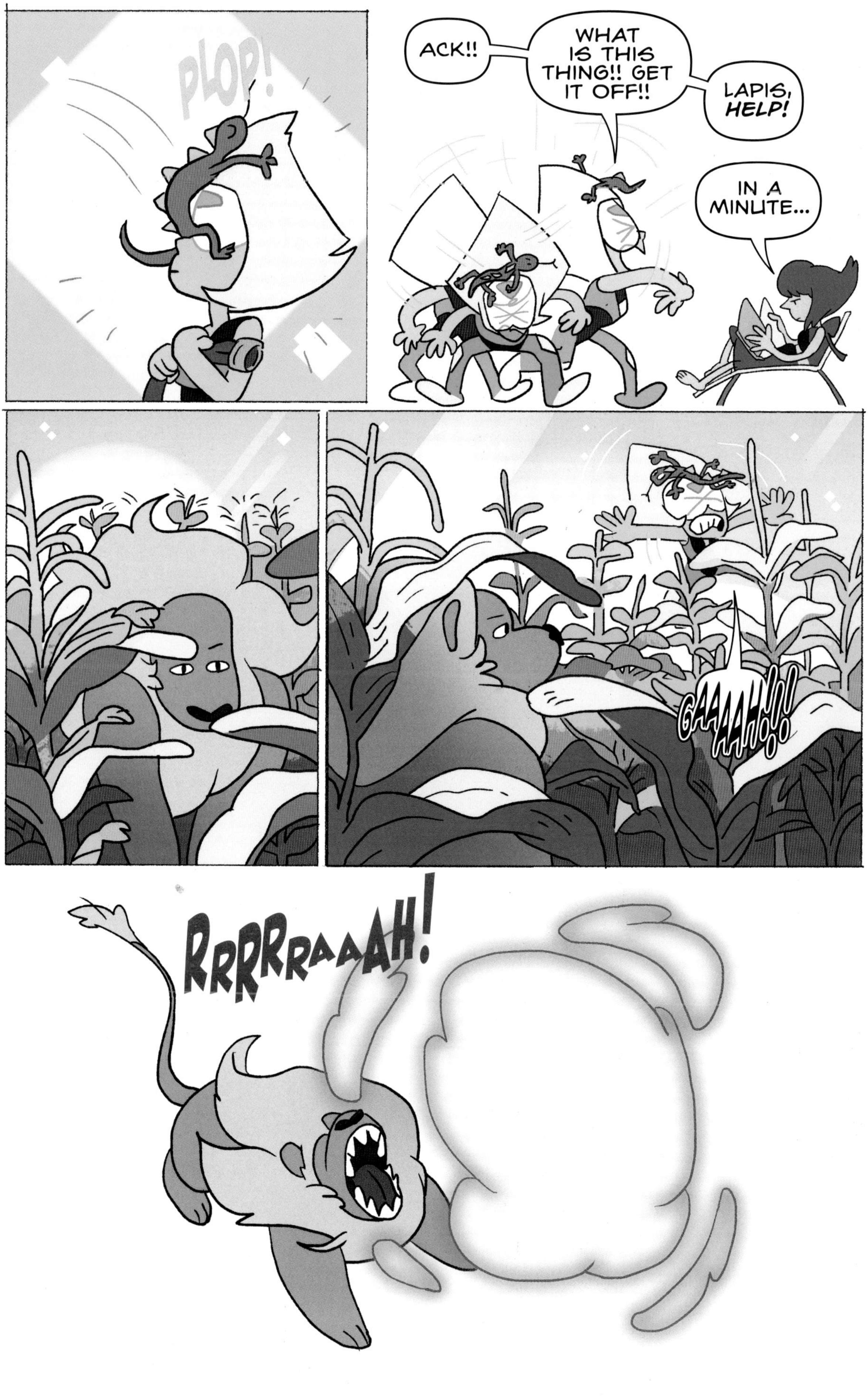
PLOP!
ACK!!
WHAT IS THIS THING!! GET IT OFF!!
LAPIS, HELP!
IN A MINUTE...
GAAAAHH!!!
RRRRRAAAH!

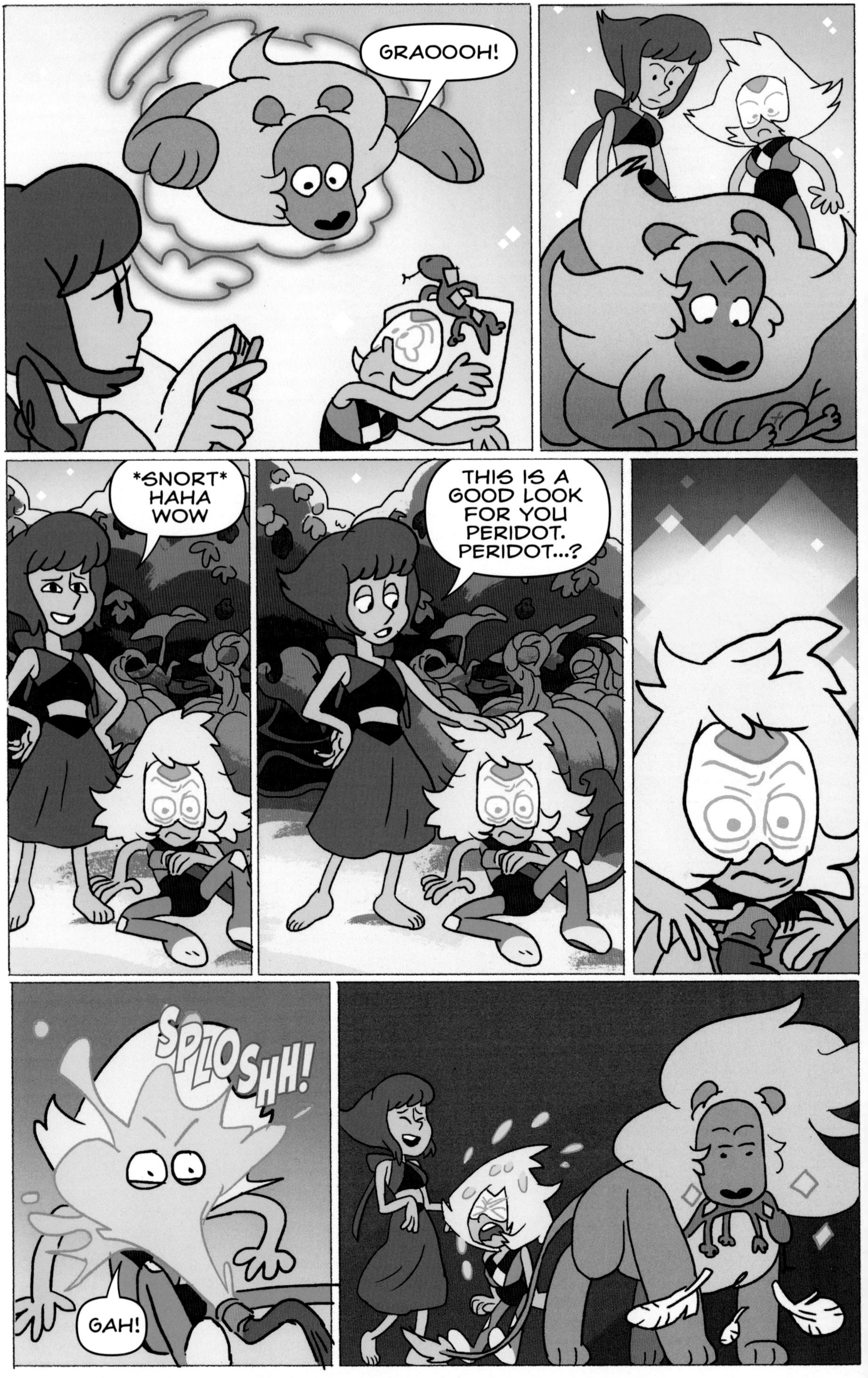
GRAOOOH!
*SNORT* HAHA WOW
THIS IS A GOOD LOOK FOR YOU PERIDOT. PERIDOT...?
SPLOSHH!
GAH!

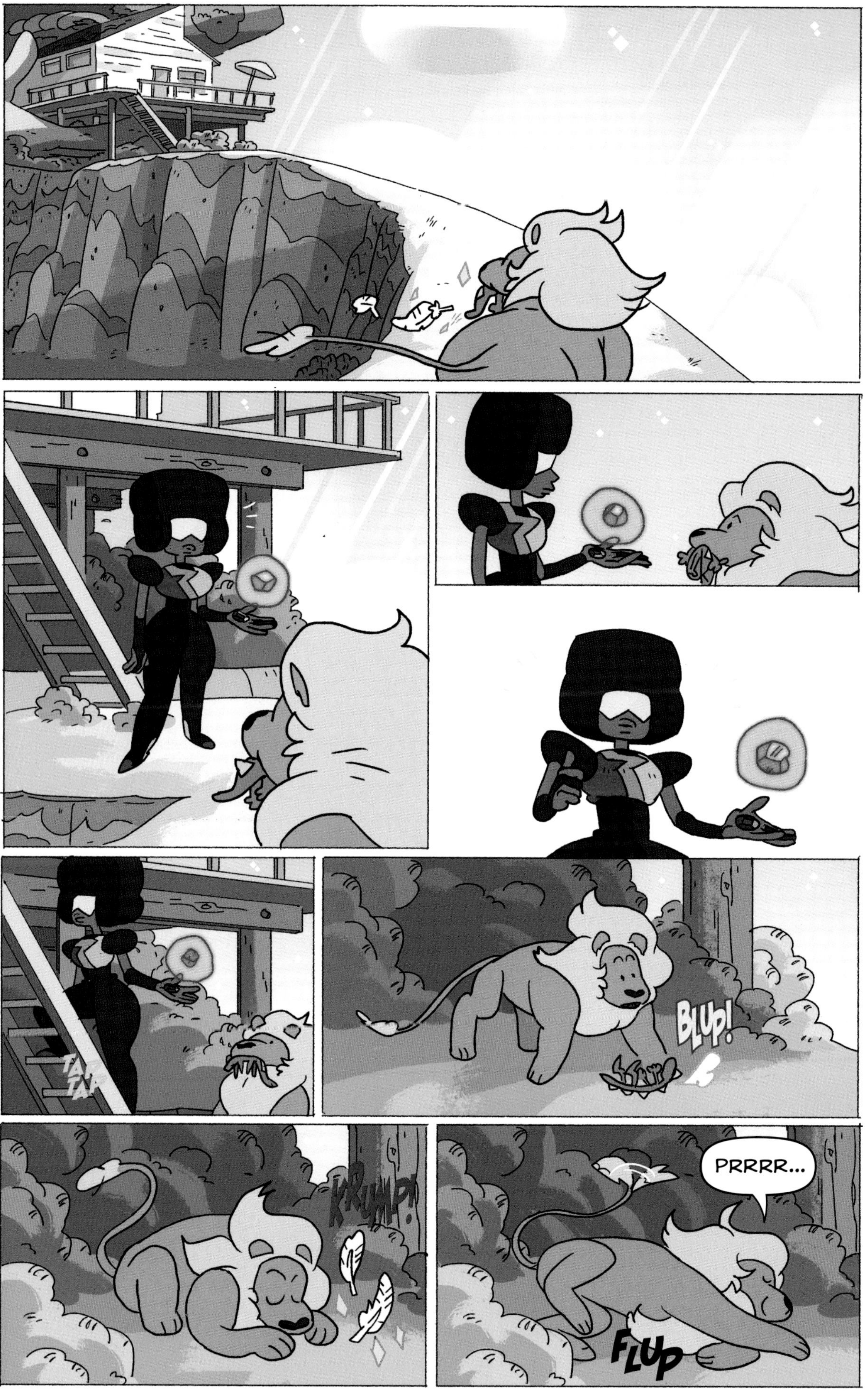
TAP TAP
BLUP!
KRUMP!
PRRRR...
FLUP

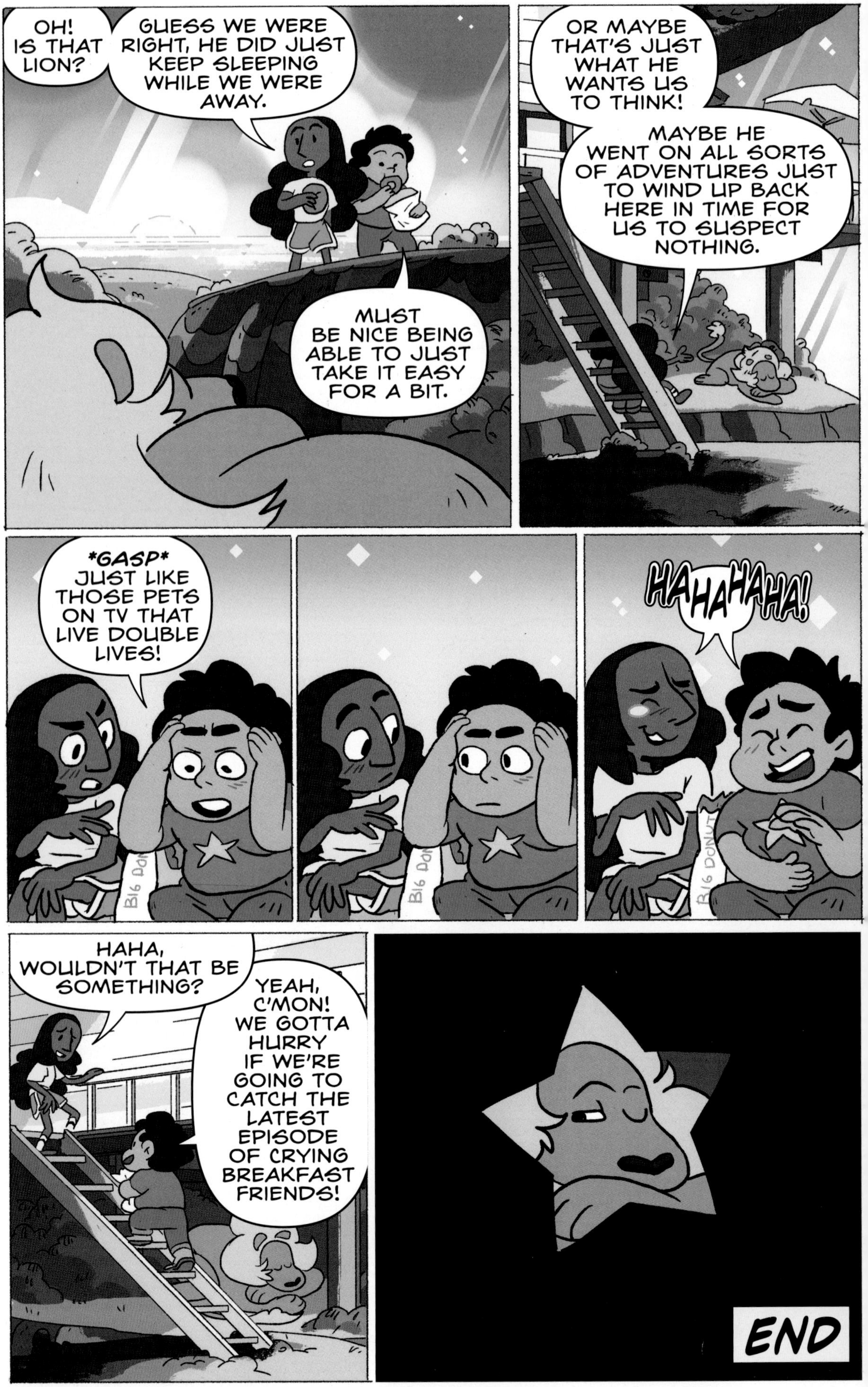
OH! IS THAT LION?
GUESS WE WERE RIGHT, HE DID JUST KEEP SLEEPING WHILE WE WERE AWAY.
MUST BE NICE BEING ABLE TO JUST TAKE IT EASY FOR A BIT.
OR MAYBE THAT'S JUST WHAT HE WANTS US TO THINK!
MAYBE HE WENT ON ALL SORTS OF ADVENTURES JUST TO WIND UP BACK HERE IN TIME FOR US TO SUSPECT NOTHING.
*GASP* JUST LIKE THOSE PETS ON TV THAT LIVE DOUBLE LIVES!
HAHAHAHAHA!
HAHA, WOULDN'T THAT BE SOMETHING?
YEAH, C'MON! WE GOTTA HURRY IF WE'RE GOING TO CATCH THE LATEST EPISODE OF CRYING BREAKFAST FRIENDS!
END

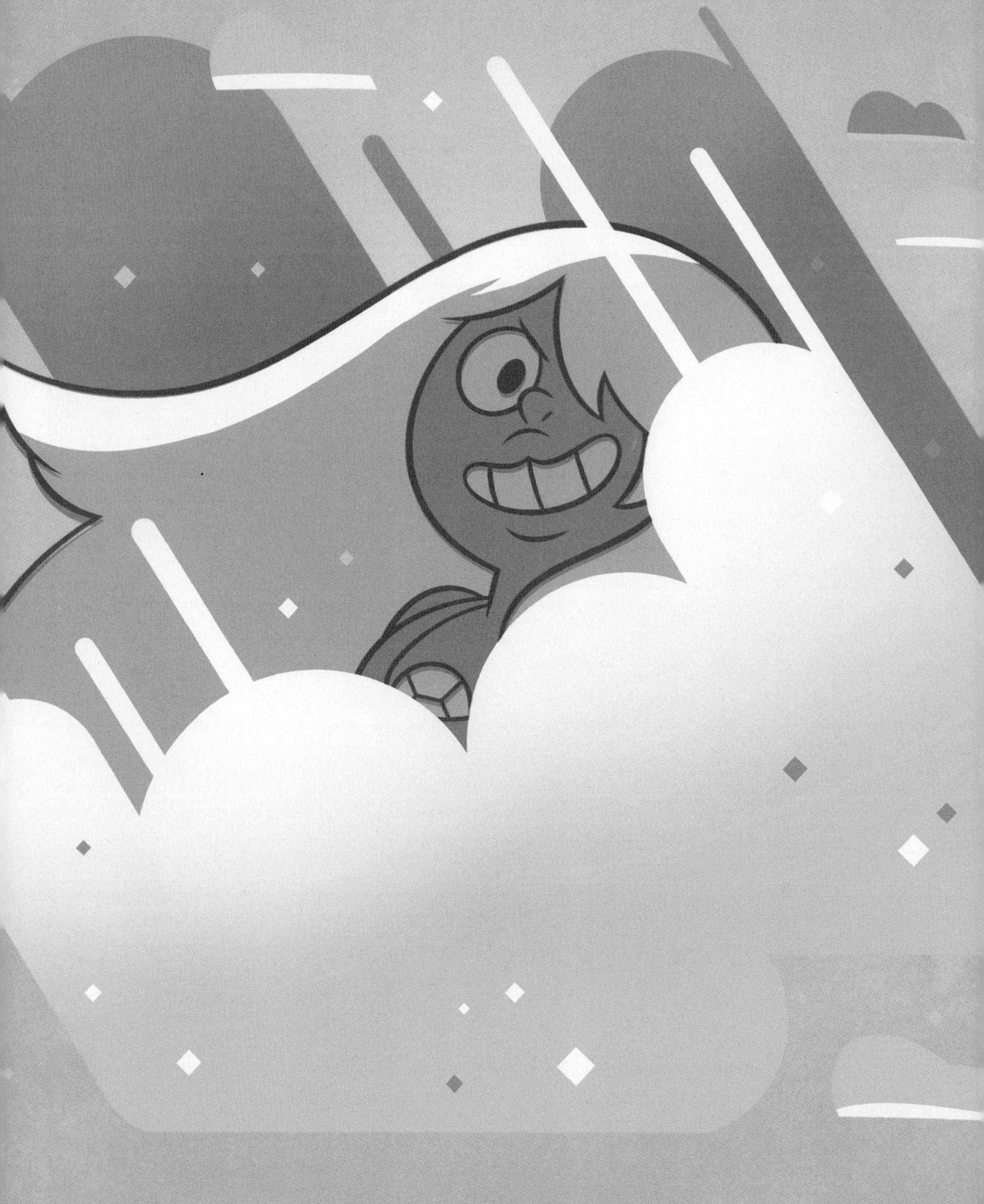

# CHAPTER SIX

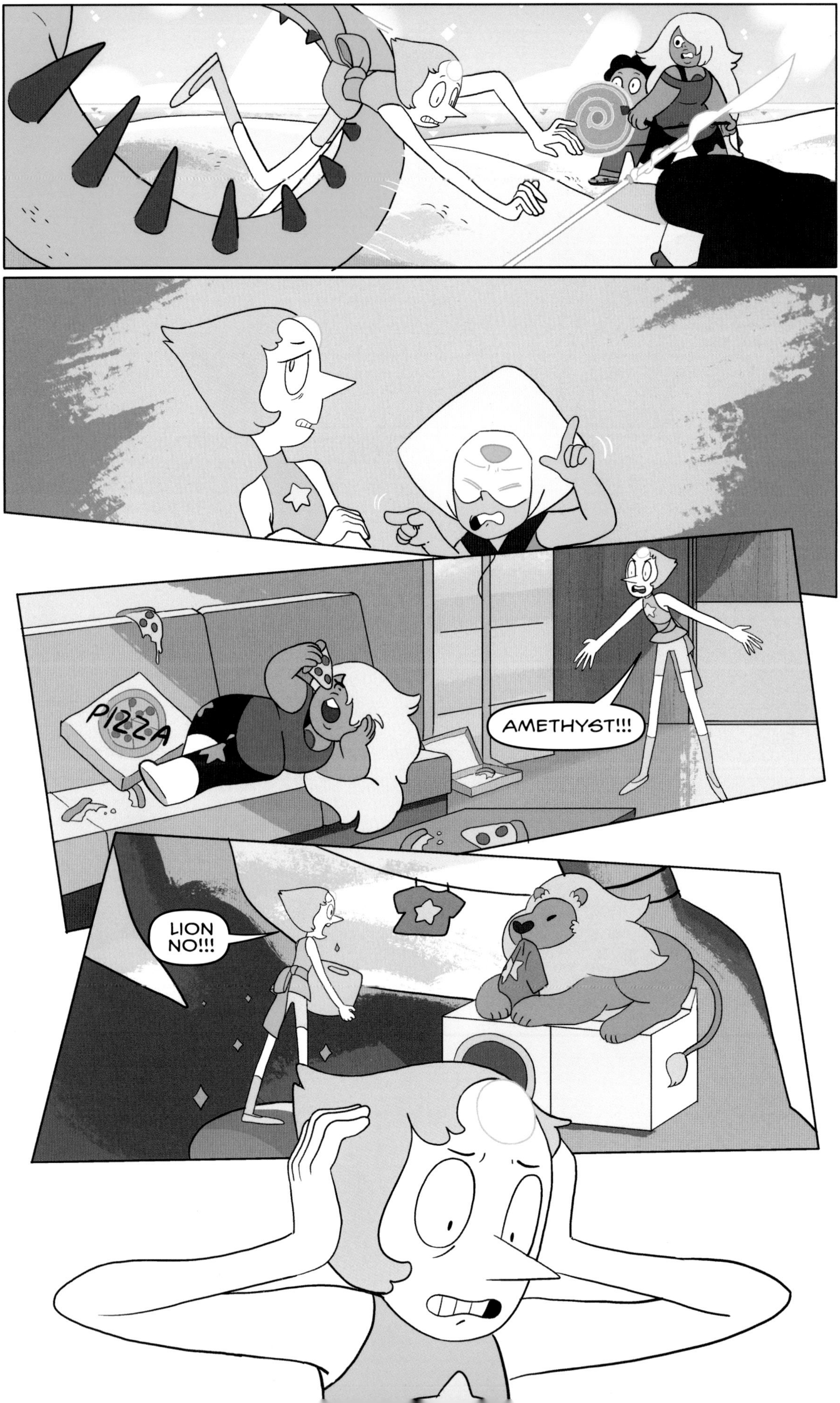

PIZZA
AMETHYST!!!
LION NO!!!

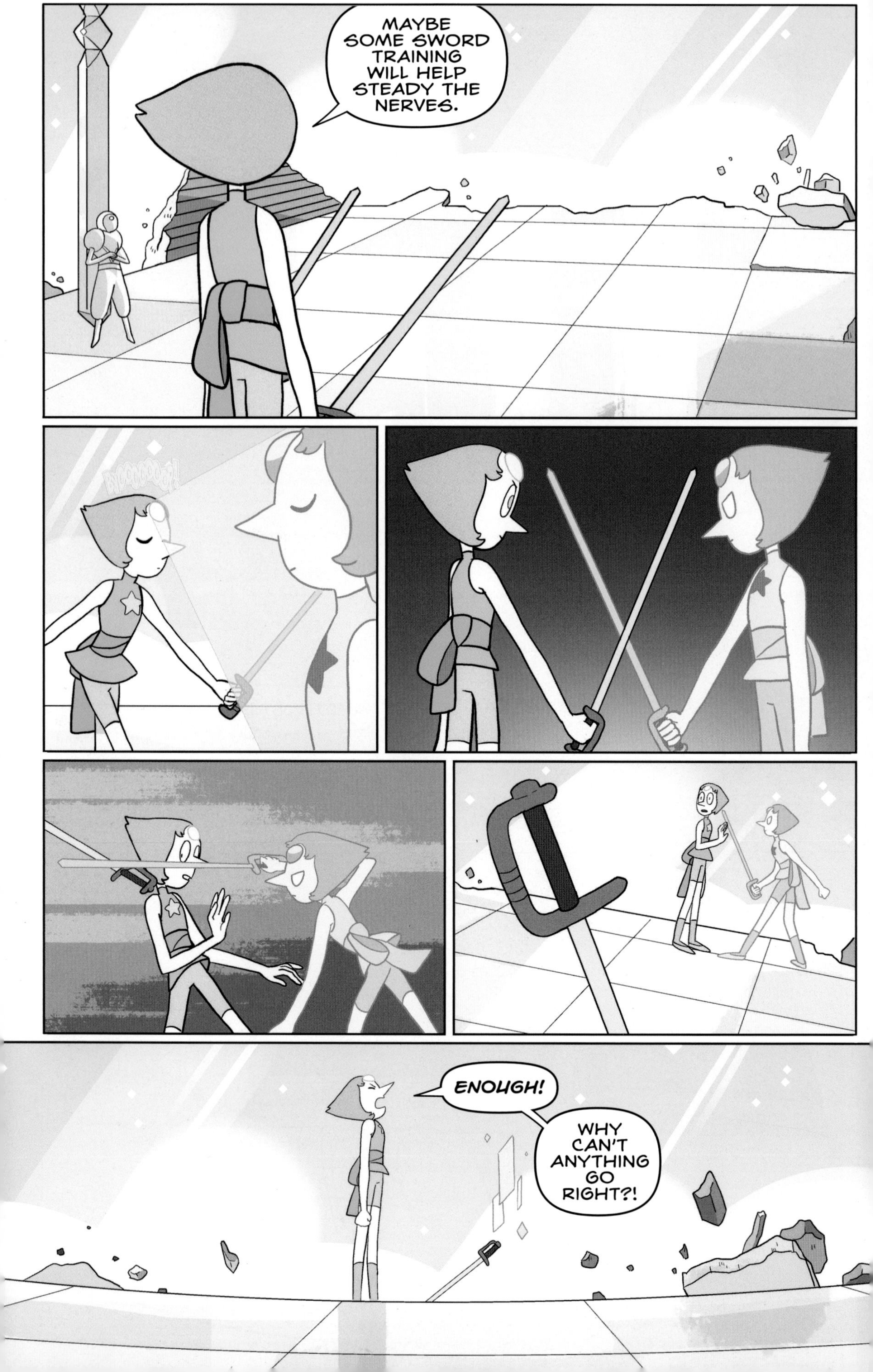
MAYBE SOME SWORD TRAINING WILL HELP STEADY THE NERVES.
ENOUGH!
WHY CAN'T ANYTHING GO RIGHT?!

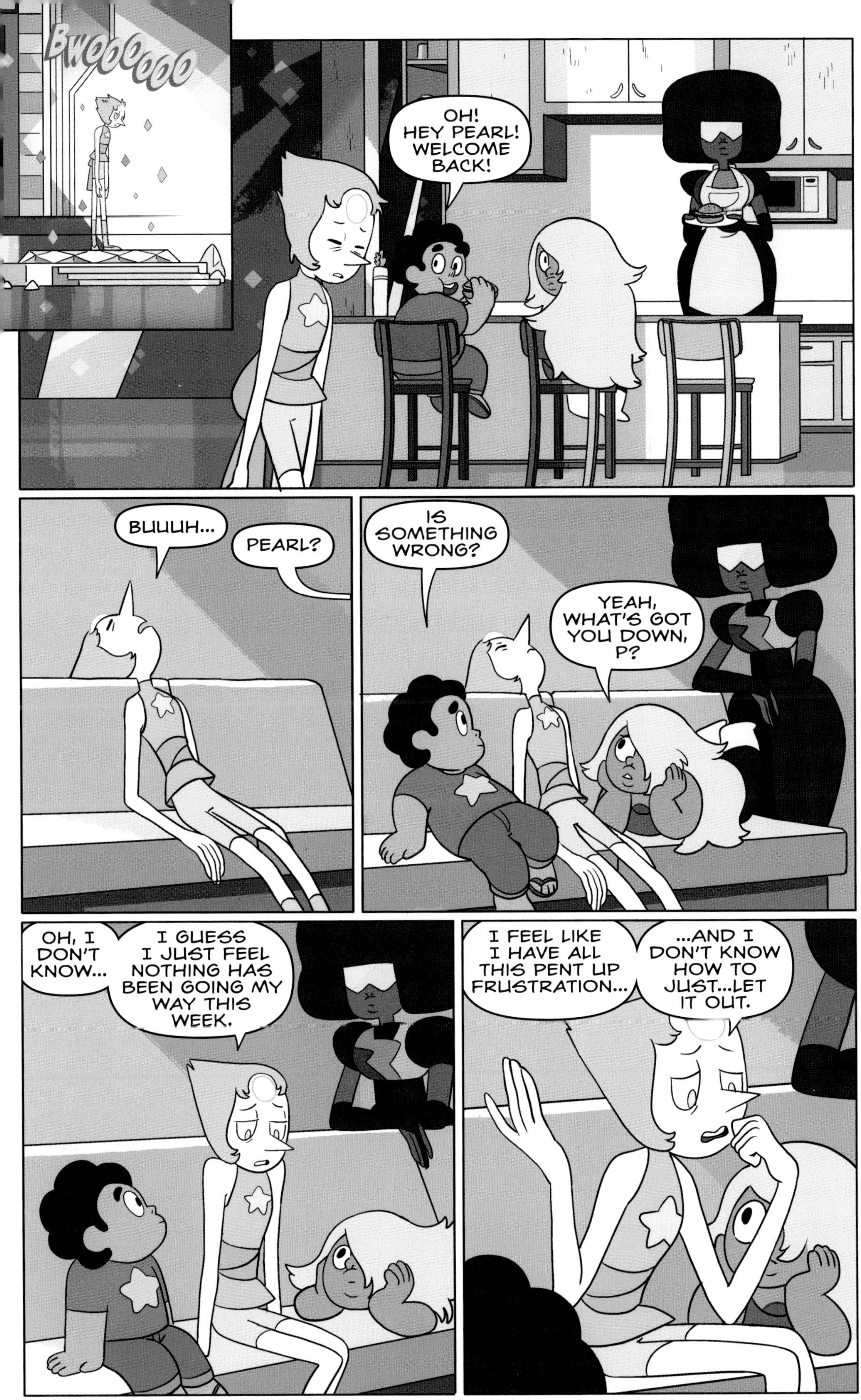
BWOOOOOO
OH! HEY PEARL! WELCOME BACK!
BUUUH...
PEARL?
IS SOMETHING WRONG?
YEAH, WHAT'S GOT YOU DOWN, P?
OH, I DON'T KNOW...
I GUESS I JUST FEEL NOTHING HAS BEEN GOING MY WAY THIS WEEK.
I FEEL LIKE I HAVE ALL THIS PENT UP FRUSTRATION...
...AND I DON'T KNOW HOW TO JUST...LET IT OUT.

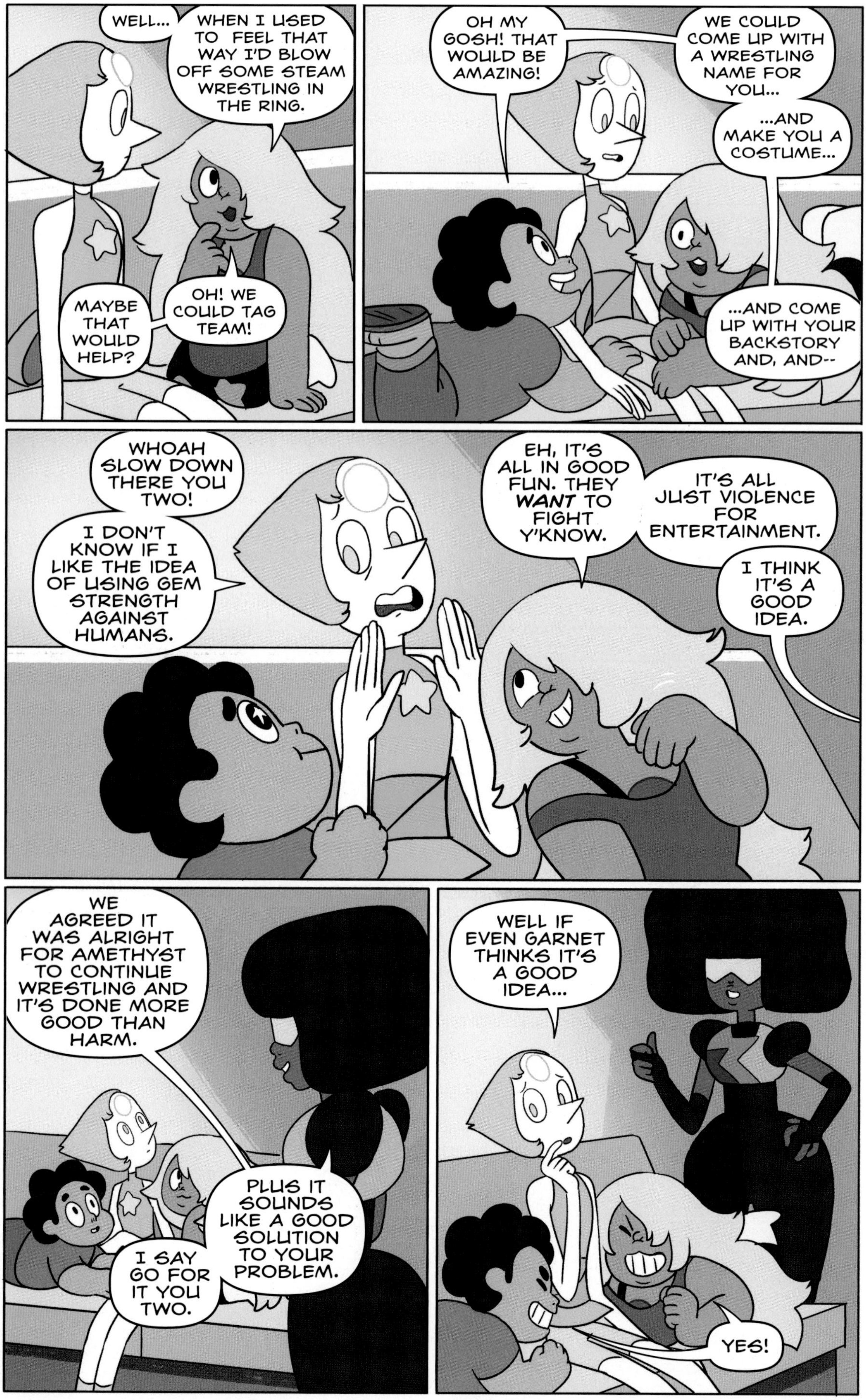
WELL...
WHEN I USED TO FEEL THAT WAY I'D BLOW OFF SOME STEAM WRESTLING IN THE RING.
MAYBE THAT WOULD HELP?
OH! WE COULD TAG TEAM!
OH MY GOSH! THAT WOULD BE AMAZING!
WE COULD COME UP WITH A WRESTLING NAME FOR YOU...
...AND MAKE YOU A COSTUME...
...AND COME UP WITH YOUR BACKSTORY AND, AND--
WHOAH SLOW DOWN THERE YOU TWO!
I DON'T KNOW IF I LIKE THE IDEA OF USING GEM STRENGTH AGAINST HUMANS.
EH, IT'S ALL IN GOOD FUN. THEY *WANT* TO FIGHT Y'KNOW.
IT'S ALL JUST VIOLENCE FOR ENTERTAINMENT.
I THINK IT'S A GOOD IDEA.
WE AGREED IT WAS ALRIGHT FOR AMETHYST TO CONTINUE WRESTLING AND IT'S DONE MORE GOOD THAN HARM.
PLUS IT SOUNDS LIKE A GOOD SOLUTION TO YOUR PROBLEM.
I SAY GO FOR IT YOU TWO.
WELL IF EVEN GARNET THINKS IT'S A GOOD IDEA...
YES!

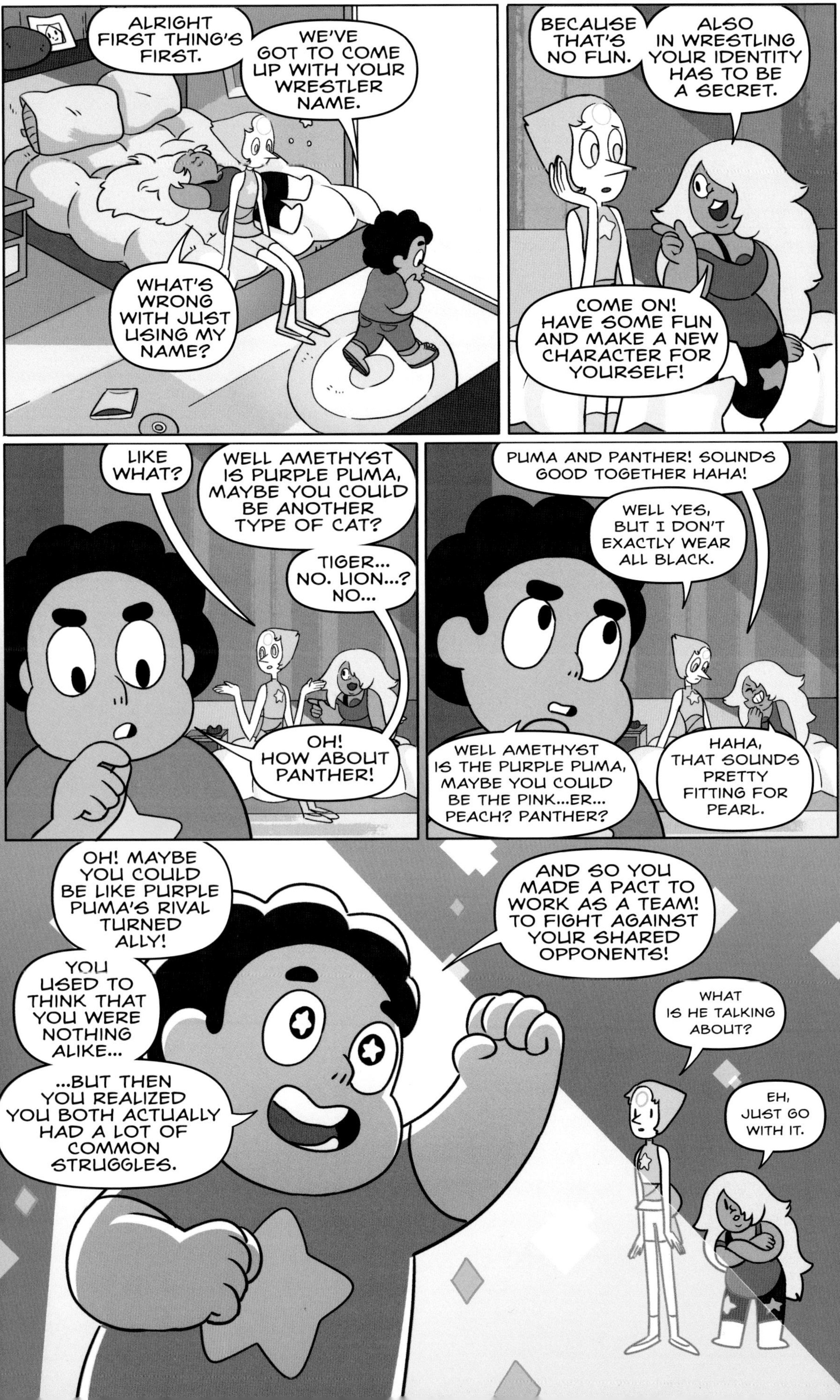
ALRIGHT FIRST THING'S FIRST.
WE'VE GOT TO COME UP WITH YOUR WRESTLER NAME.
WHAT'S WRONG WITH JUST USING MY NAME?
BECAUSE THAT'S NO FUN.
ALSO IN WRESTLING YOUR IDENTITY HAS TO BE A SECRET.
COME ON! HAVE SOME FUN AND MAKE A NEW CHARACTER FOR YOURSELF!
LIKE WHAT?
WELL AMETHYST IS PURPLE PUMA, MAYBE YOU COULD BE ANOTHER TYPE OF CAT?
TIGER... NO. LION...? NO...
OH! HOW ABOUT PANTHER!
PUMA AND PANTHER! SOUNDS GOOD TOGETHER HAHA!
WELL YES, BUT I DON'T EXACTLY WEAR ALL BLACK.
WELL AMETHYST IS THE PURPLE PUMA, MAYBE YOU COULD BE THE PINK...ER... PEACH? PANTHER?
HAHA, THAT SOUNDS PRETTY FITTING FOR PEARL.
OH! MAYBE YOU COULD BE LIKE PURPLE PUMA'S RIVAL TURNED ALLY!
YOU USED TO THINK THAT YOU WERE NOTHING ALIKE...
...BUT THEN YOU REALIZED YOU BOTH ACTUALLY HAD A LOT OF COMMON STRUGGLES.
AND SO YOU MADE A PACT TO WORK AS A TEAM! TO FIGHT AGAINST YOUR SHARED OPPONENTS!
WHAT IS HE TALKING ABOUT?
EH, JUST GO WITH IT.

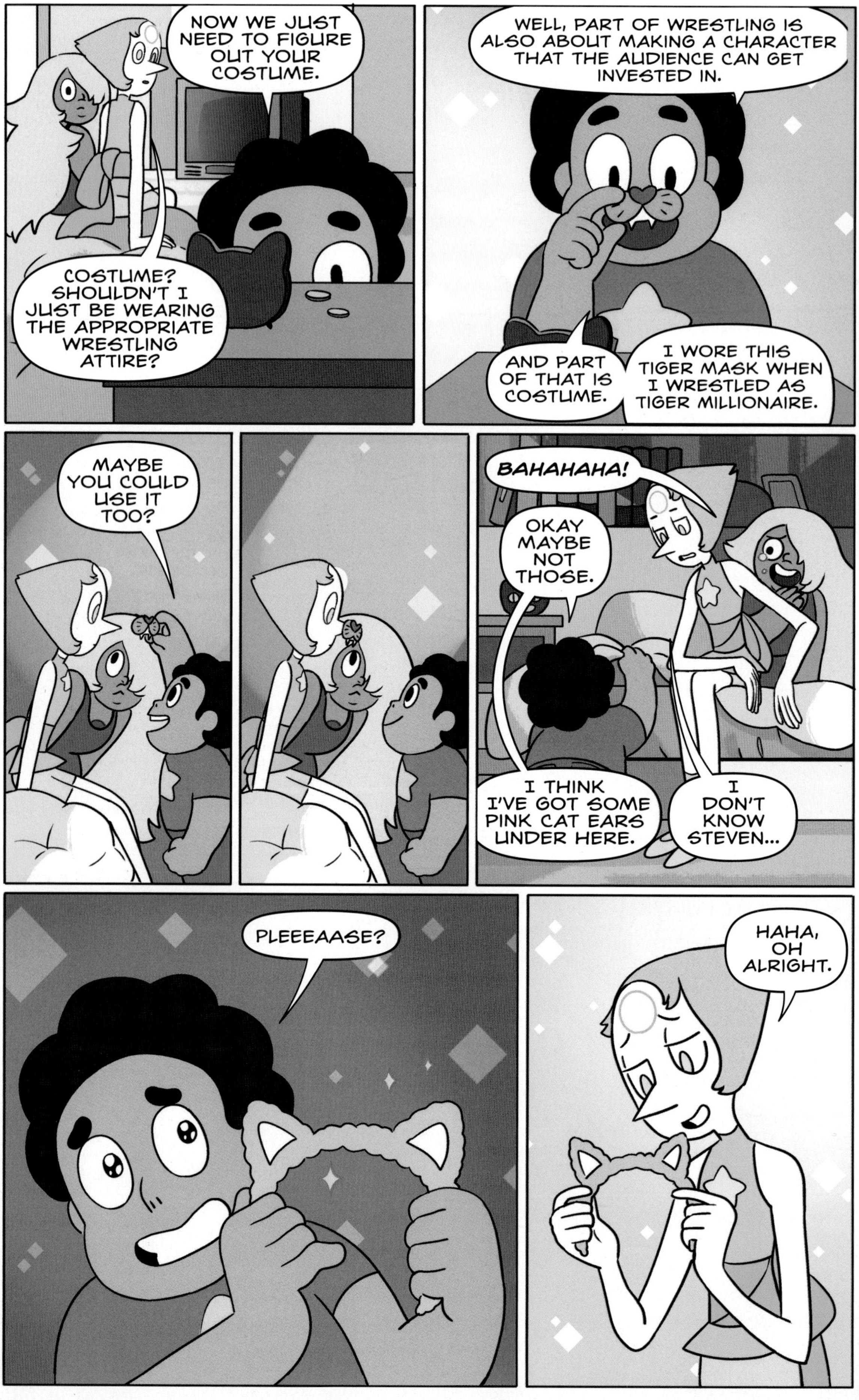
NOW WE JUST NEED TO FIGURE OUT YOUR COSTUME.
COSTUME? SHOULDN'T I JUST BE WEARING THE APPROPRIATE WRESTLING ATTIRE?
WELL, PART OF WRESTLING IS ALSO ABOUT MAKING A CHARACTER THAT THE AUDIENCE CAN GET INVESTED IN.
AND PART OF THAT IS COSTUME.
I WORE THIS TIGER MASK WHEN I WRESTLED AS TIGER MILLIONAIRE.
MAYBE YOU COULD USE IT TOO?
BAHAHAHA!
OKAY MAYBE NOT THOSE.
I THINK I'VE GOT SOME PINK CAT EARS UNDER HERE.
I DON'T KNOW STEVEN...
PLEEEAAASE?
HAHA, OH ALRIGHT.

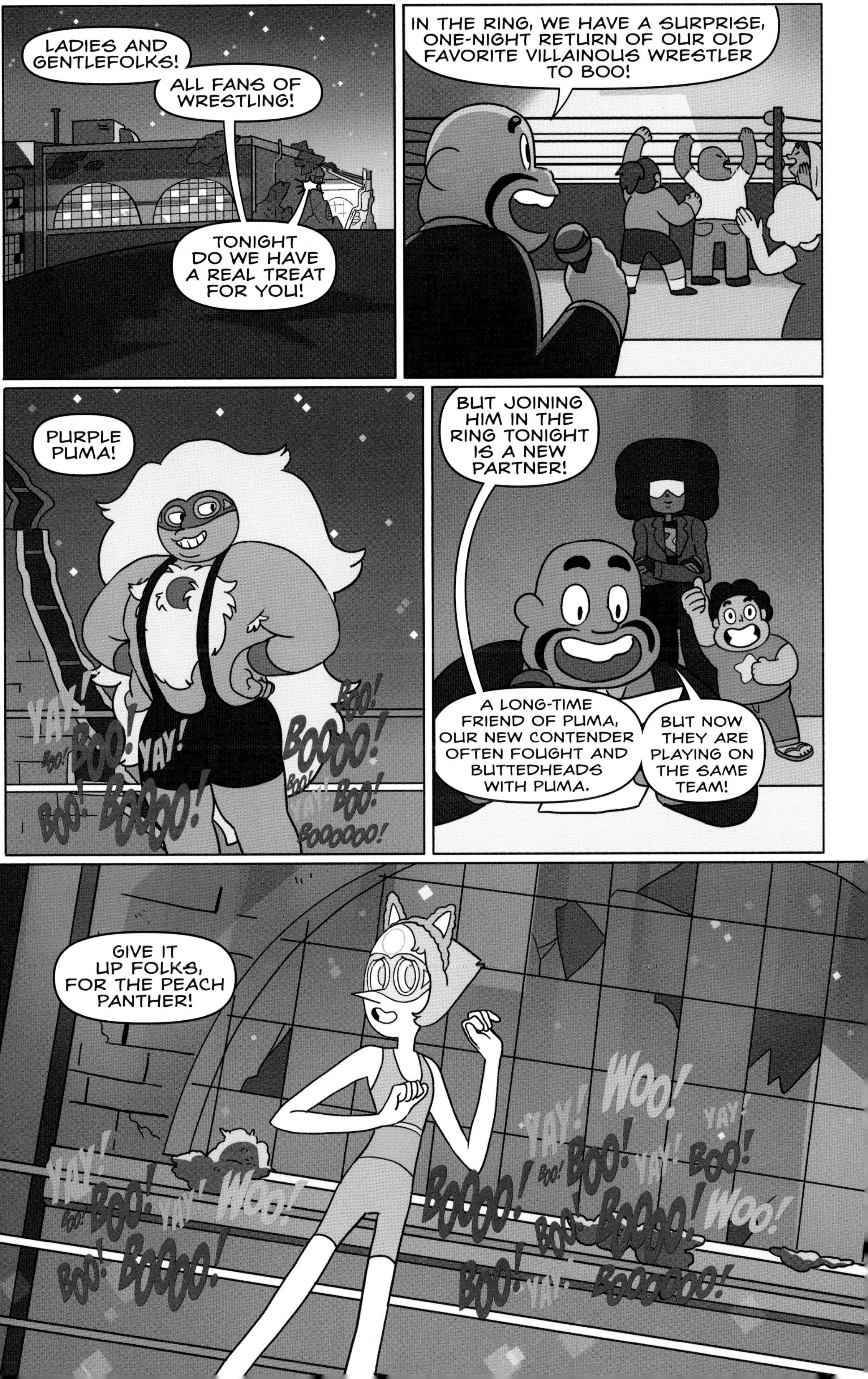
LADIES AND GENTLEFOLKS!
ALL FANS OF WRESTLING!
TONIGHT DO WE HAVE A REAL TREAT FOR YOU!
IN THE RING, WE HAVE A SURPRISE, ONE-NIGHT RETURN OF OUR OLD FAVORITE VILLAINOUS WRESTLER TO BOO!
PURPLE PUMA!
YAY!
BOO!
BOO!
YAY!
BOO!
BOOOO!
BOO!
BOOOO!
BOO!
YAY!
BOO!
BOOOOOO!
BUT JOINING HIM IN THE RING TONIGHT IS A NEW PARTNER!
A LONG-TIME FRIEND OF PUMA, OUR NEW CONTENDER OFTEN FOUGHT AND BUTTEDHEADS WITH PUMA.
BUT NOW THEY ARE PLAYING ON THE SAME TEAM!
GIVE IT UP FOLKS, FOR THE PEACH PANTHER!
YAY!
BOO!
BOO!
YAY!
WOO!
BOO!
BOOOO!
WOO!
YAY!
YAY!
BOO!
BOO!
YAY!
BOO!
BOOOO!
BOO!
BOO!
BOOOO!
WOO!
BOO!
YAY!
BOOOOOO!

GO PUMA AND PANTHER

GO PUMA AND PANTHER!

WOO!

I DON'T KNOW ABOUT THIS...

AH DON'T WORRY PANTHER, YOU'RE GONNA DO GREAT!

NOW REMEMBER, NO PUNCHING OR KICKING.

YOU GOTTA BEAT YOUR OPPONENT BY LIKE GRAPPLING THEM AND THROWING THEM AND FLIPPING THEM AND STUFF.

AND IT HELPS TO LIKE USE THE ROPES TO GIVE YOU MORE MOMENTUM.

GOT ALL THAT?

UUUUH... YES I THINK SO...?

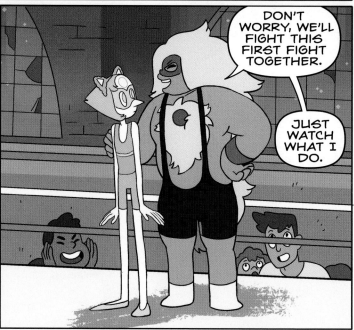

DON'T WORRY, WE'LL FIGHT THIS FIRST FIGHT TOGETHER.

JUST WATCH WHAT I DO.

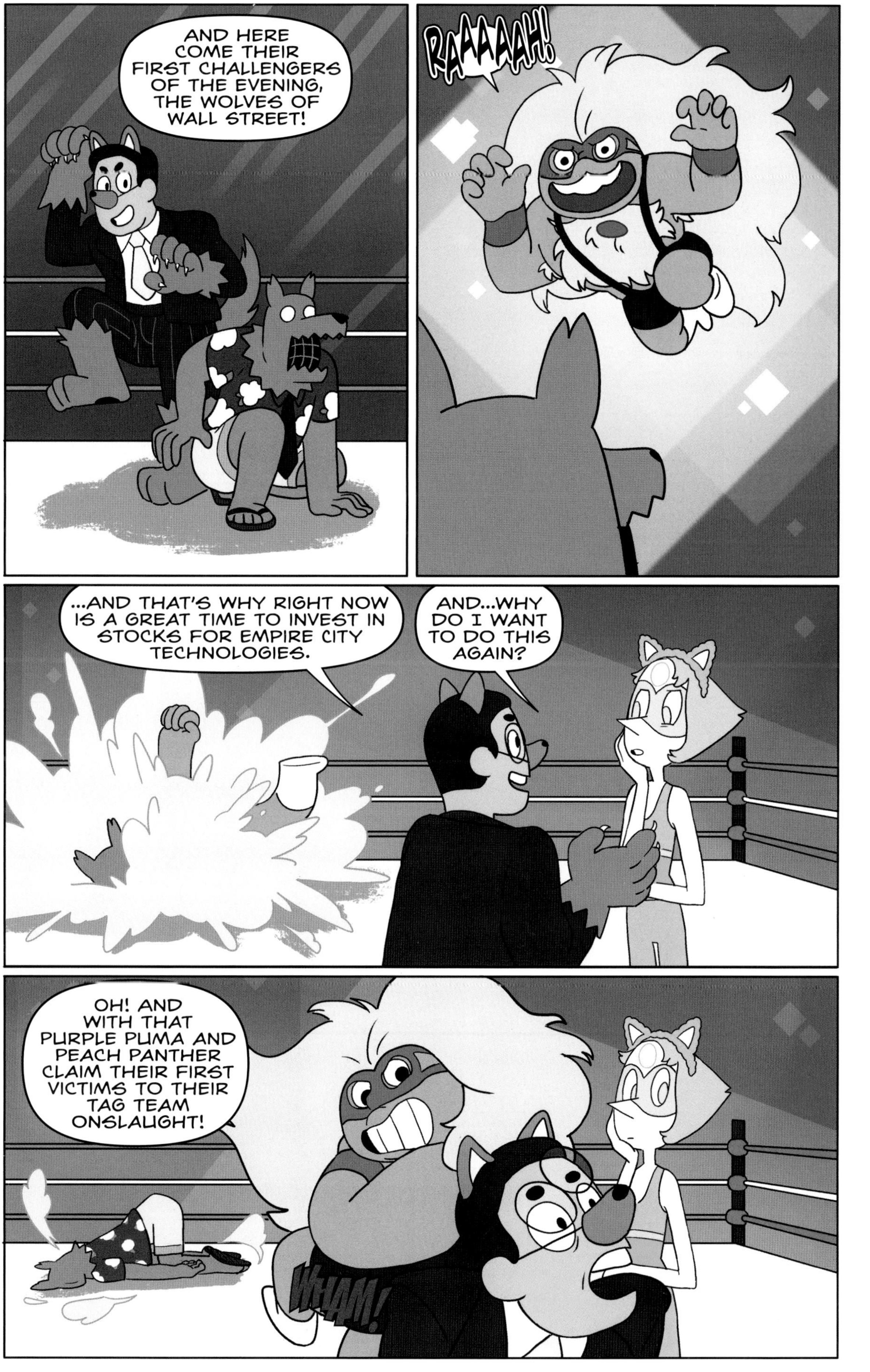
AND HERE COME THEIR FIRST CHALLENGERS OF THE EVENING, THE WOLVES OF WALL STREET!
RAAAAAH!
...AND THAT'S WHY RIGHT NOW IS A GREAT TIME TO INVEST IN STOCKS FOR EMPIRE CITY TECHNOLOGIES.
AND...WHY DO I WANT TO DO THIS AGAIN?
OH! AND WITH THAT PURPLE PUMA AND PEACH PANTHER CLAIM THEIR FIRST VICTIMS TO THEIR TAG TEAM ONSLAUGHT!
WHAM!

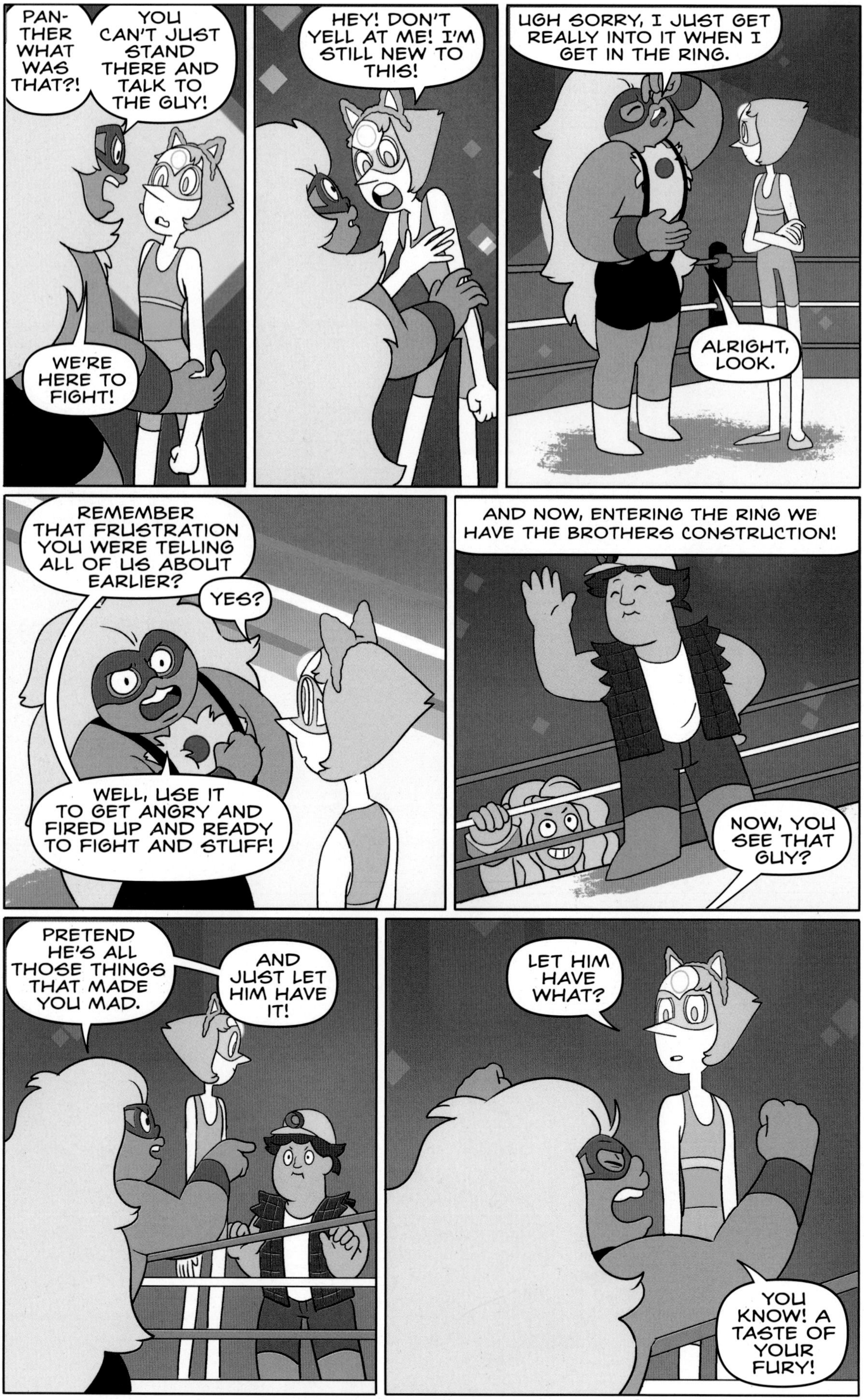
PAN-THER WHAT WAS THAT?!
YOU CAN'T JUST STAND THERE AND TALK TO THE GUY!
WE'RE HERE TO FIGHT!
HEY! DON'T YELL AT ME! I'M STILL NEW TO THIS!
UGH SORRY, I JUST GET REALLY INTO IT WHEN I GET IN THE RING.
ALRIGHT, LOOK.
REMEMBER THAT FRUSTRATION YOU WERE TELLING ALL OF US ABOUT EARLIER?
YES?
WELL, USE IT TO GET ANGRY AND FIRED UP AND READY TO FIGHT AND STUFF!
AND NOW, ENTERING THE RING WE HAVE THE BROTHERS CONSTRUCTION!
NOW, YOU SEE THAT GUY?
PRETEND HE'S ALL THOSE THINGS THAT MADE YOU MAD.
AND JUST LET HIM HAVE IT!
LET HIM HAVE WHAT?
YOU KNOW! A TASTE OF YOUR FURY!

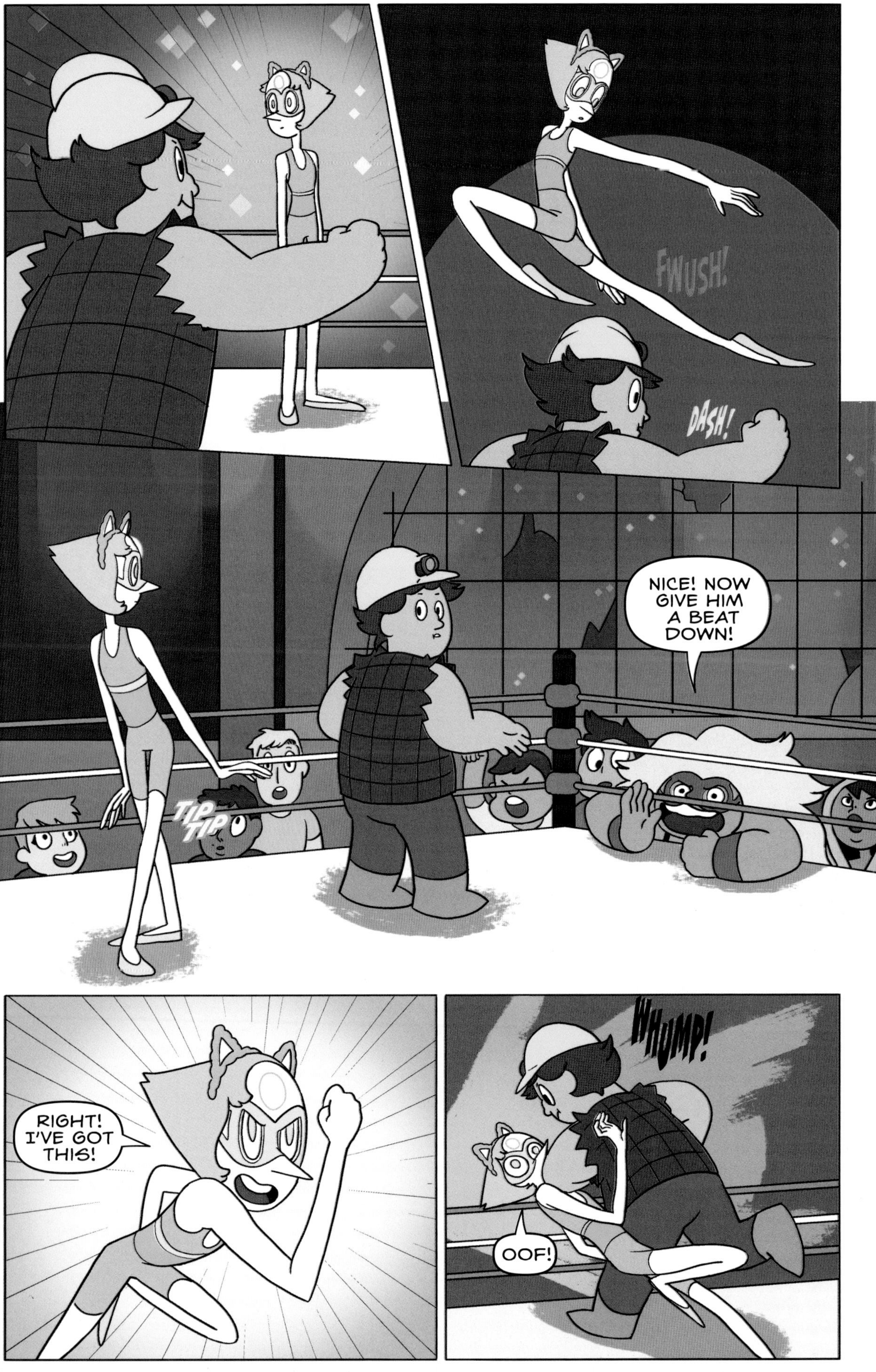
FWUSH!
DASH!
NICE! NOW GIVE HIM A BEAT DOWN!
TIP TIP
RIGHT! I'VE GOT THIS!
WHUMP!
OOF!

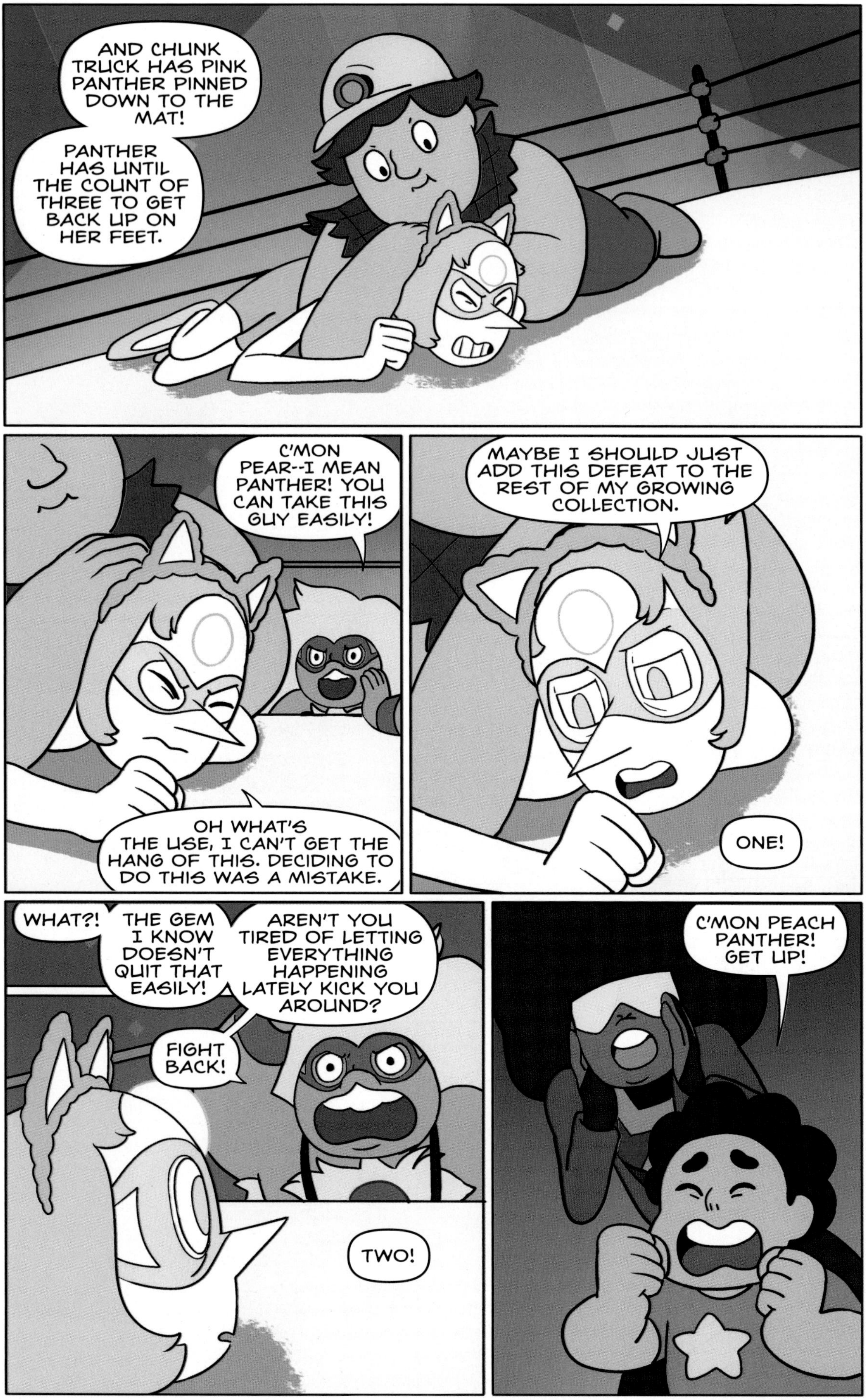
AND CHUNK TRUCK HAS PINK PANTHER PINNED DOWN TO THE MAT!
PANTHER HAS UNTIL THE COUNT OF THREE TO GET BACK UP ON HER FEET.
C'MON PEAR--I MEAN PANTHER! YOU CAN TAKE THIS GUY EASILY!
OH WHAT'S THE USE, I CAN'T GET THE HANG OF THIS. DECIDING TO DO THIS WAS A MISTAKE.
MAYBE I SHOULD JUST ADD THIS DEFEAT TO THE REST OF MY GROWING COLLECTION.
ONE!
WHAT?!
THE GEM I KNOW DOESN'T QUIT THAT EASILY!
AREN'T YOU TIRED OF LETTING EVERYTHING HAPPENING LATELY KICK YOU AROUND?
FIGHT BACK!
TWO!
C'MON PEACH PANTHER! GET UP!

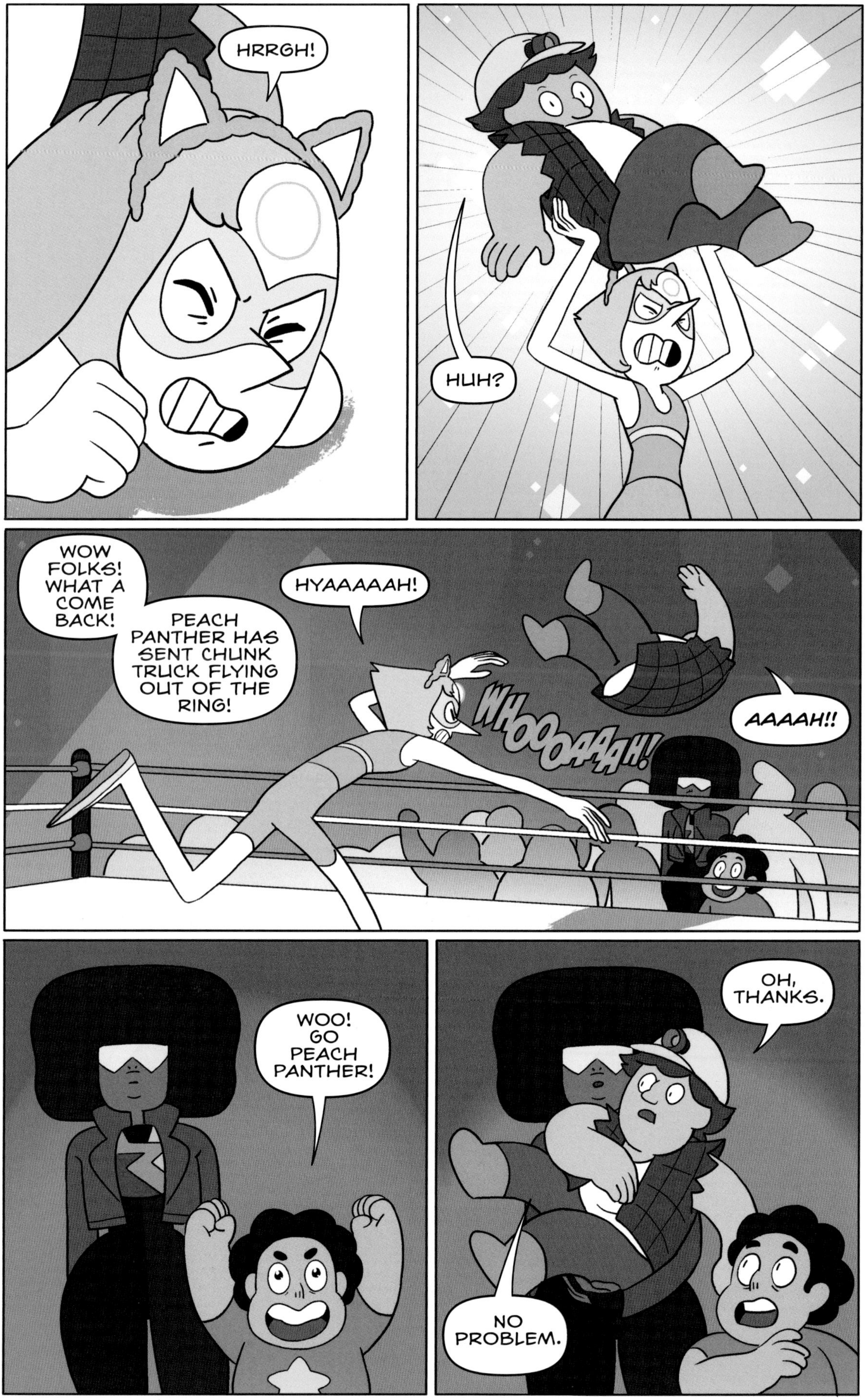

HRRGH!
HUH?
WOW FOLKS! WHAT A COME BACK!
PEACH PANTHER HAS SENT CHUNK TRUCK FLYING OUT OF THE RING!
HYAAAAAH!
WHOOOAAAH!
AAAAH!!
WOO! GO PEACH PANTHER!
OH, THANKS.
NO PROBLEM.

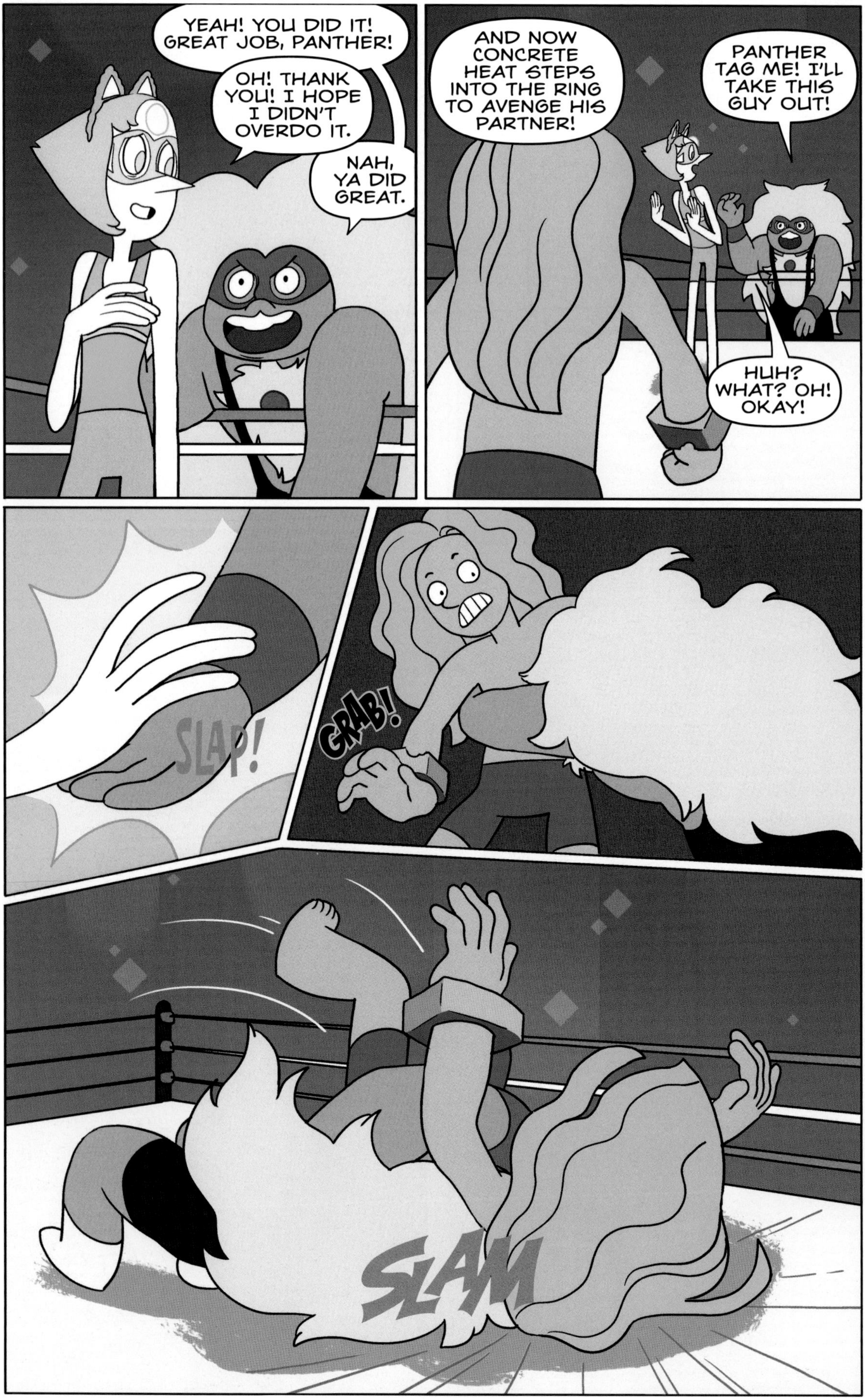

YEAH! YOU DID IT! GREAT JOB, PANTHER!
OH! THANK YOU! I HOPE I DIDN'T OVERDO IT.
NAH, YA DID GREAT.
AND NOW CONCRETE HEAT STEPS INTO THE RING TO AVENGE HIS PARTNER!
PANTHER TAG ME! I'LL TAKE THIS GUY OUT!
HUH? WHAT? OH! OKAY!
SLAP!
GRAB!
SLAM

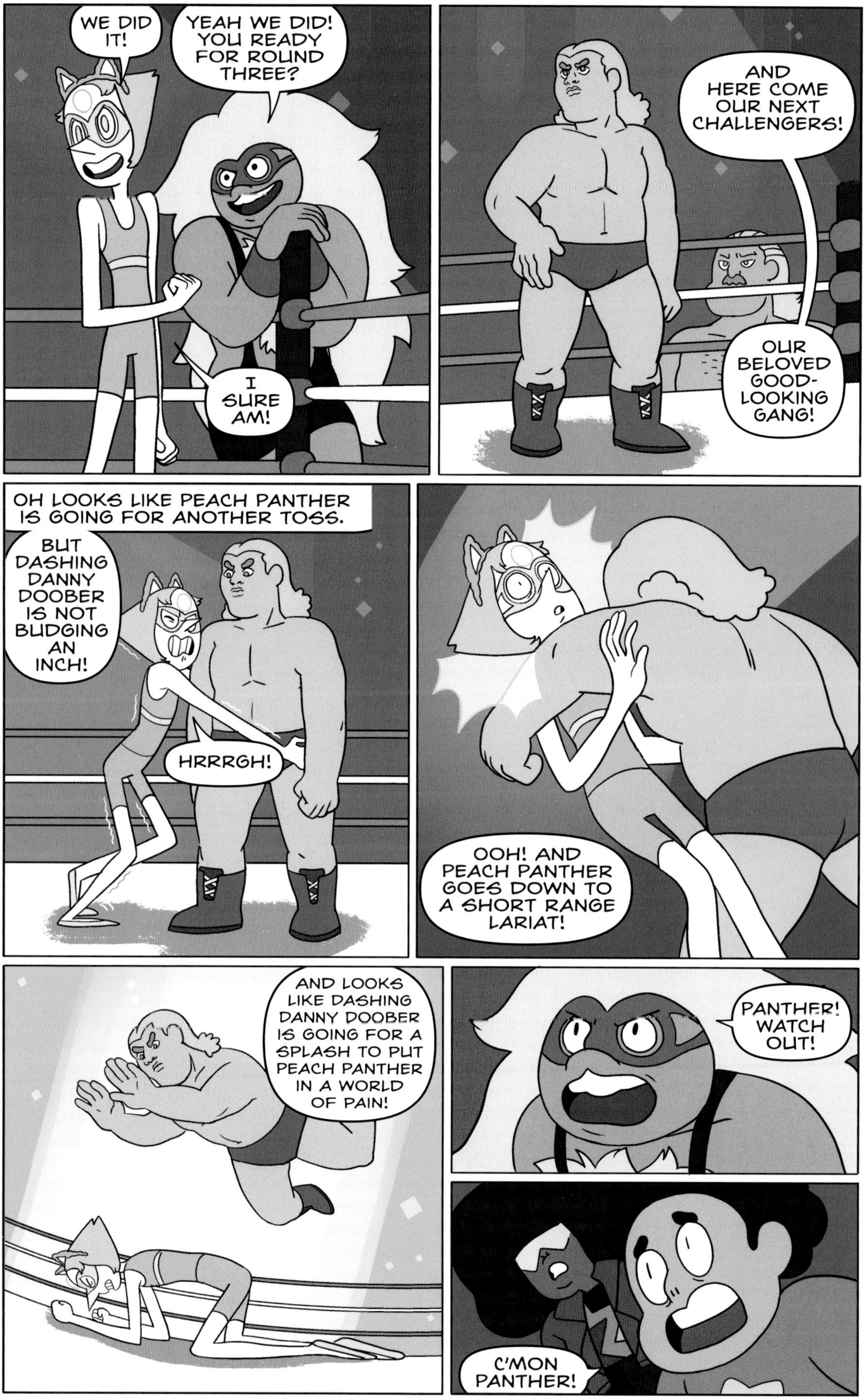
WE DID IT!
YEAH WE DID! YOU READY FOR ROUND THREE?
I SURE AM!
AND HERE COME OUR NEXT CHALLENGERS!
OUR BELOVED GOOD-LOOKING GANG!
OH LOOKS LIKE PEACH PANTHER IS GOING FOR ANOTHER TOSS.
BUT DASHING DANNY DOOBER IS NOT BUDGING AN INCH!
HRRRGH!
OOH! AND PEACH PANTHER GOES DOWN TO A SHORT RANGE LARIAT!
AND LOOKS LIKE DASHING DANNY DOOBER IS GOING FOR A SPLASH TO PUT PEACH PANTHER IN A WORLD OF PAIN!
PANTHER! WATCH OUT!
C'MON PANTHER!

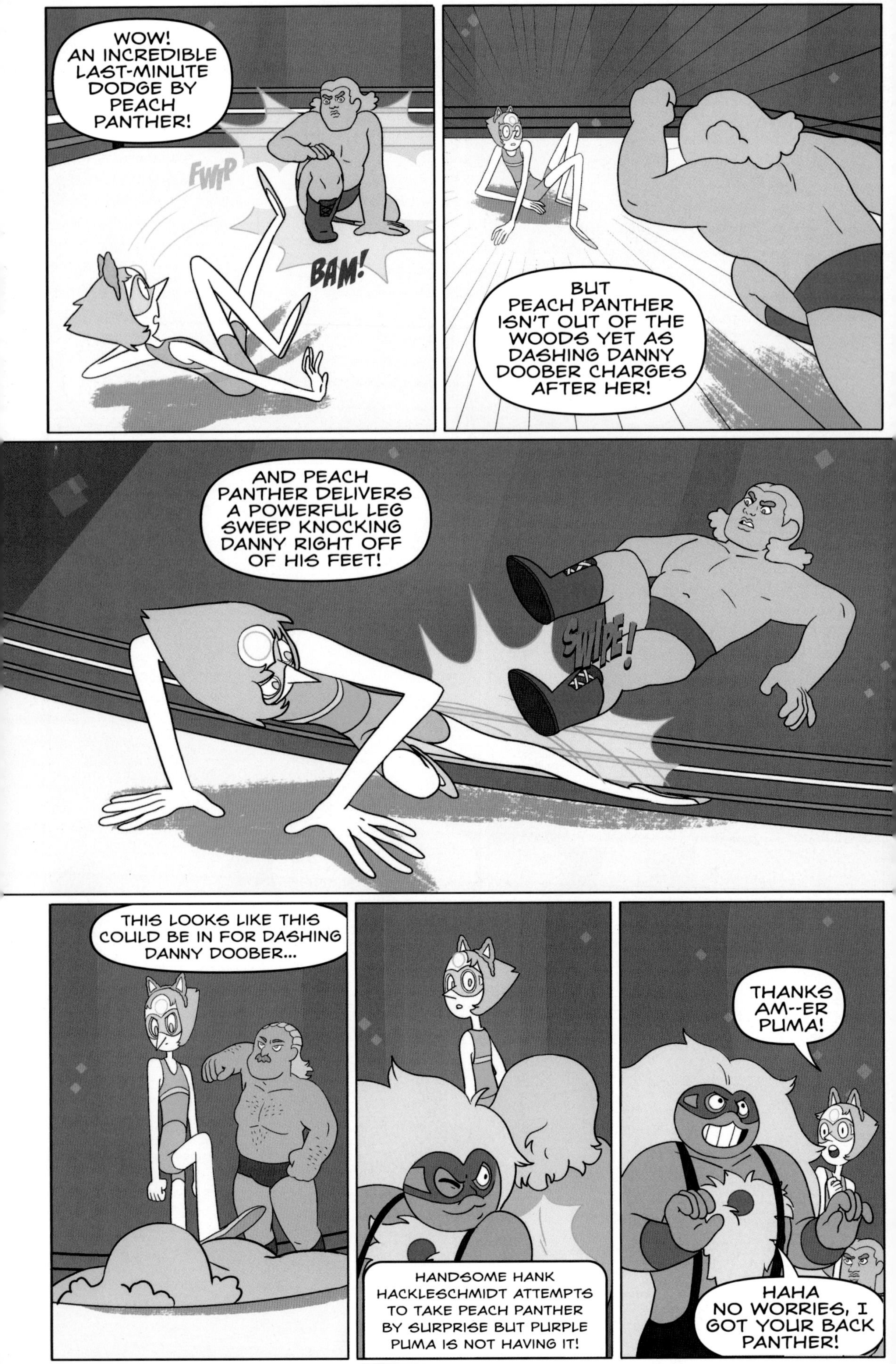
WOW! AN INCREDIBLE LAST-MINUTE DODGE BY PEACH PANTHER!
FWIP
BAM!
BUT PEACH PANTHER ISN'T OUT OF THE WOODS YET AS DASHING DANNY DOOBER CHARGES AFTER HER!
AND PEACH PANTHER DELIVERS A POWERFUL LEG SWEEP KNOCKING DANNY RIGHT OFF OF HIS FEET!
SWIPE!
THIS LOOKS LIKE THIS COULD BE IN FOR DASHING DANNY DOOBER...
HANDSOME HANK HACKLESCHMIDT ATTEMPTS TO TAKE PEACH PANTHER BY SURPRISE BUT PURPLE PUMA IS NOT HAVING IT!
THANKS AM--ER PUMA!
HAHA NO WORRIES, I GOT YOUR BACK PANTHER!

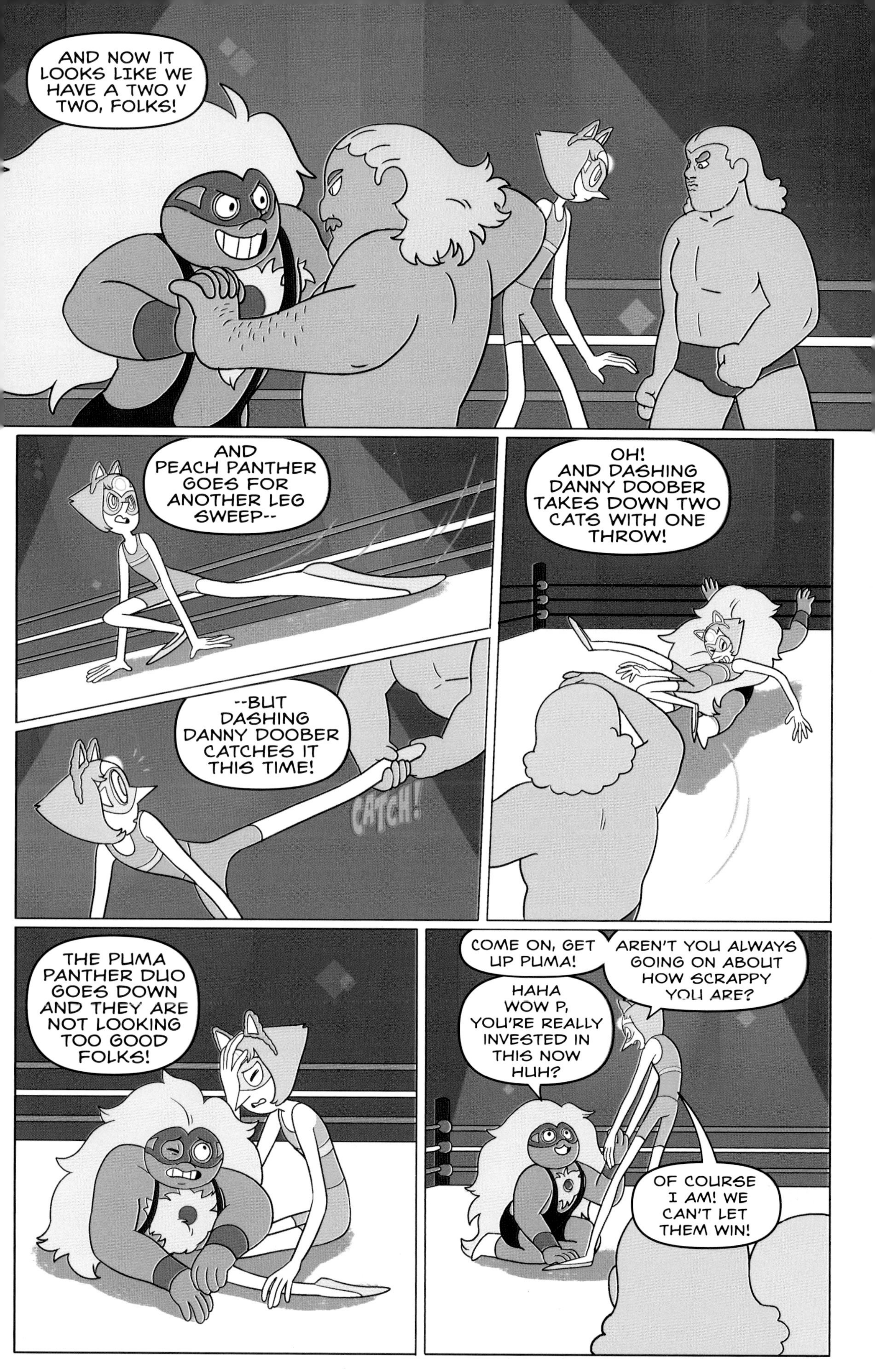
AND NOW IT LOOKS LIKE WE HAVE A TWO V TWO, FOLKS!
AND PEACH PANTHER GOES FOR ANOTHER LEG SWEEP--
--BUT DASHING DANNY DOOBER CATCHES IT THIS TIME!
CATCH!
OH! AND DASHING DANNY DOOBER TAKES DOWN TWO CATS WITH ONE THROW!
THE PUMA PANTHER DUO GOES DOWN AND THEY ARE NOT LOOKING TOO GOOD FOLKS!
COME ON, GET UP PUMA!
AREN'T YOU ALWAYS GOING ON ABOUT HOW SCRAPPY YOU ARE?
HAHA WOW P, YOU'RE REALLY INVESTED IN THIS NOW HUH?
OF COURSE I AM! WE CAN'T LET THEM WIN!

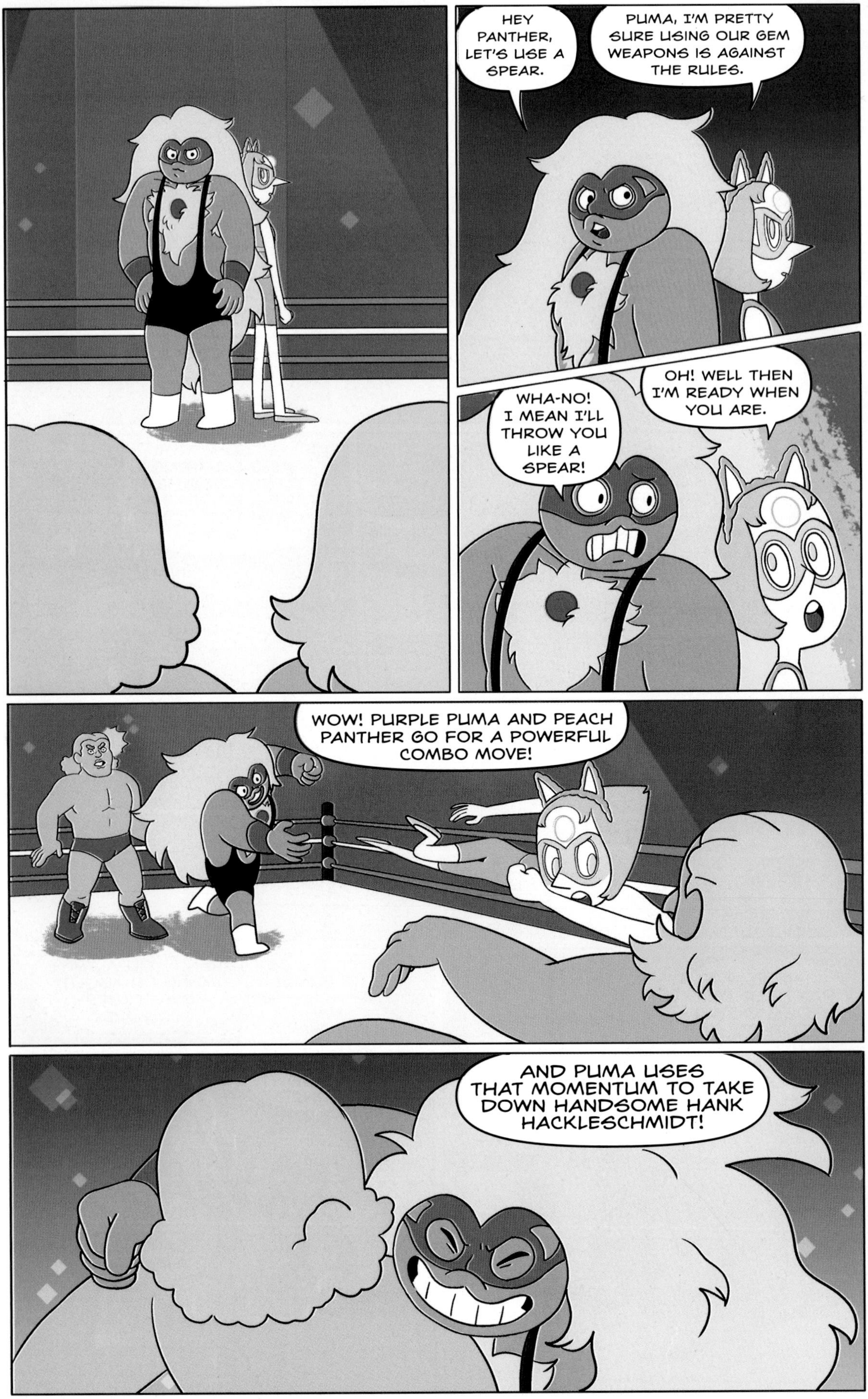
HEY PANTHER, LET'S USE A SPEAR.
PUMA, I'M PRETTY SURE USING OUR GEM WEAPONS IS AGAINST THE RULES.
WHA-NO! I MEAN I'LL THROW YOU LIKE A SPEAR!
OH! WELL THEN I'M READY WHEN YOU ARE.
WOW! PURPLE PUMA AND PEACH PANTHER GO FOR A POWERFUL COMBO MOVE!
AND PUMA USES THAT MOMENTUM TO TAKE DOWN HANDSOME HANK HACKLESCHMIDT!

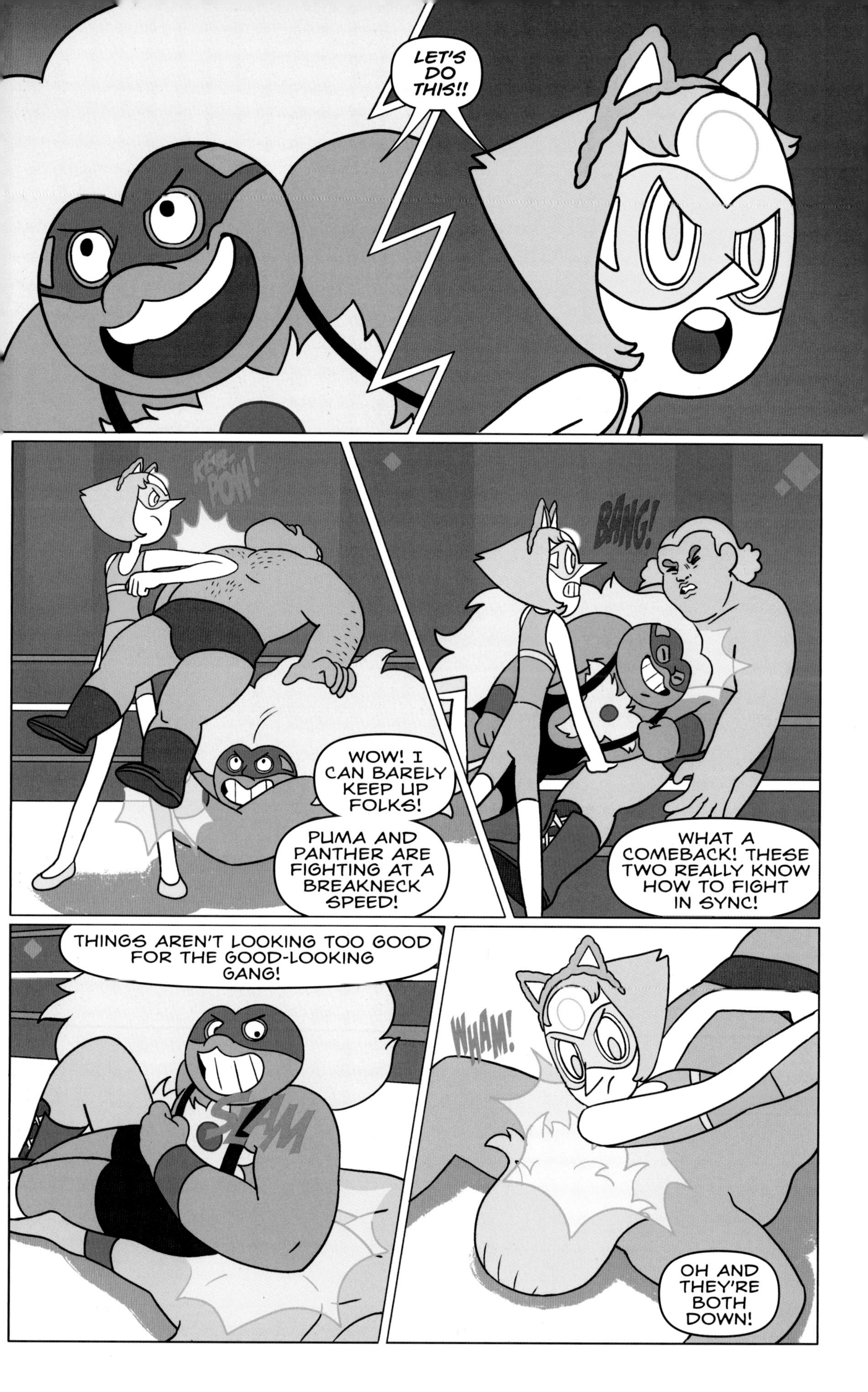
LET'S DO THIS!!
K-FA-POW!
WOW! I CAN BARELY KEEP UP FOLKS!
PUMA AND PANTHER ARE FIGHTING AT A BREAKNECK SPEED!
BANG!
WHAT A COMEBACK! THESE TWO REALLY KNOW HOW TO FIGHT IN SYNC!
THINGS AREN'T LOOKING TOO GOOD FOR THE GOOD-LOOKING GANG!
SLAM
WHAM!
OH AND THEY'RE BOTH DOWN!

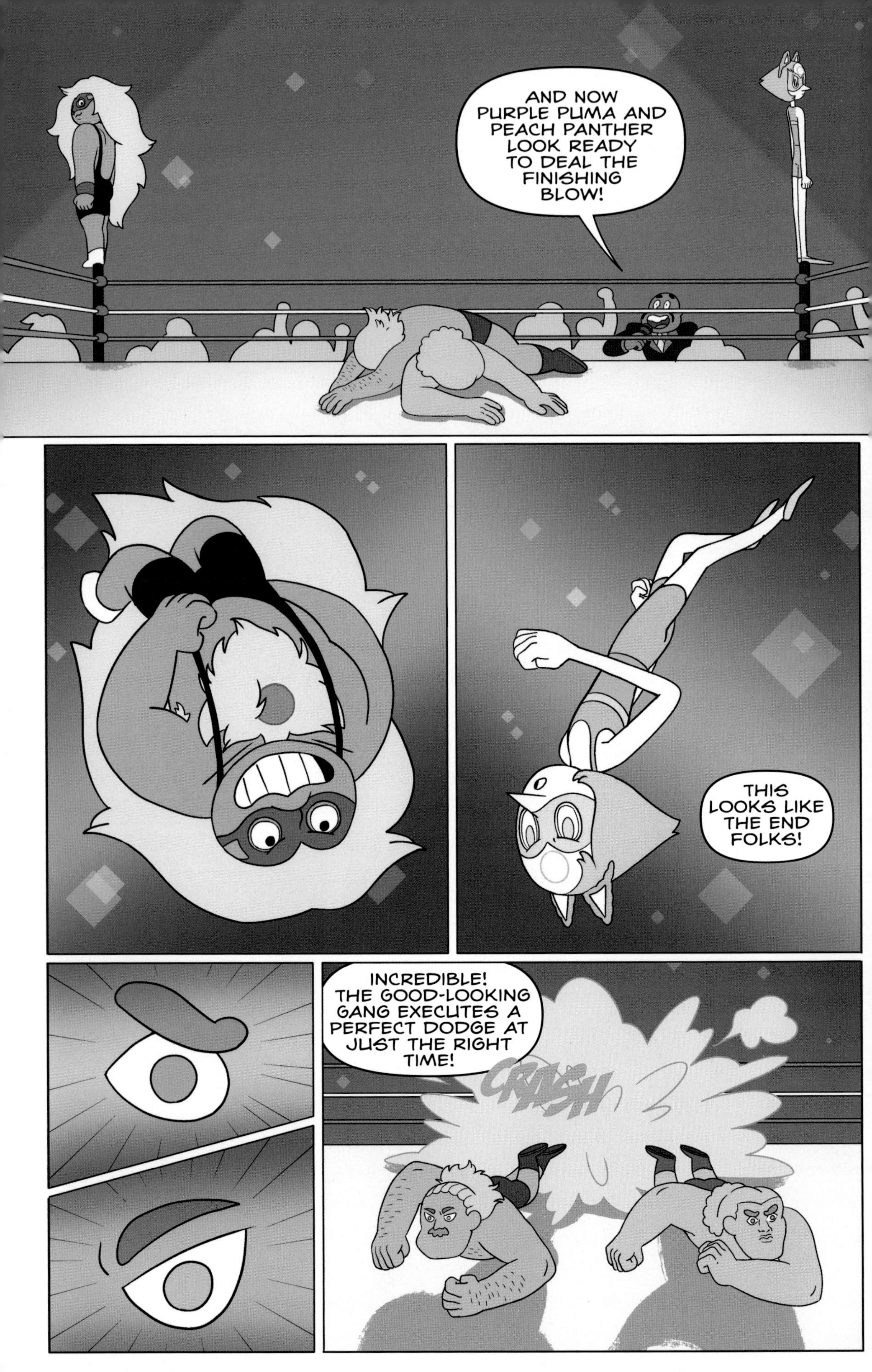
AND NOW PURPLE PUMA AND PEACH PANTHER LOOK READY TO DEAL THE FINISHING BLOW!
THIS LOOKS LIKE THE END FOLKS!
INCREDIBLE! THE GOOD-LOOKING GANG EXECUTES A PERFECT DODGE AT JUST THE RIGHT TIME!
CRASH

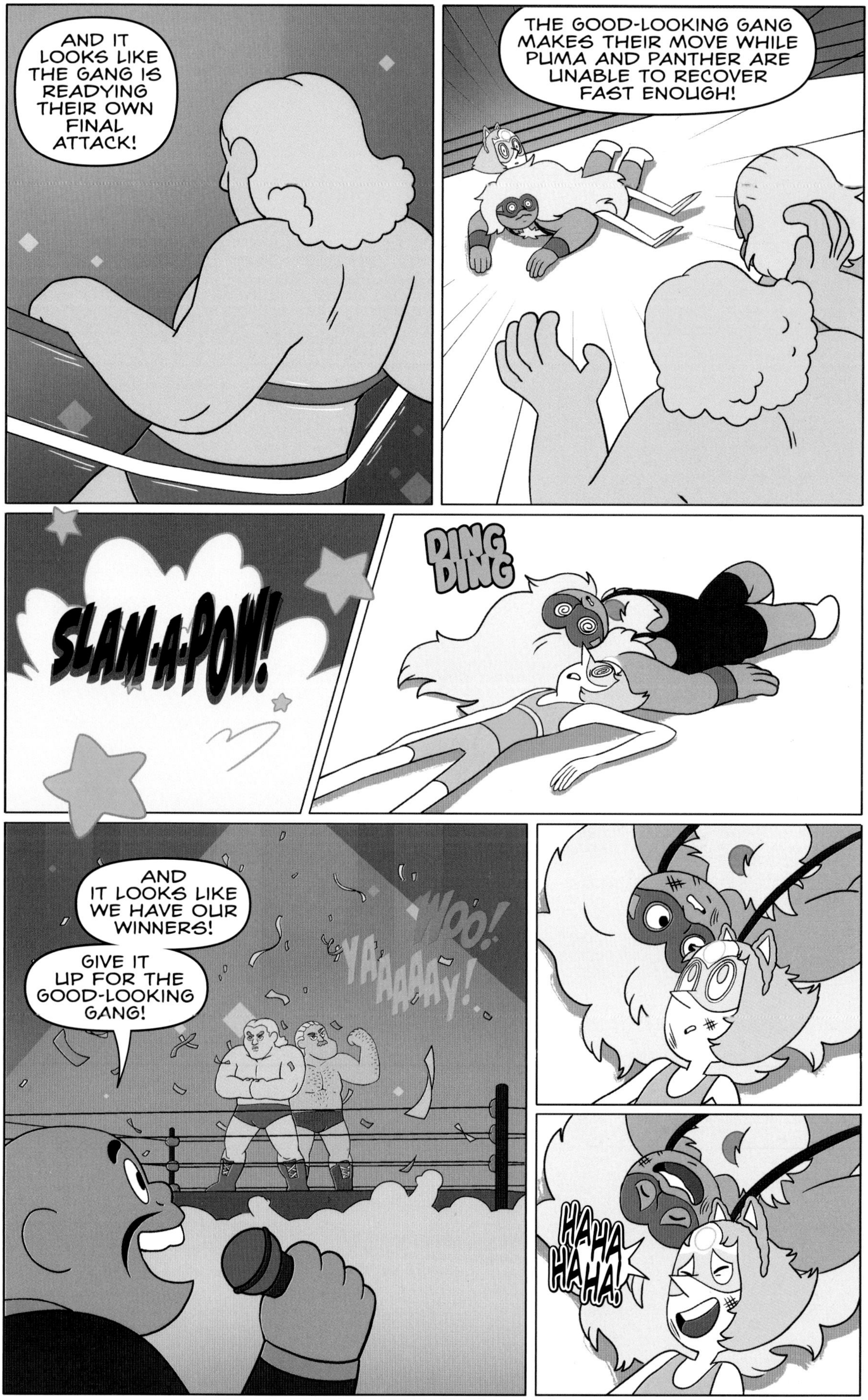
AND IT LOOKS LIKE THE GANG IS READYING THEIR OWN FINAL ATTACK!
THE GOOD-LOOKING GANG MAKES THEIR MOVE WHILE PUMA AND PANTHER ARE UNABLE TO RECOVER FAST ENOUGH!
SLAM-A-POW!
DING DING
AND IT LOOKS LIKE WE HAVE OUR WINNERS!
GIVE IT UP FOR THE GOOD-LOOKING GANG!
WOO!
YAAAAAY!
HAHA HAHA!

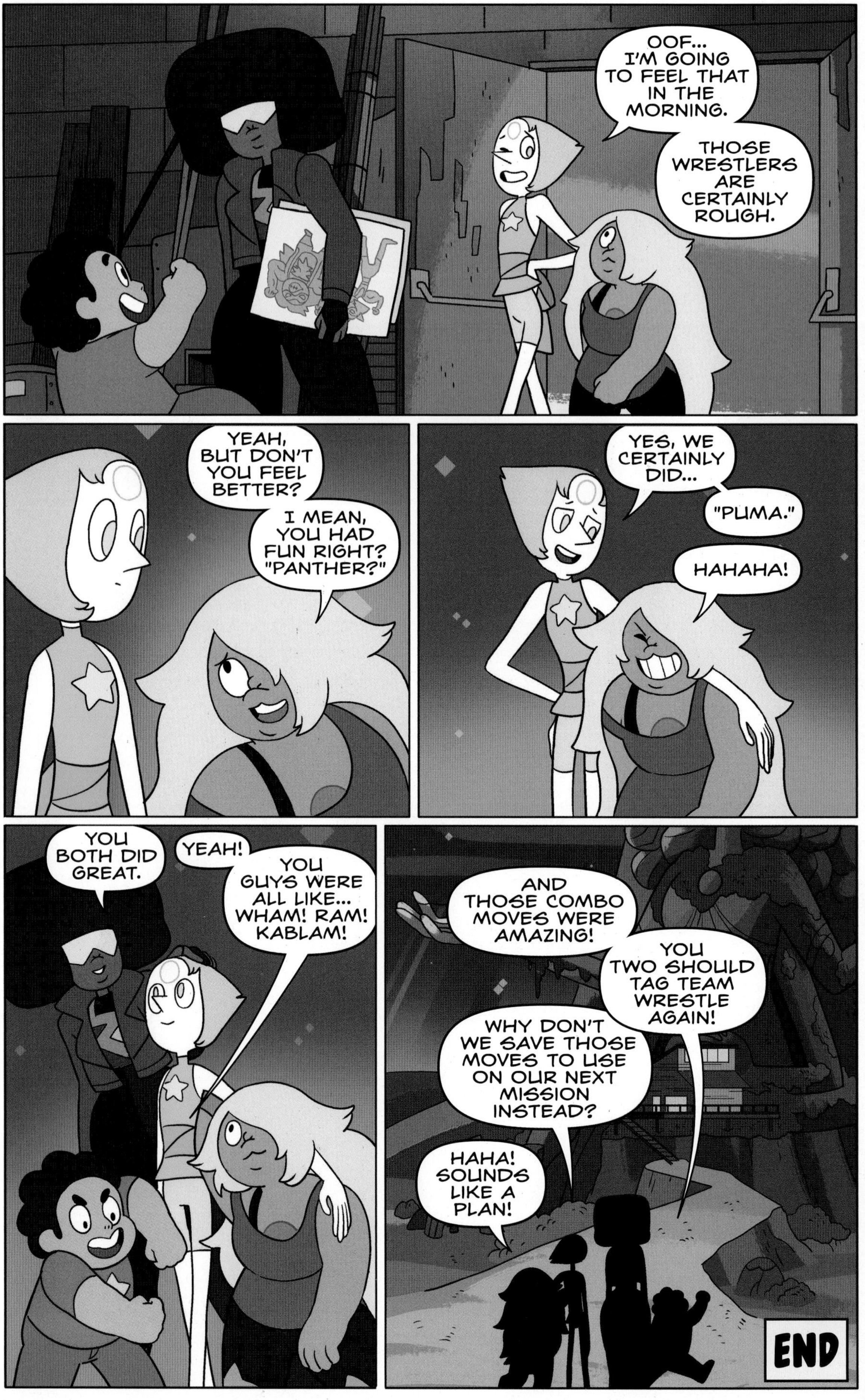
OOF... I'M GOING TO FEEL THAT IN THE MORNING.
THOSE WRESTLERS ARE CERTAINLY ROUGH.
YEAH, BUT DON'T YOU FEEL BETTER?
I MEAN, YOU HAD FUN RIGHT? "PANTHER?"
YES, WE CERTAINLY DID...
"PUMA."
HAHAHA!
YOU BOTH DID GREAT.
YEAH!
YOU GUYS WERE ALL LIKE... WHAM! RAM! KABLAM!
AND THOSE COMBO MOVES WERE AMAZING!
YOU TWO SHOULD TAG TEAM WRESTLE AGAIN!
WHY DON'T WE SAVE THOSE MOVES TO USE ON OUR NEXT MISSION INSTEAD?
HAHA! SOUNDS LIKE A PLAN!
END

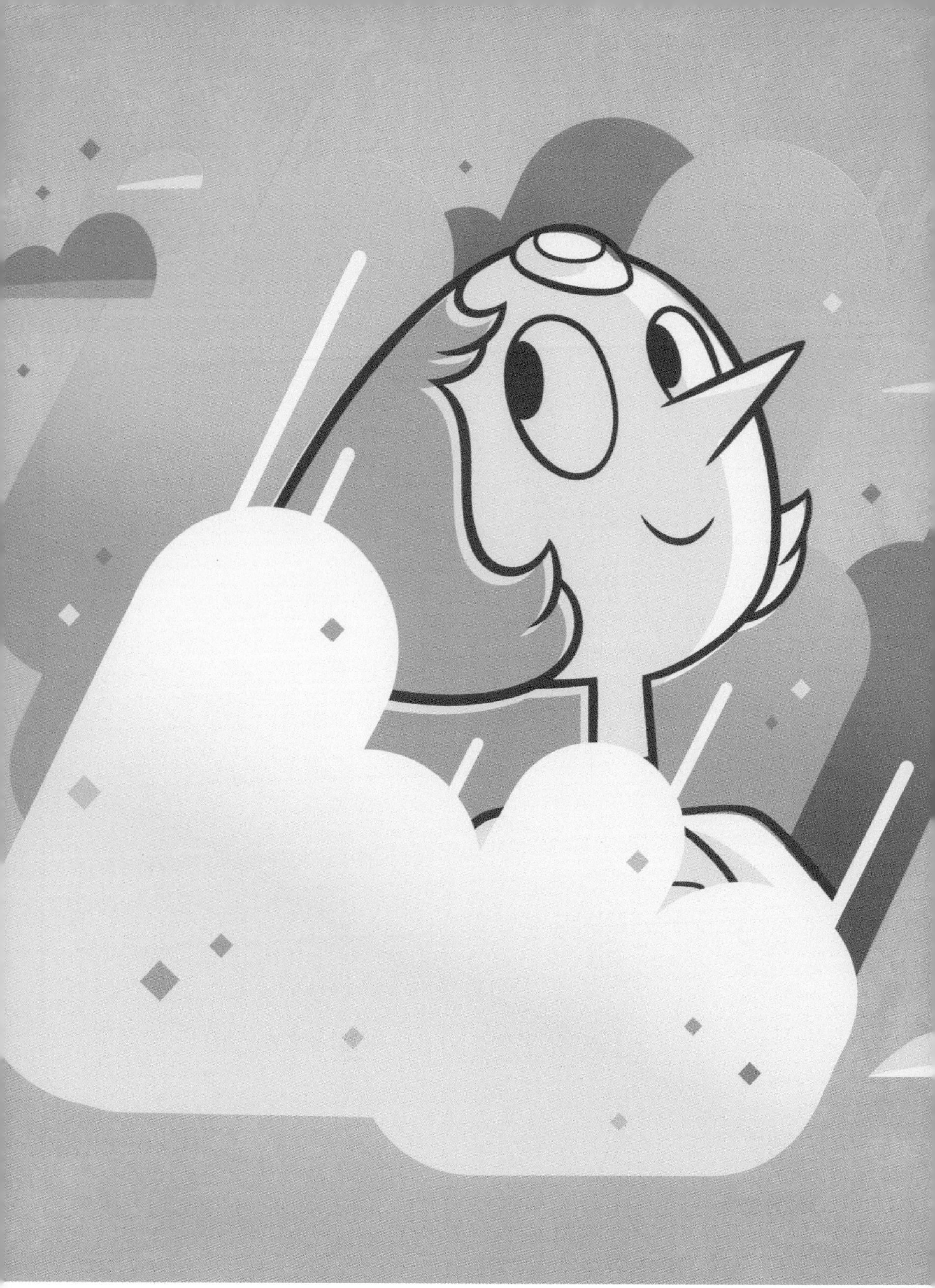

# CHAPTER SEVEN

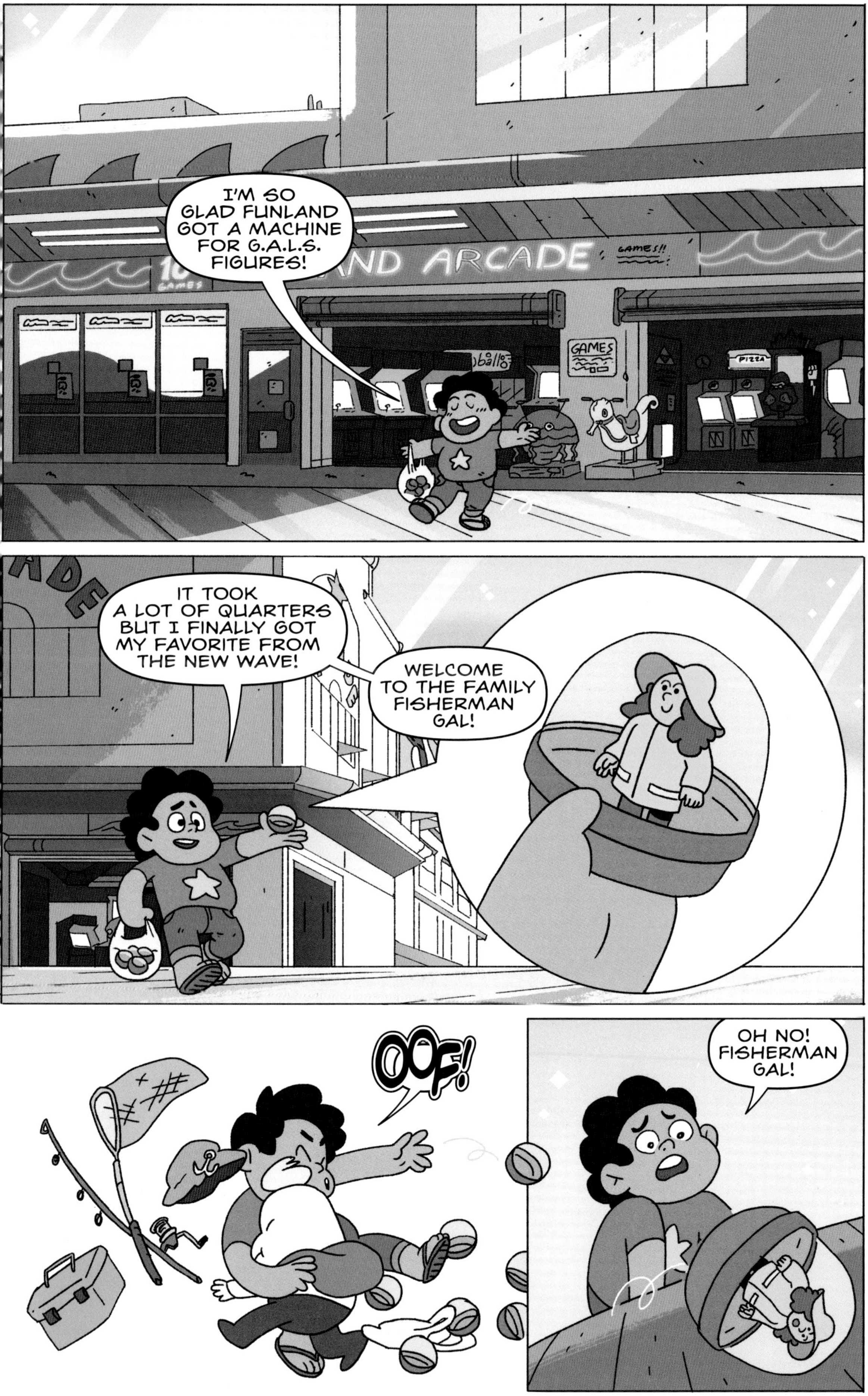
I'M SO GLAD FUNLAND GOT A MACHINE FOR G.A.L.S. FIGURES!
GAMES
PIZZA
IT TOOK A LOT OF QUARTERS BUT I FINALLY GOT MY FAVORITE FROM THE NEW WAVE!
WELCOME TO THE FAMILY FISHERMAN GAL!
OOF!
OH NO! FISHERMAN GAL!

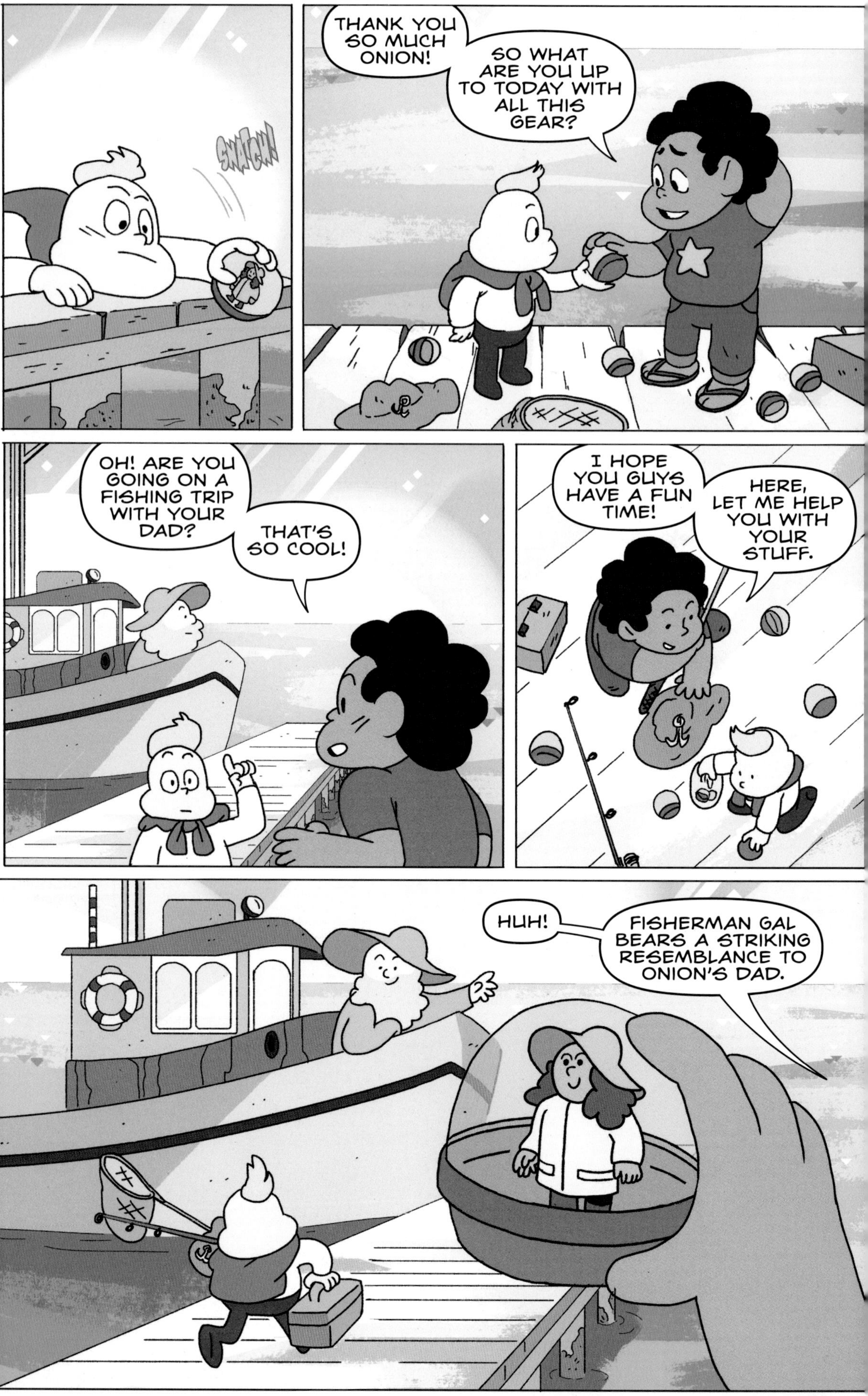
SNATCH!
THANK YOU SO MUCH ONION!
SO WHAT ARE YOU UP TO TODAY WITH ALL THIS GEAR?
OH! ARE YOU GOING ON A FISHING TRIP WITH YOUR DAD?
THAT'S SO COOL!
I HOPE YOU GUYS HAVE A FUN TIME!
HERE, LET ME HELP YOU WITH YOUR STUFF.
HUH!
FISHERMAN GAL BEARS A STRIKING RESEMBLANCE TO ONION'S DAD.

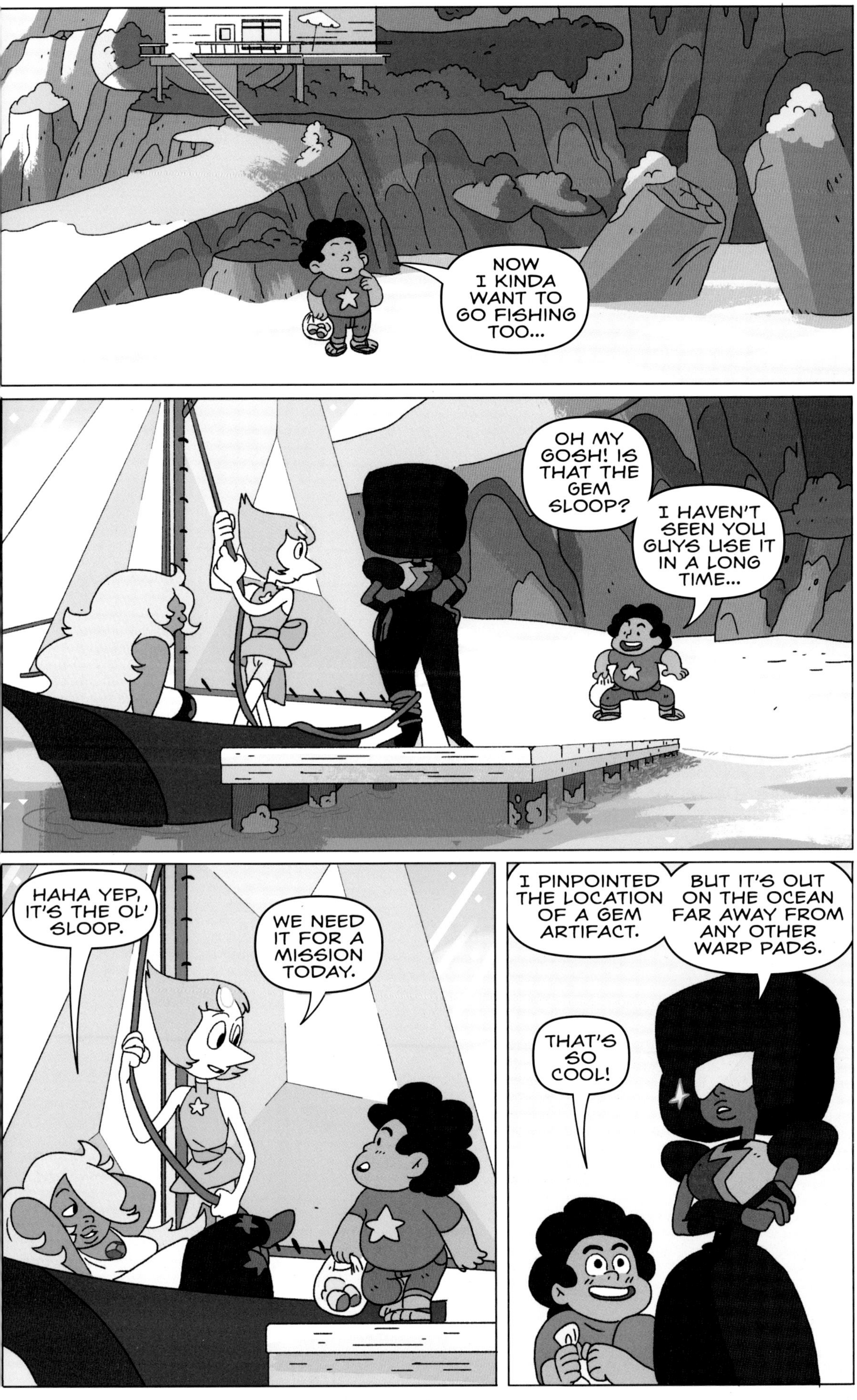
NOW I KINDA WANT TO GO FISHING TOO...
OH MY GOSH! IS THAT THE GEM SLOOP?
I HAVEN'T SEEN YOU GUYS USE IT IN A LONG TIME...
HAHA YEP, IT'S THE OL' SLOOP.
WE NEED IT FOR A MISSION TODAY.
I PINPOINTED THE LOCATION OF A GEM ARTIFACT.
BUT IT'S OUT ON THE OCEAN FAR AWAY FROM ANY OTHER WARP PADS.
THAT'S SO COOL!

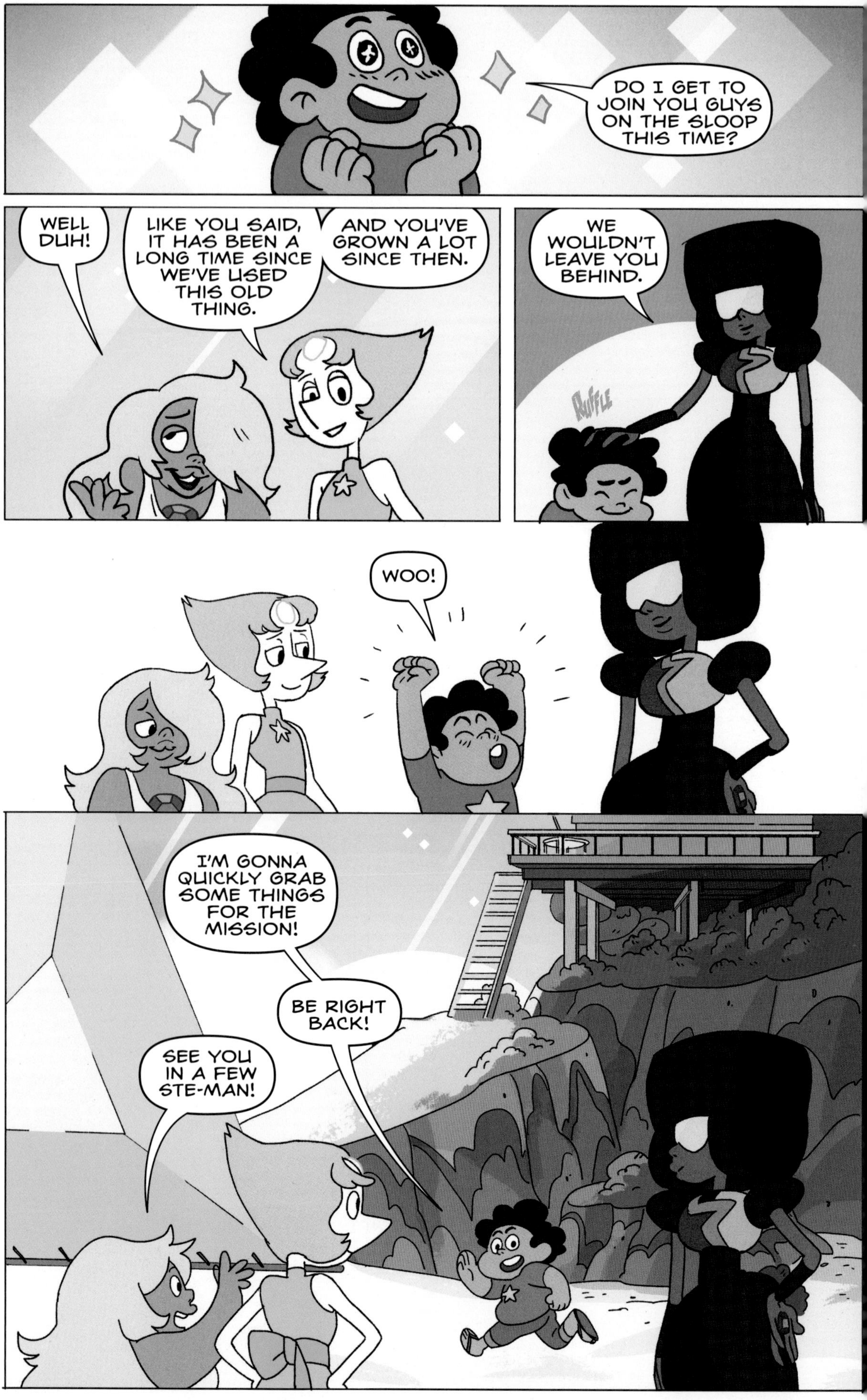
DO I GET TO JOIN YOU GUYS ON THE SLOOP THIS TIME?
WELL DUH!
LIKE YOU SAID, IT HAS BEEN A LONG TIME SINCE WE'VE USED THIS OLD THING.
AND YOU'VE GROWN A LOT SINCE THEN.
WE WOULDN'T LEAVE YOU BEHIND.
RUFFLE
WOO!
I'M GONNA QUICKLY GRAB SOME THINGS FOR THE MISSION!
BE RIGHT BACK!
SEE YOU IN A FEW STE-MAN!

HOW MUCH LONGER UNTIL WE GET THERE?

MMM... IT'S STILL GOING TO BE A WHILE.

WELL IN THAT CASE, I'M GONNA DO A LITTLE FISHING!

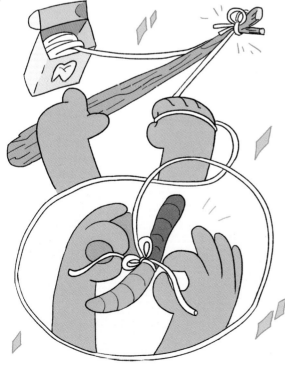

ZOOP!

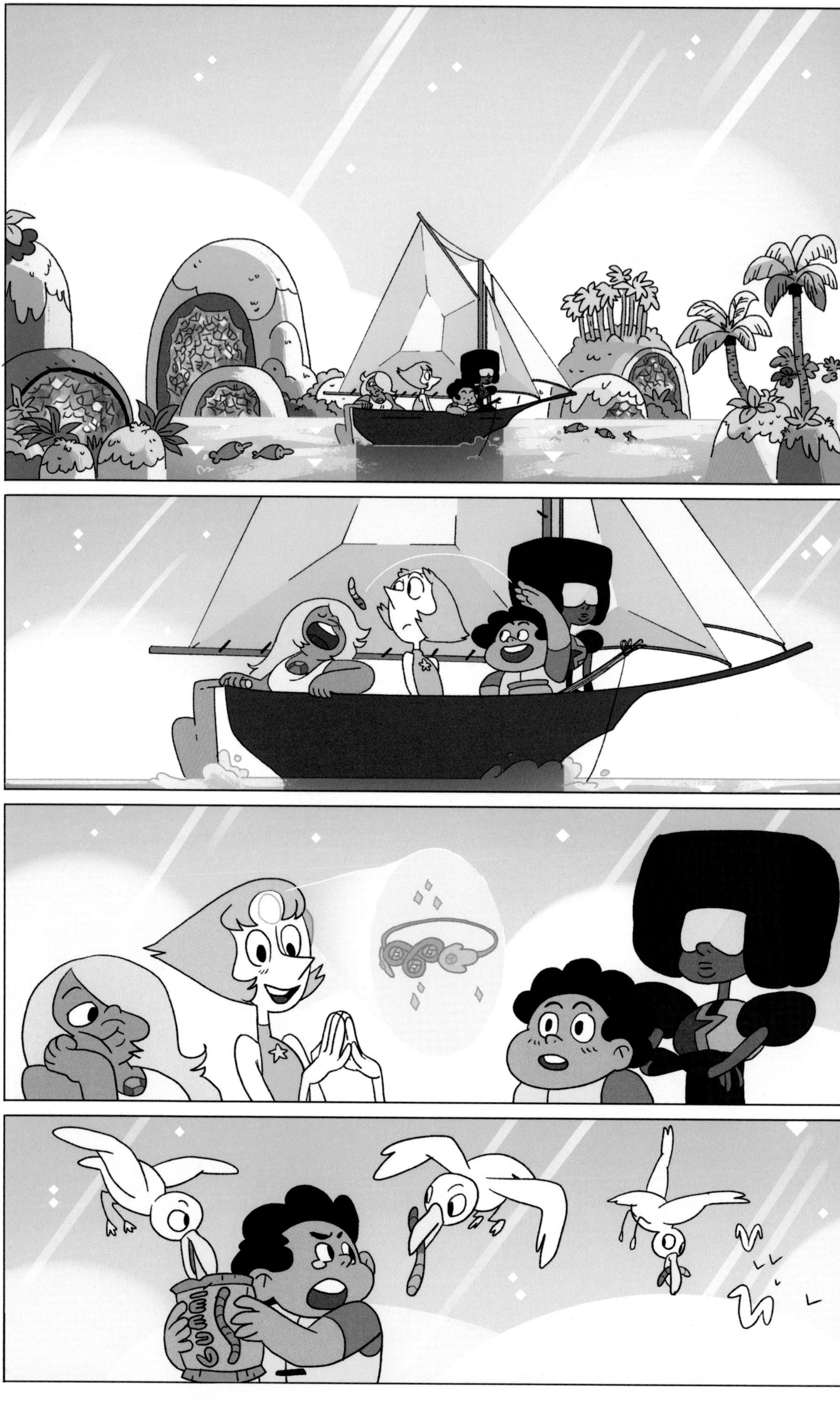

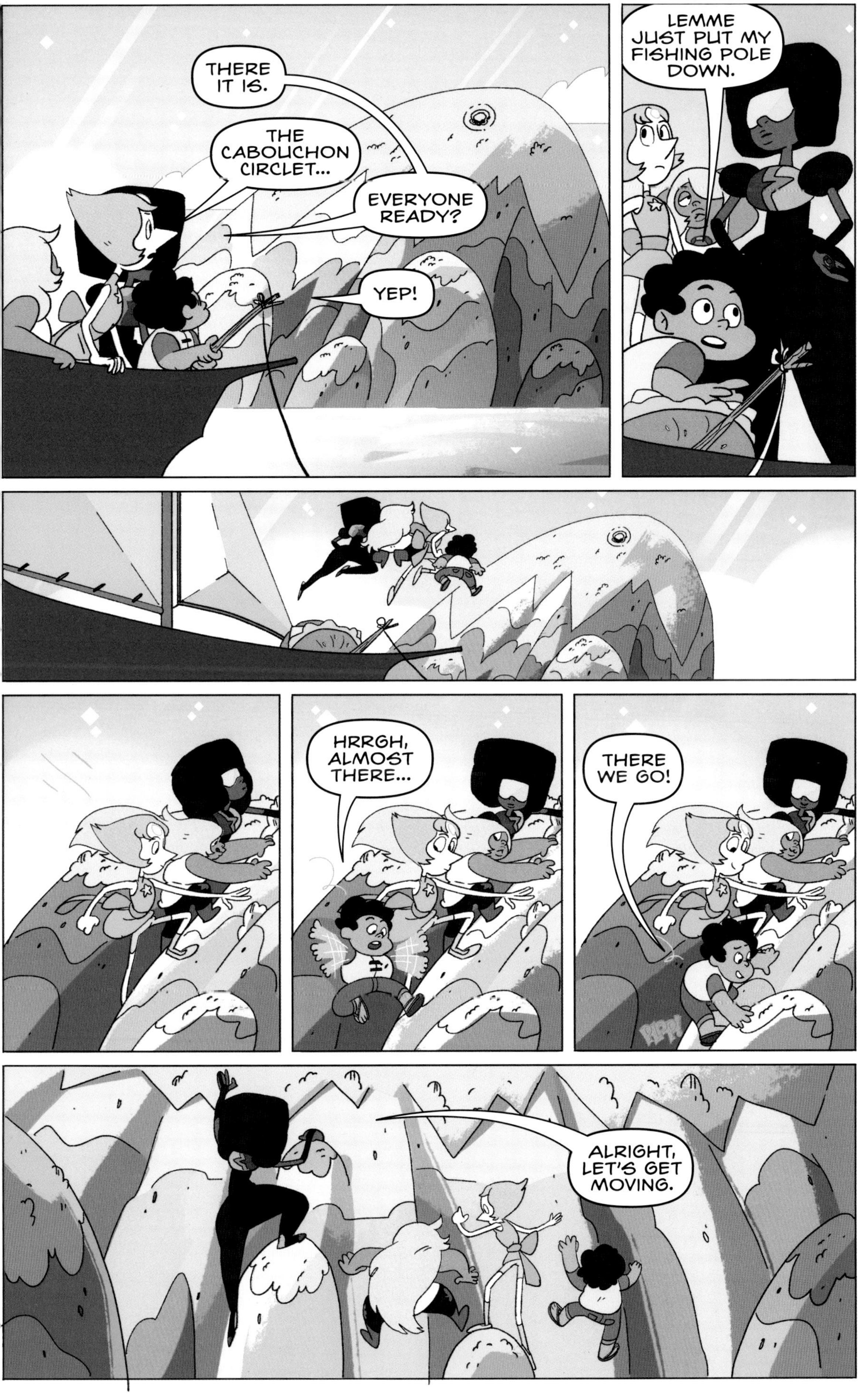
THERE IT IS.
THE CABOUCHON CIRCLET...
EVERYONE READY?
YEP!
LEMME JUST PUT MY FISHING POLE DOWN.
HRRGH, ALMOST THERE...
THERE WE GO!
ALRIGHT, LET'S GET MOVING.

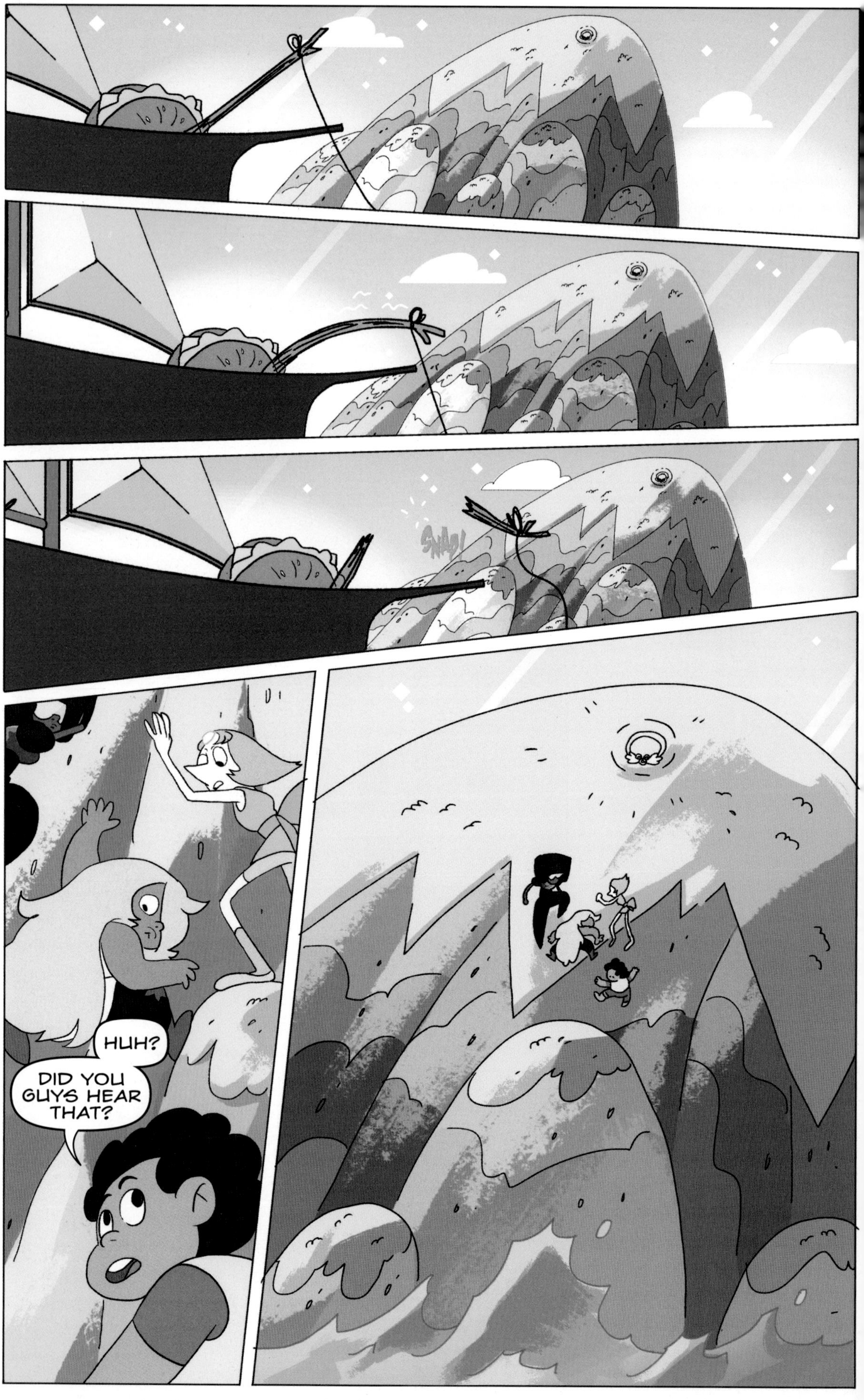
SNAP!
HUH?
DID YOU GUYS HEAR THAT?

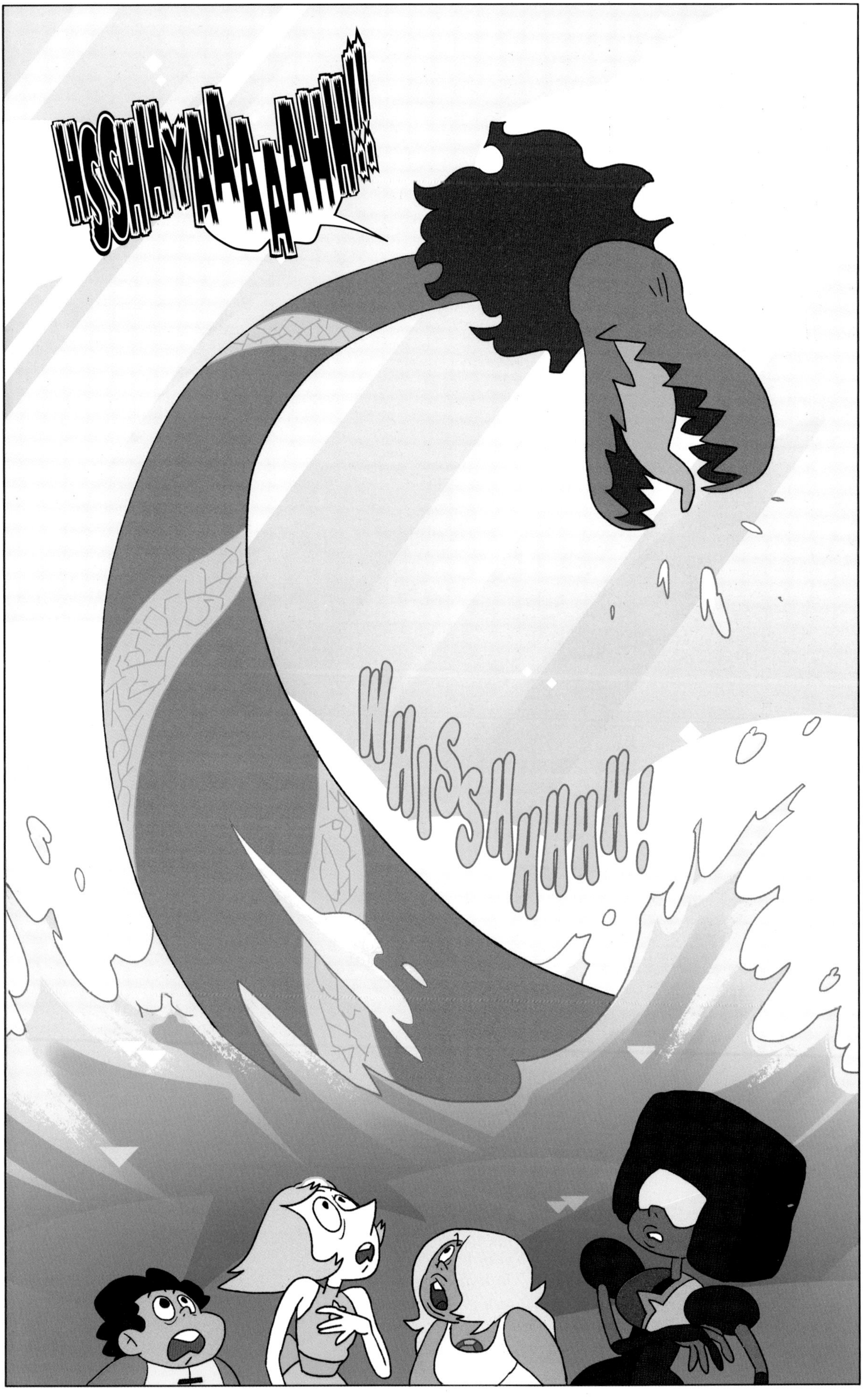
HSSHHYAAAAAHH!!
WHISSHHHHH!

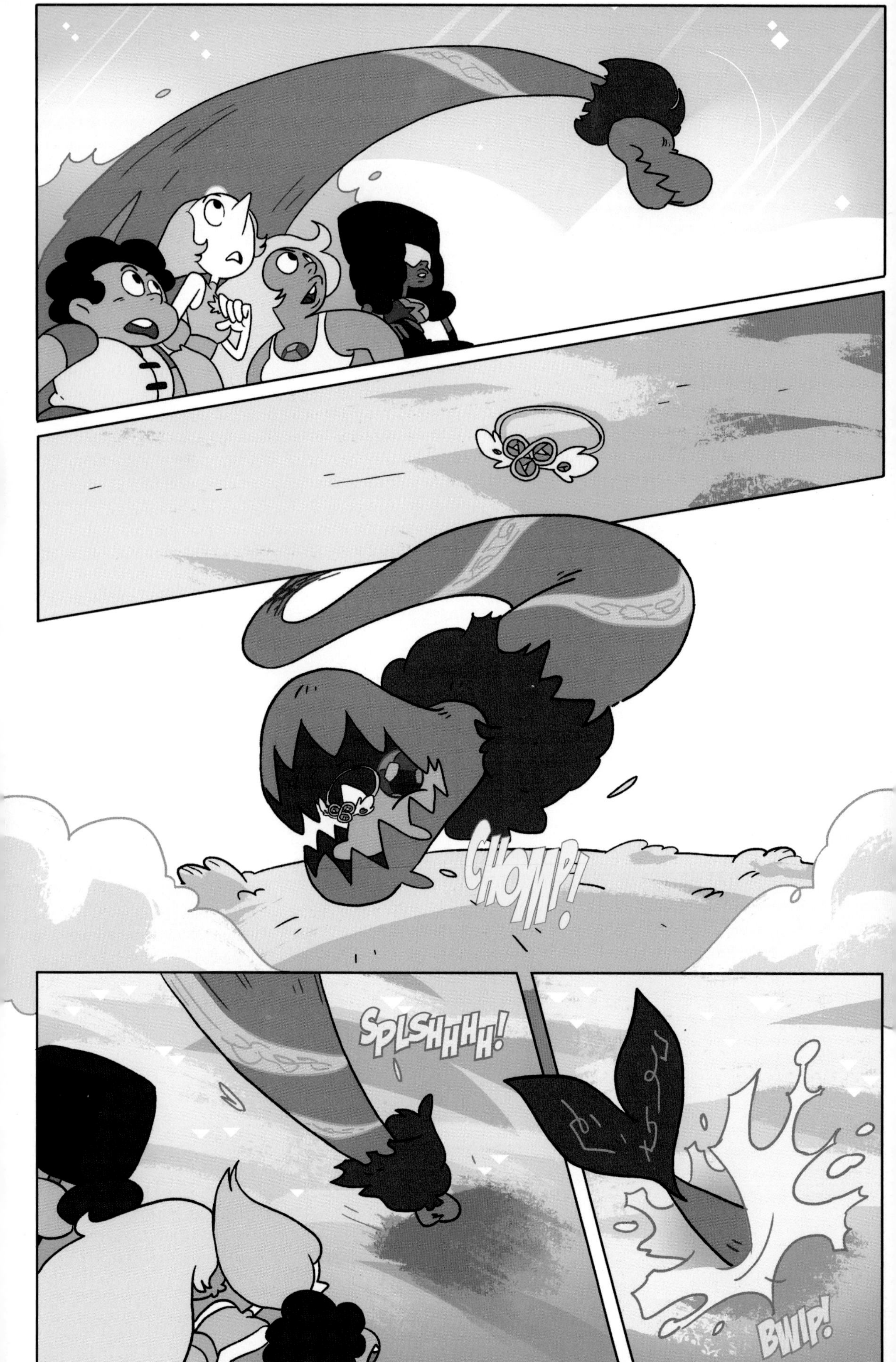
CHOMP!
SPLSHHHH!
BWIP!

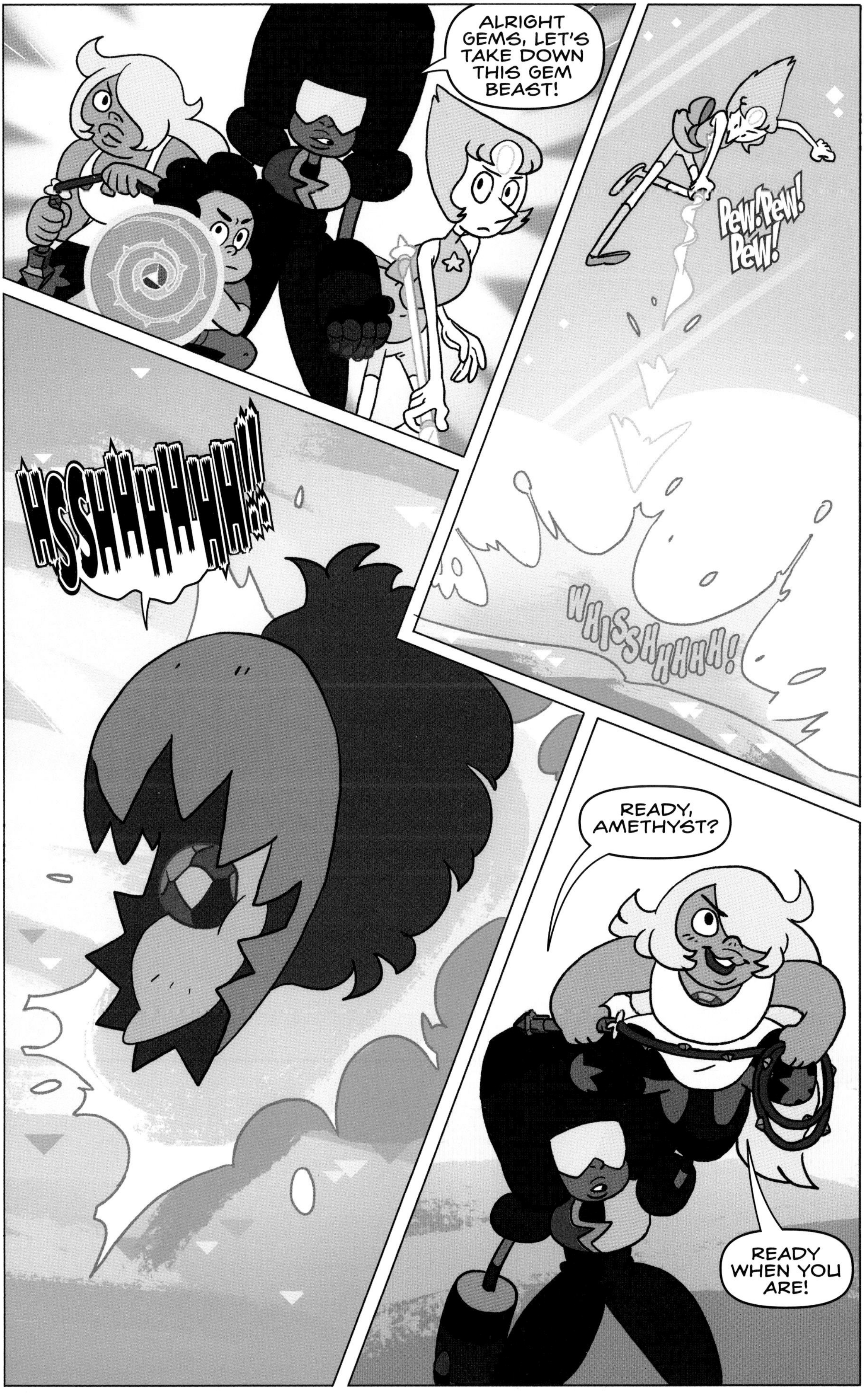
ALRIGHT GEMS, LET'S TAKE DOWN THIS GEM BEAST!
PEW! PEW! PEW!
HSSHHHHHHHH!!
WHISSHHHHH!
READY, AMETHYST?
READY WHEN YOU ARE!

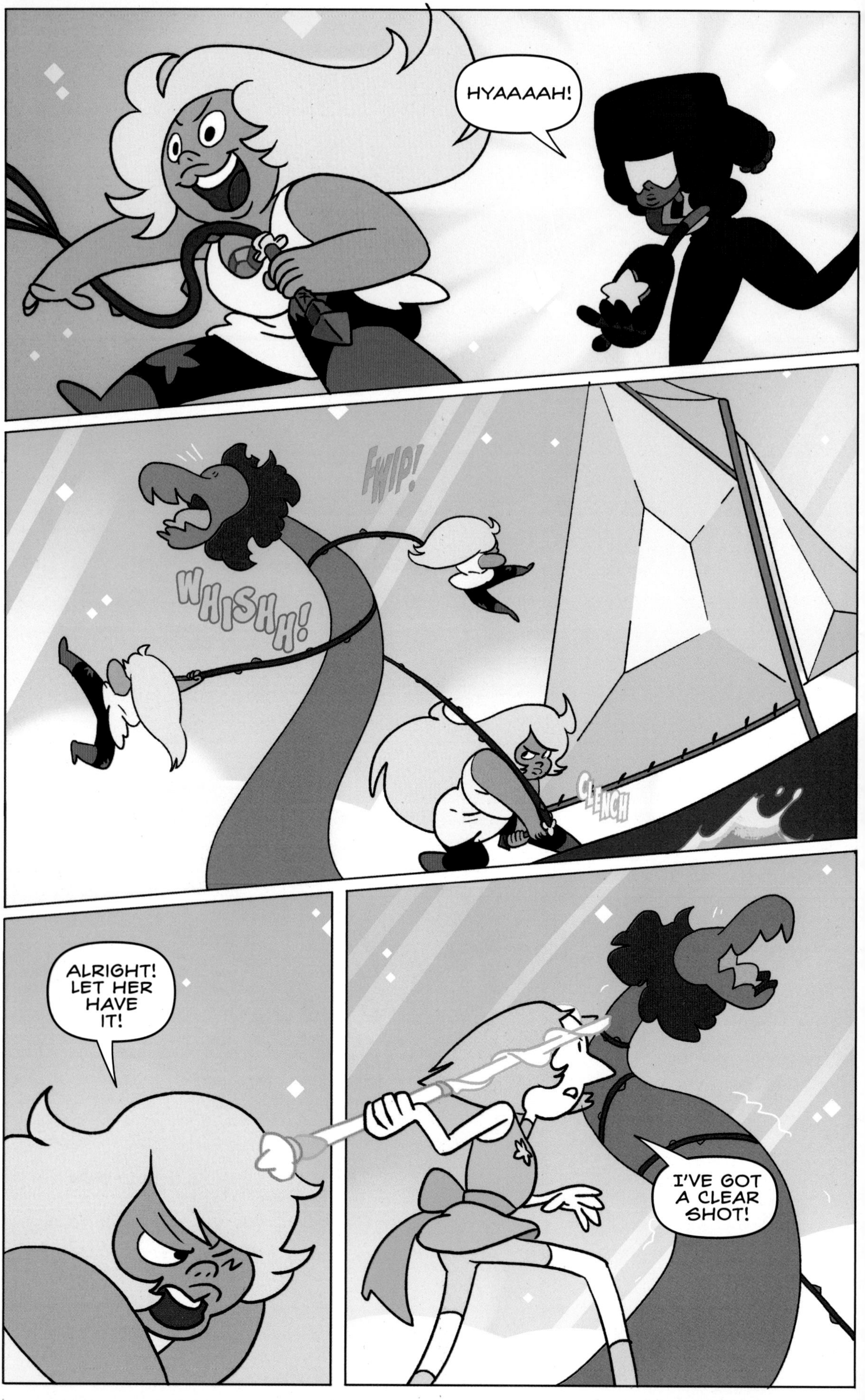
HYAAAAH!
FWIP!
WHISHH!
CLENCH
ALRIGHT! LET HER HAVE IT!
I'VE GOT A CLEAR SHOT!

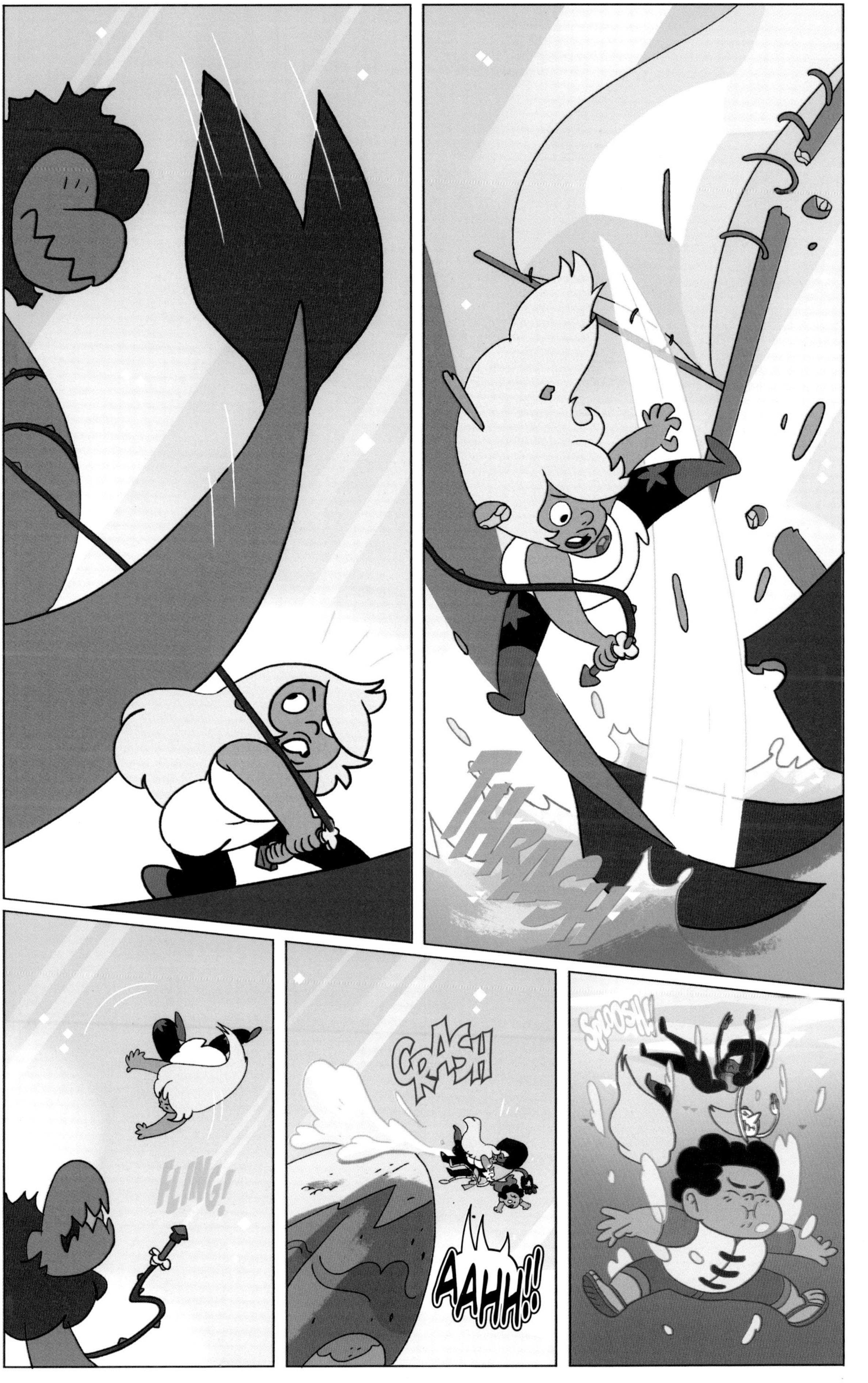
THRASH
FLING!
CRASH
AAHH!!
SPLOOSH!

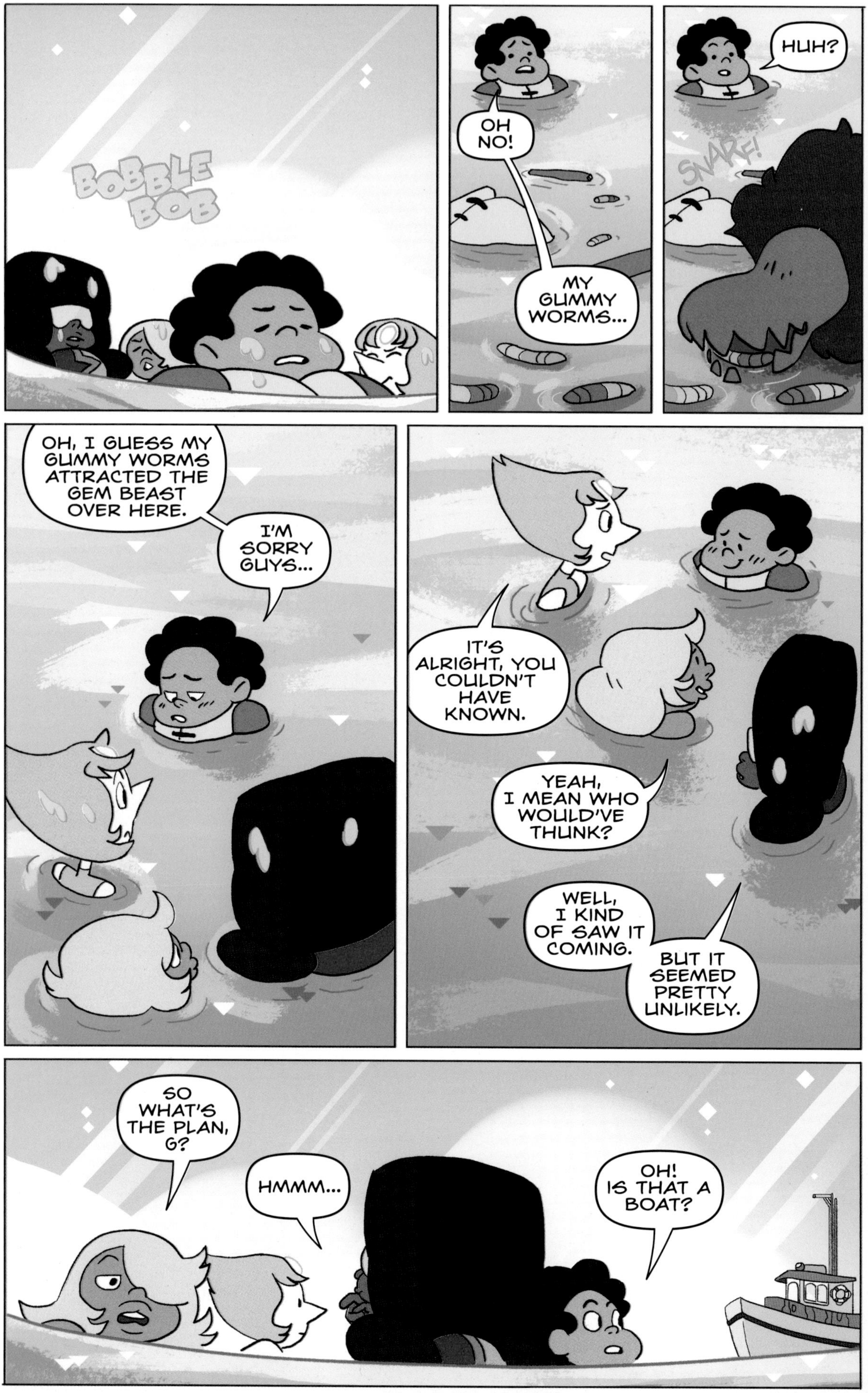
BOBBLE BOB
OH NO!
MY GLUMMY WORMS...
HUH?
SNARF!
OH, I GUESS MY GLUMMY WORMS ATTRACTED THE GEM BEAST OVER HERE.
I'M SORRY GUYS...
IT'S ALRIGHT, YOU COULDN'T HAVE KNOWN.
YEAH, I MEAN WHO WOULD'VE THUNK?
WELL, I KIND OF SAW IT COMING.
BUT IT SEEMED PRETTY UNLIKELY.
SO WHAT'S THE PLAN, G?
HMMM...
OH! IS THAT A BOAT?

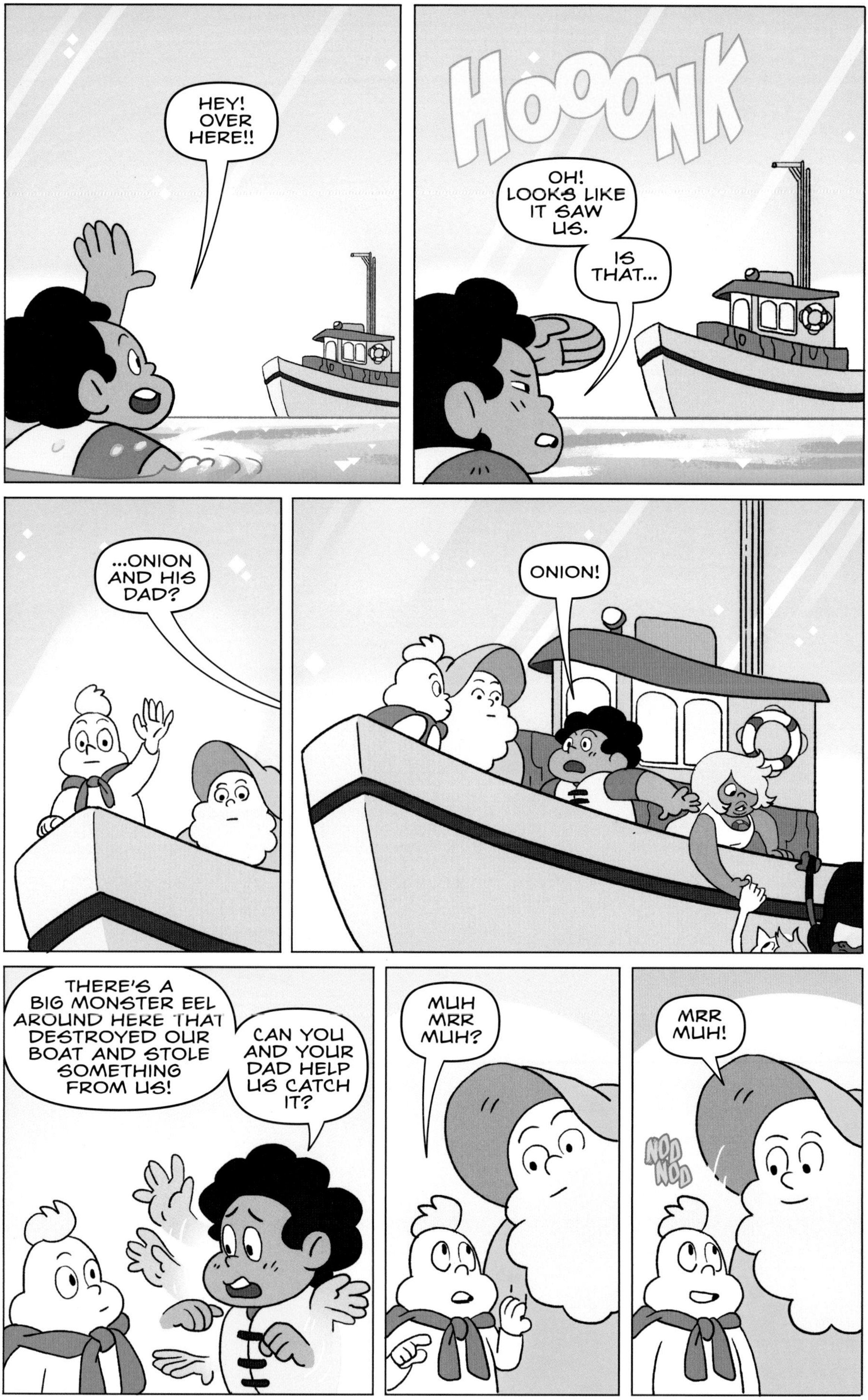

HEY! OVER HERE!!
HOOONK
OH! LOOKS LIKE IT SAW US.
IS THAT...
...ONION AND HIS DAD?
ONION!
THERE'S A BIG MONSTER EEL AROUND HERE THAT DESTROYED OUR BOAT AND STOLE SOMETHING FROM US!
CAN YOU AND YOUR DAD HELP US CATCH IT?
MUH MRR MUH?
MRR MUH!
NOD NOD

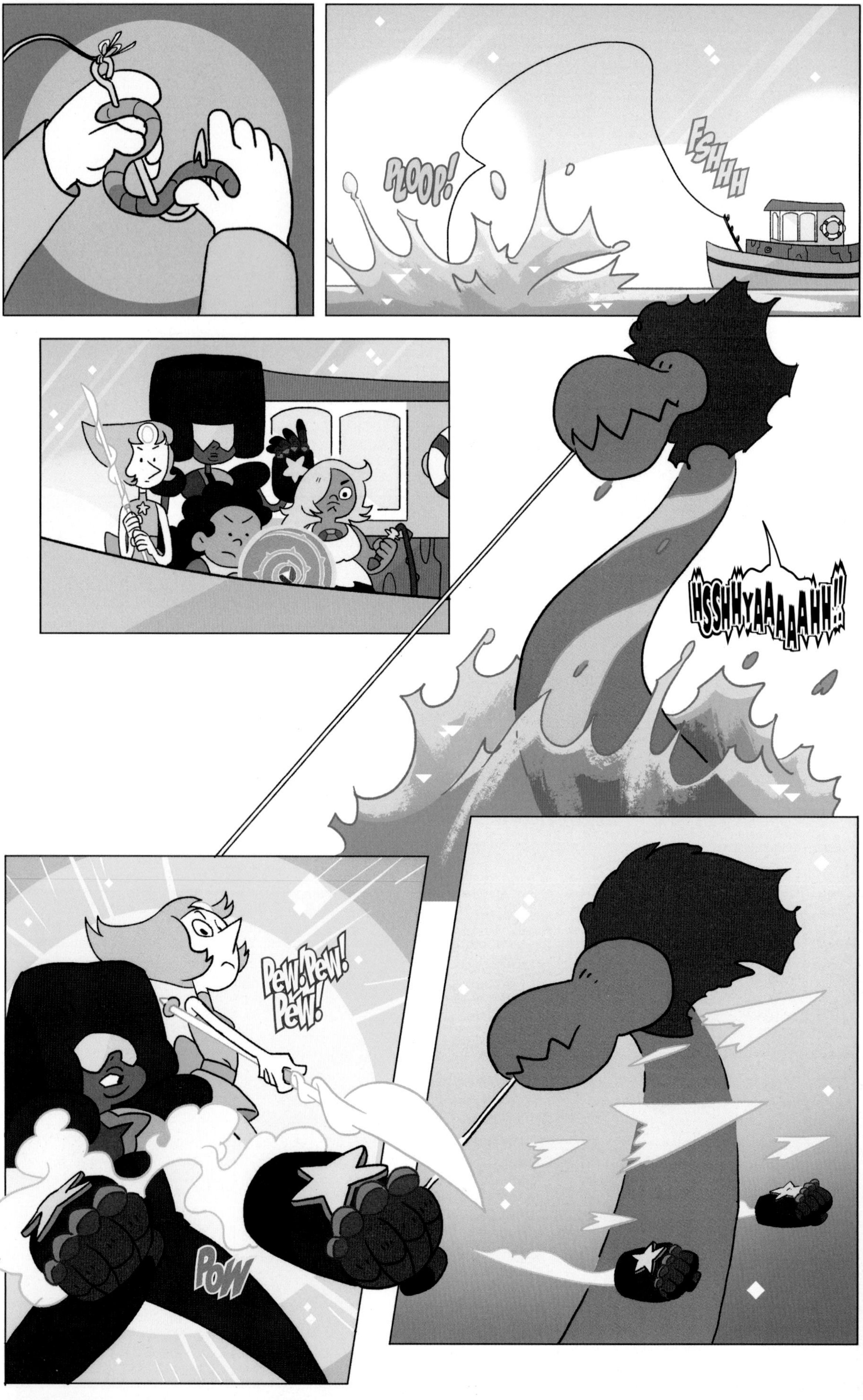
PLOOP!
FSHHH
HSSHHYAAAAAHH!!
PEW! PEW!
PEW!
POW

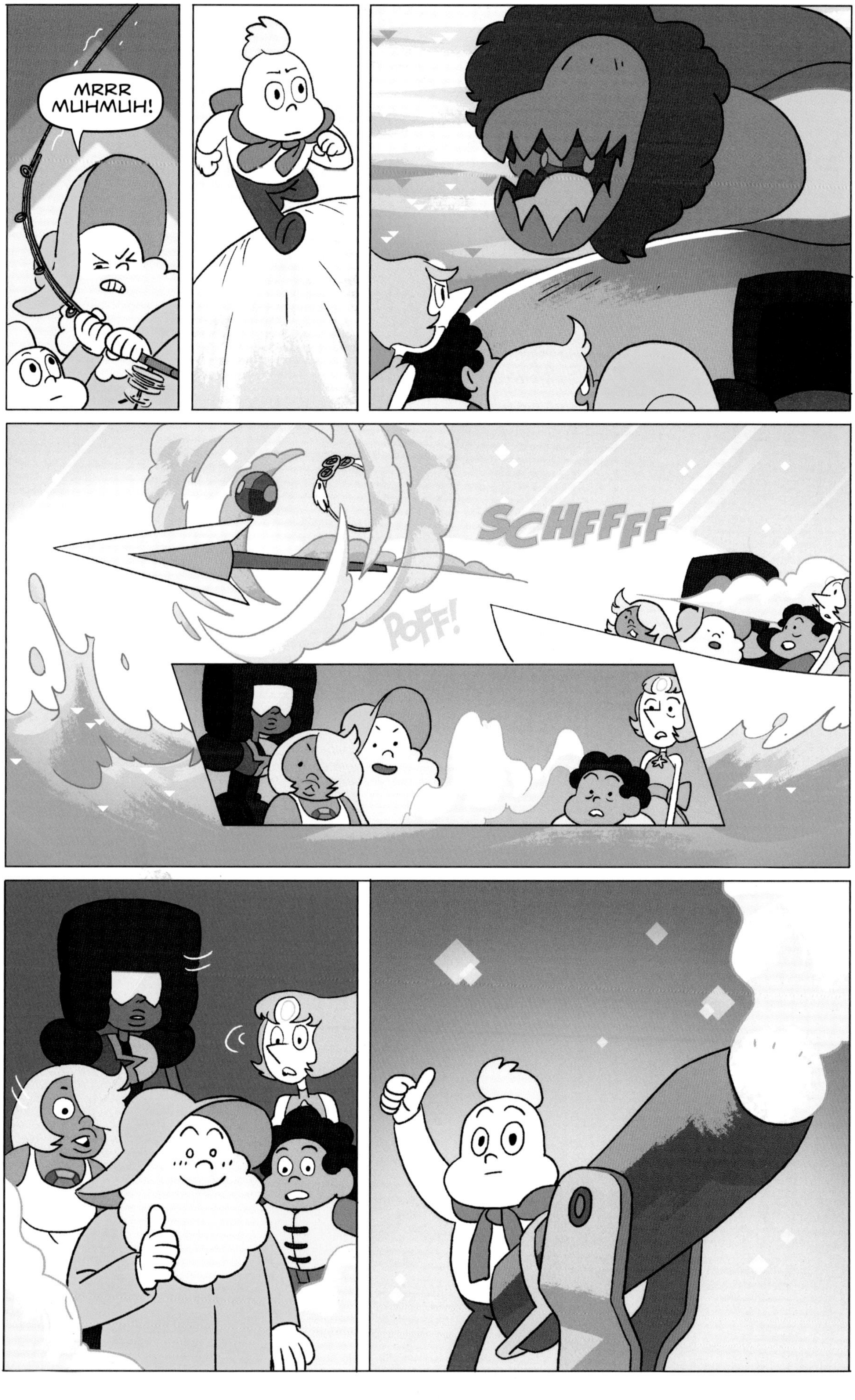
MRRR MUHMUH!
SCHFFFFF
POFF!

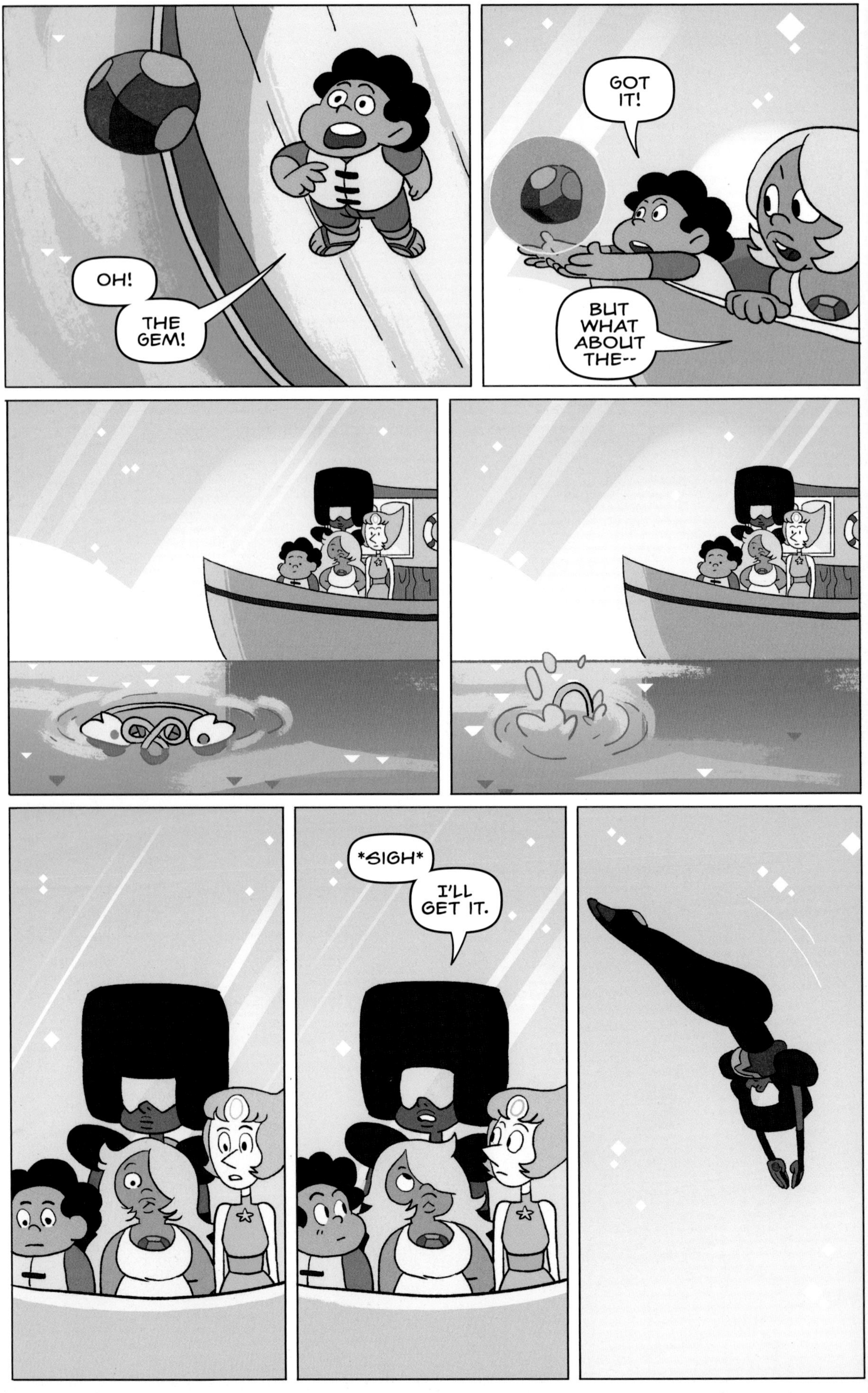
OH!
THE GEM!
GOT IT!
BUT WHAT ABOUT THE--
*SIGH*
I'LL GET IT.

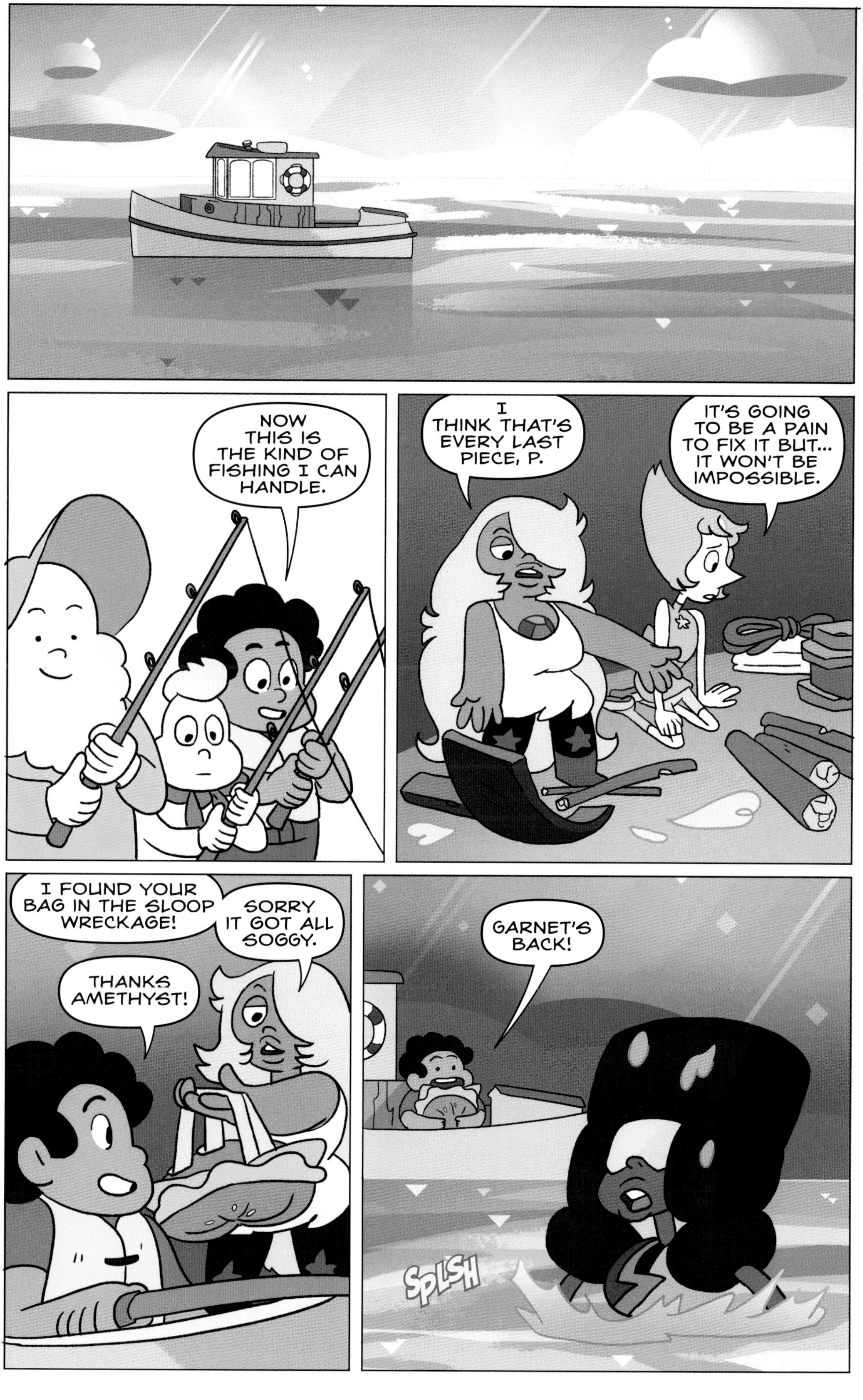
NOW THIS IS THE KIND OF FISHING I CAN HANDLE.
I THINK THAT'S EVERY LAST PIECE, P.
IT'S GOING TO BE A PAIN TO FIX IT BUT... IT WON'T BE IMPOSSIBLE.
I FOUND YOUR BAG IN THE SLOOP WRECKAGE!
SORRY IT GOT ALL SOGGY.
THANKS AMETHYST!
GARNET'S BACK!
SPLSH

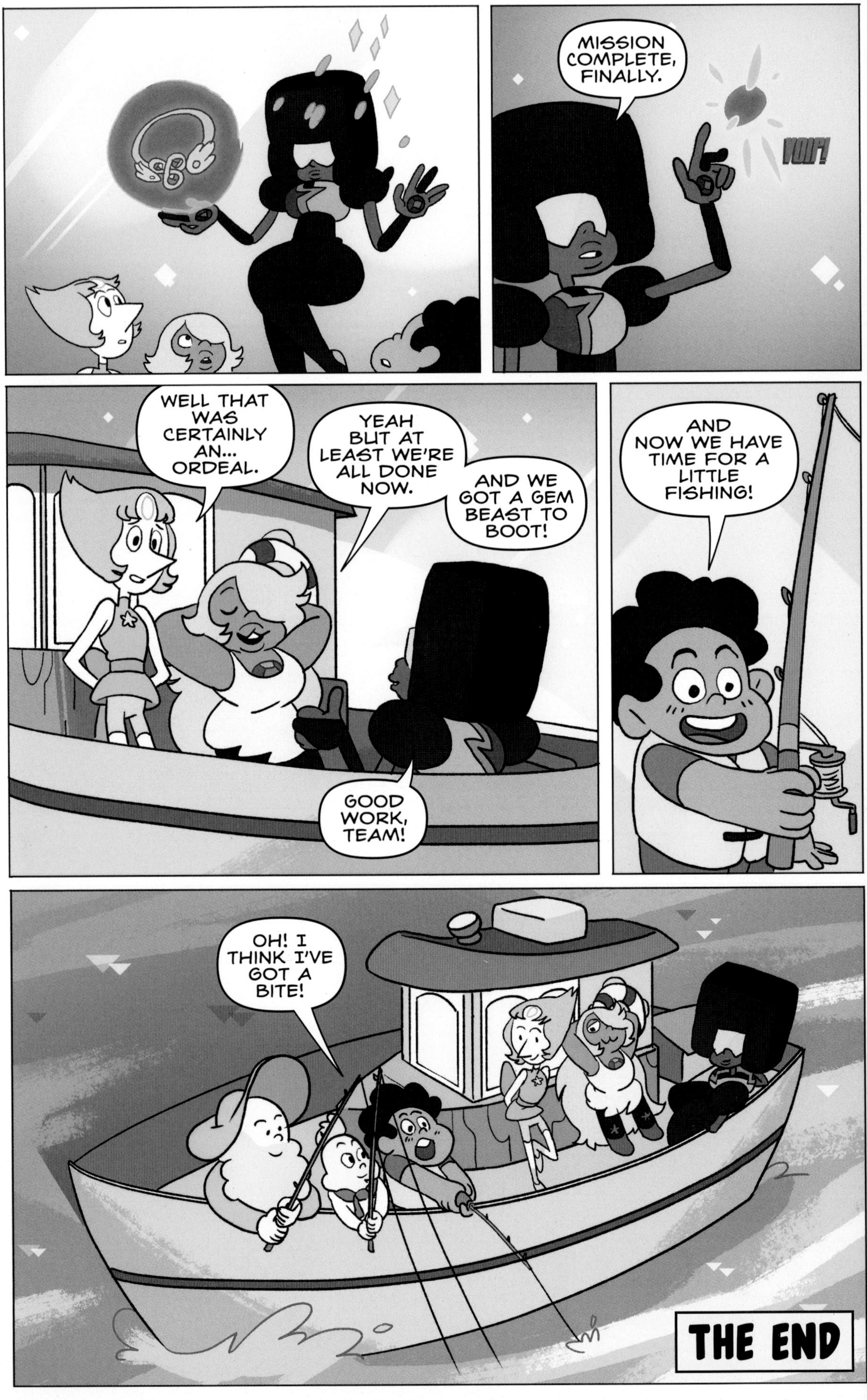
MISSION COMPLETE, FINALLY.
VWIP!
WELL THAT WAS CERTAINLY AN... ORDEAL.
YEAH BUT AT LEAST WE'RE ALL DONE NOW.
AND WE GOT A GEM BEAST TO BOOT!
GOOD WORK, TEAM!
AND NOW WE HAVE TIME FOR A LITTLE FISHING!
OH! I THINK I'VE GOT A BITE!
THE END

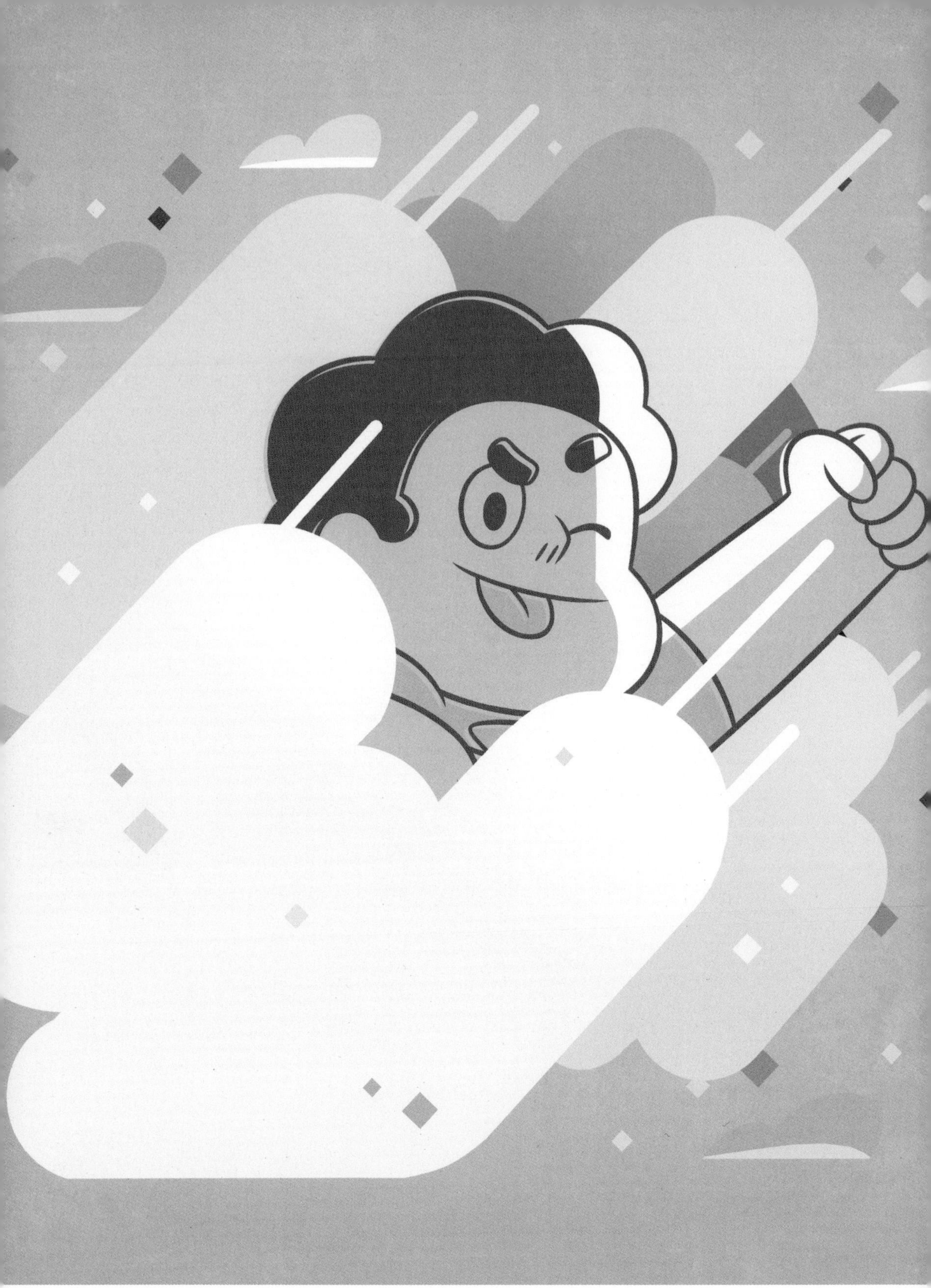

# CHAPTER EIGHT

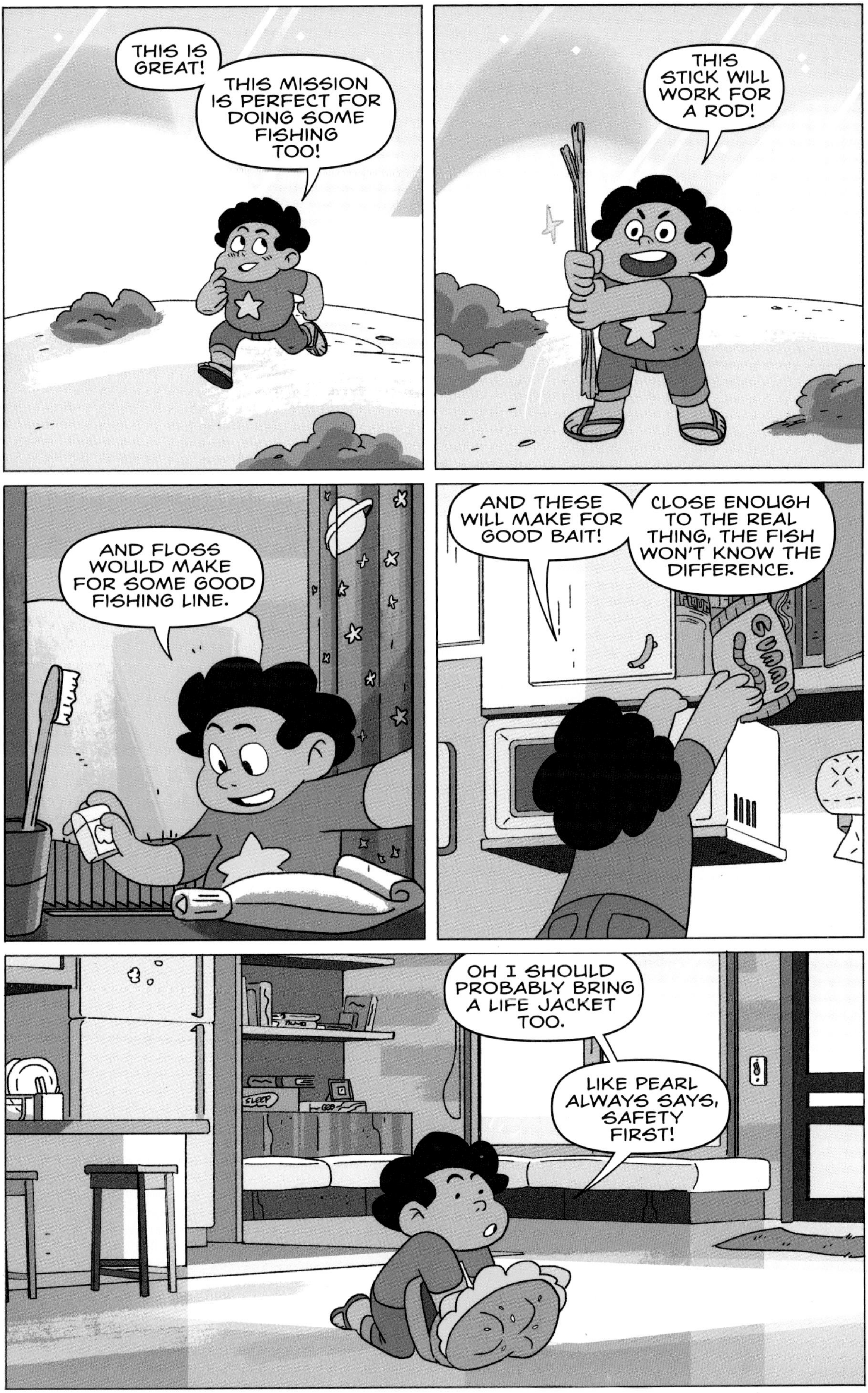
THIS IS GREAT!
THIS MISSION IS PERFECT FOR DOING SOME FISHING TOO!
THIS STICK WILL WORK FOR A ROD!
AND FLOSS WOULD MAKE FOR SOME GOOD FISHING LINE.
AND THESE WILL MAKE FOR GOOD BAIT!
CLOSE ENOUGH TO THE REAL THING, THE FISH WON'T KNOW THE DIFFERENCE.
GUMMI
OH I SHOULD PROBABLY BRING A LIFE JACKET TOO.
LIKE PEARL ALWAYS SAYS, SAFETY FIRST!

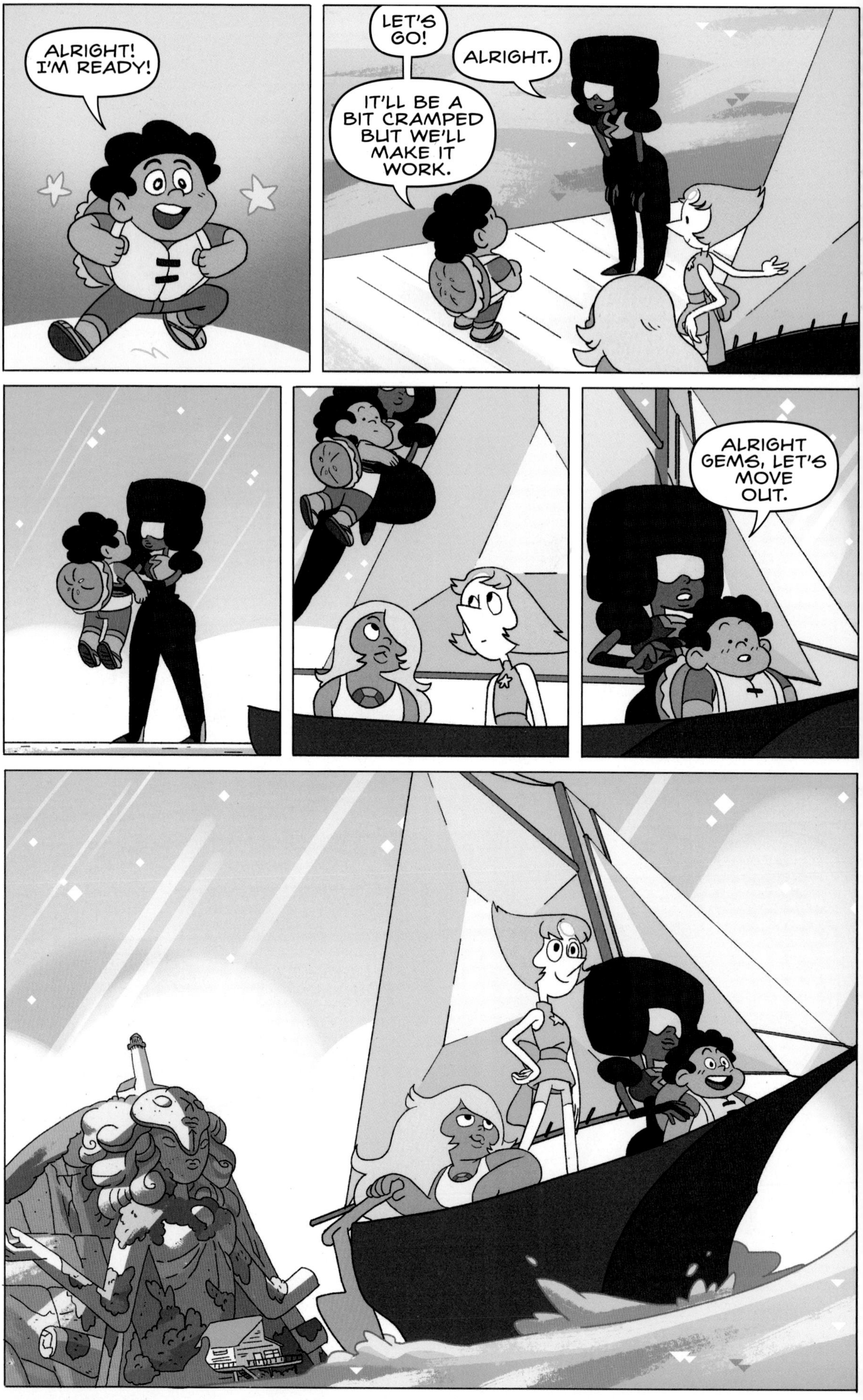
ALRIGHT! I'M READY!
LET'S GO!
IT'LL BE A BIT CRAMPED BUT WE'LL MAKE IT WORK.
ALRIGHT.
ALRIGHT GEMS, LET'S MOVE OUT.

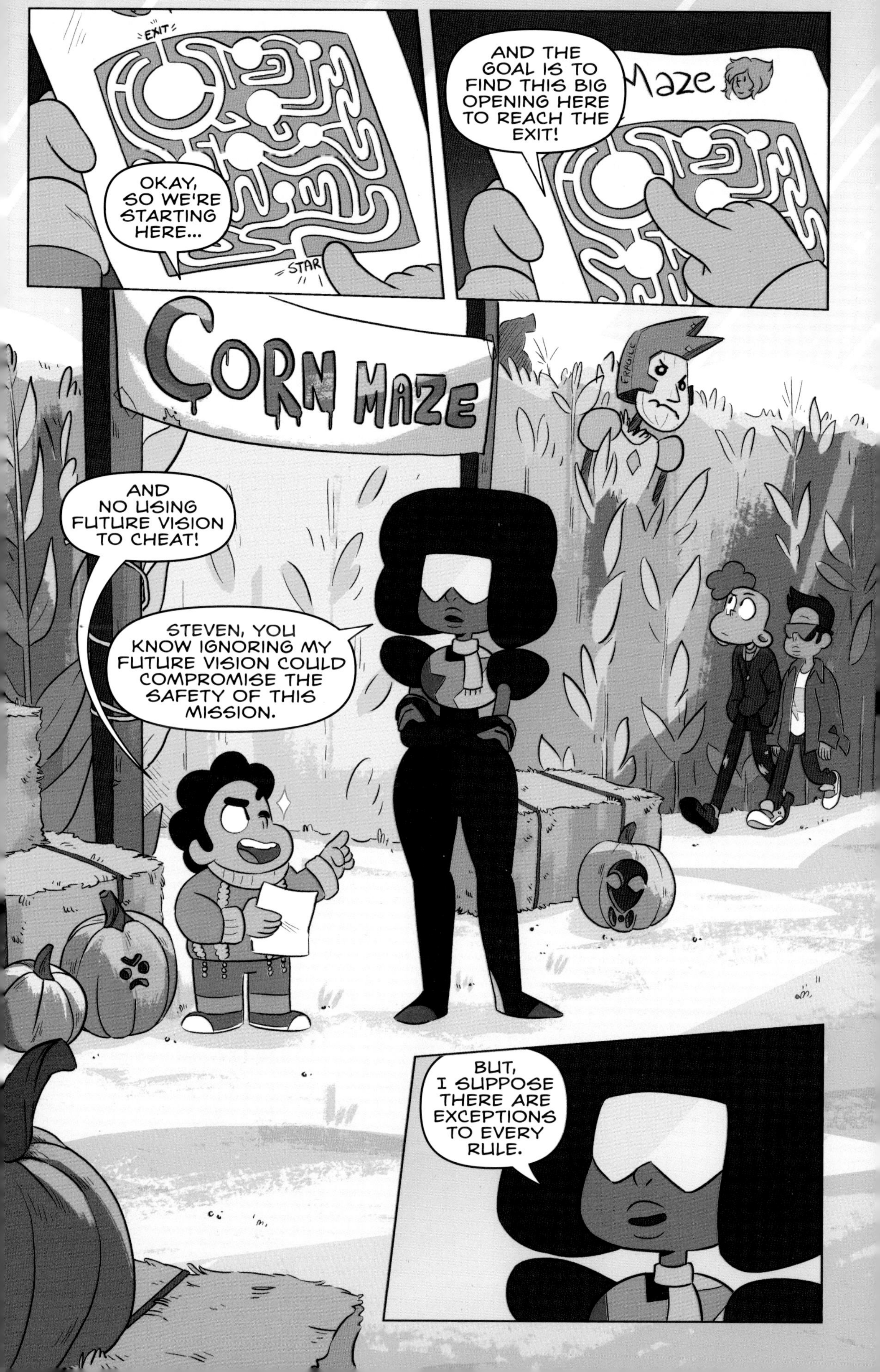
EXIT
STAR
OKAY, SO WE'RE STARTING HERE...
MAZE
AND THE GOAL IS TO FIND THIS BIG OPENING HERE TO REACH THE EXIT!
CORN MAZE
FRAGILE
AND NO USING FUTURE VISION TO CHEAT!
STEVEN, YOU KNOW IGNORING MY FUTURE VISION COULD COMPROMISE THE SAFETY OF THIS MISSION.
BUT, I SUPPOSE THERE ARE EXCEPTIONS TO EVERY RULE.

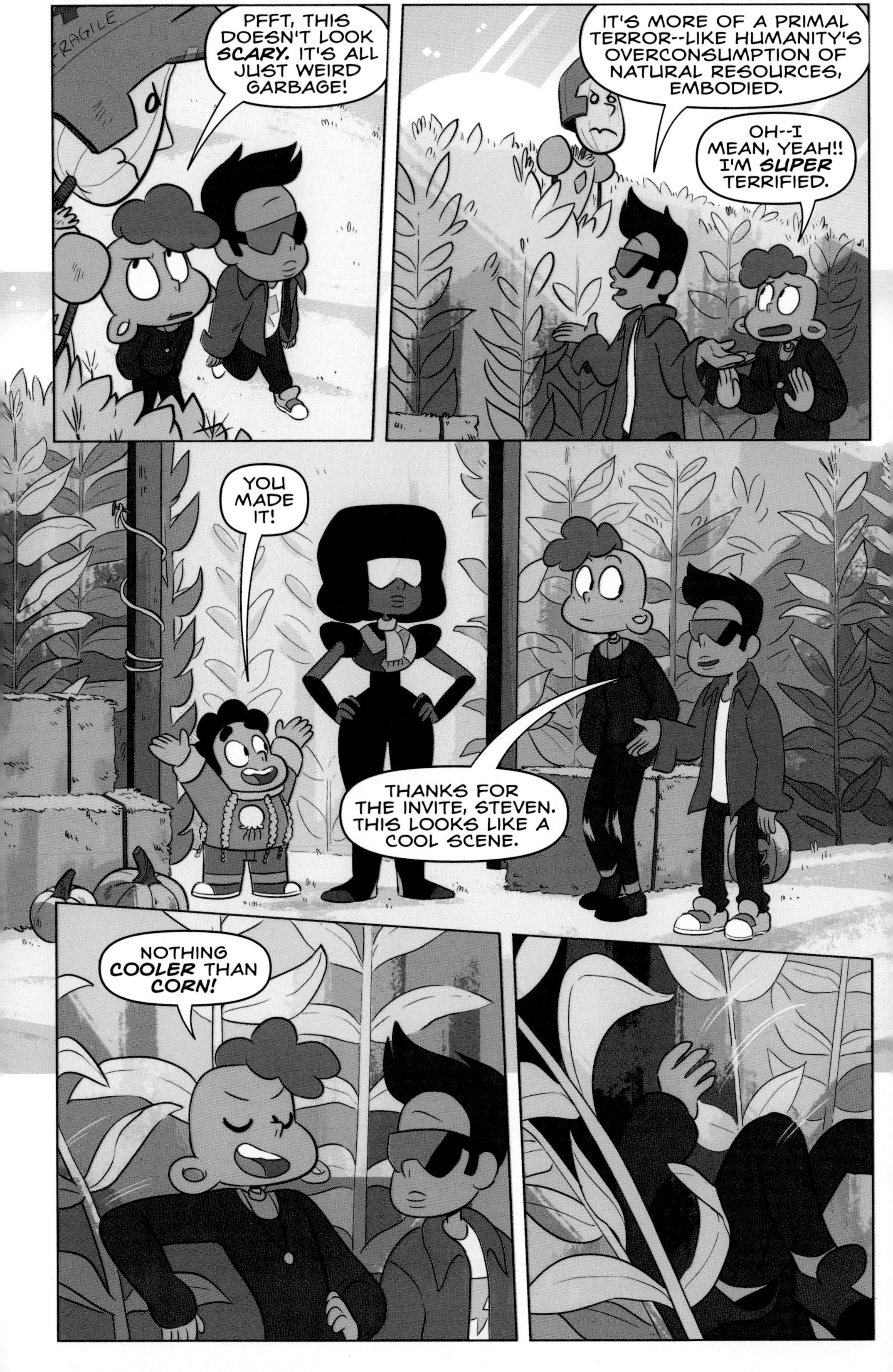
FRAGILE
PFFT, THIS DOESN'T LOOK SCARY. IT'S ALL JUST WEIRD GARBAGE!
IT'S MORE OF A PRIMAL TERROR--LIKE HUMANITY'S OVERCONSUMPTION OF NATURAL RESOURCES, EMBODIED.
OH--I MEAN, YEAH!! I'M SUPER TERRIFIED.
YOU MADE IT!
THANKS FOR THE INVITE, STEVEN. THIS LOOKS LIKE A COOL SCENE.
NOTHING COOLER THAN CORN!

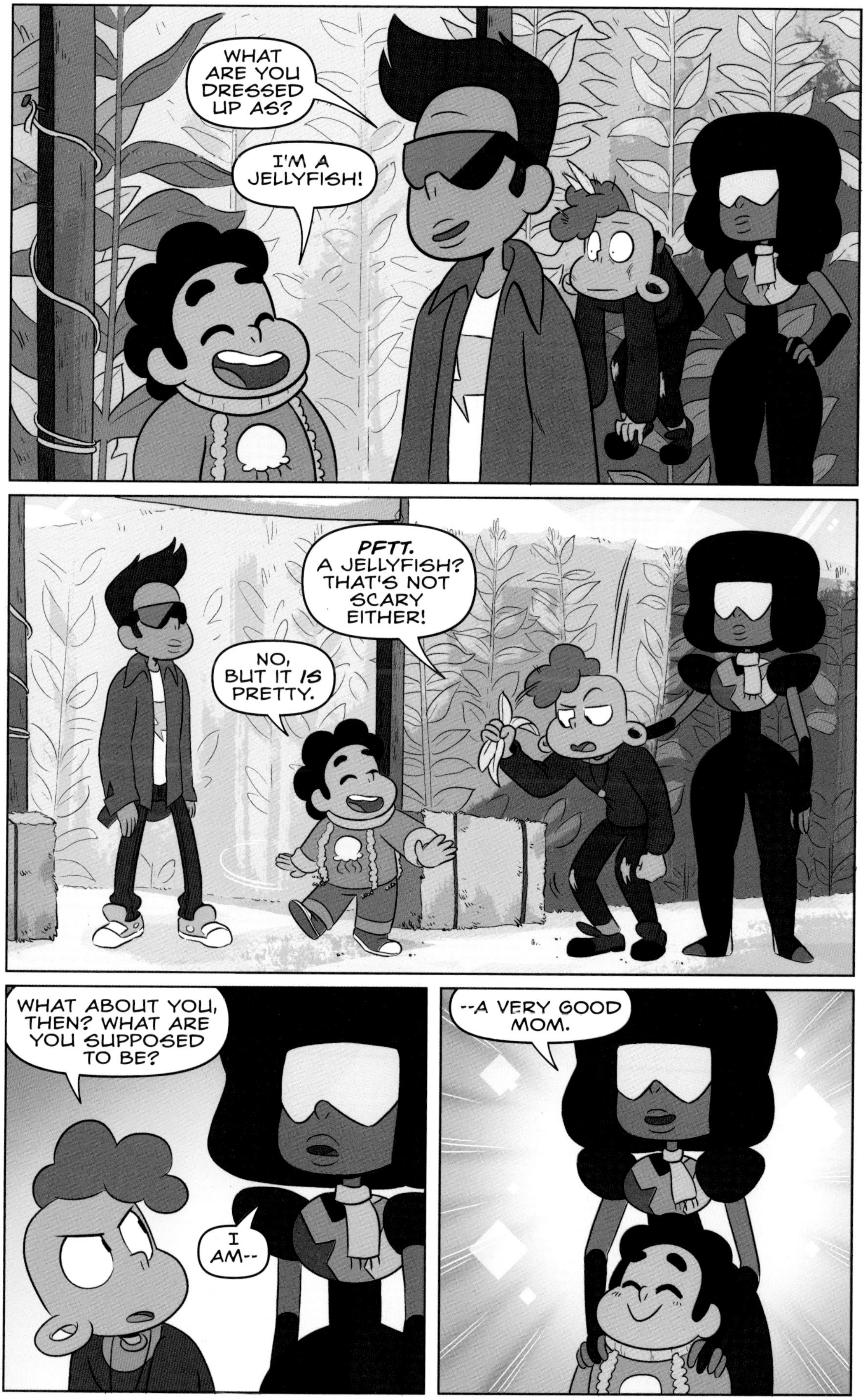
WHAT ARE YOU DRESSED UP AS?
I'M A JELLYFISH!
PFTT. A JELLYFISH? THAT'S NOT SCARY EITHER!
NO, BUT IT *IS* PRETTY.
WHAT ABOUT YOU, THEN? WHAT ARE YOU SUPPOSED TO BE?
I AM--
--A VERY GOOD MOM.

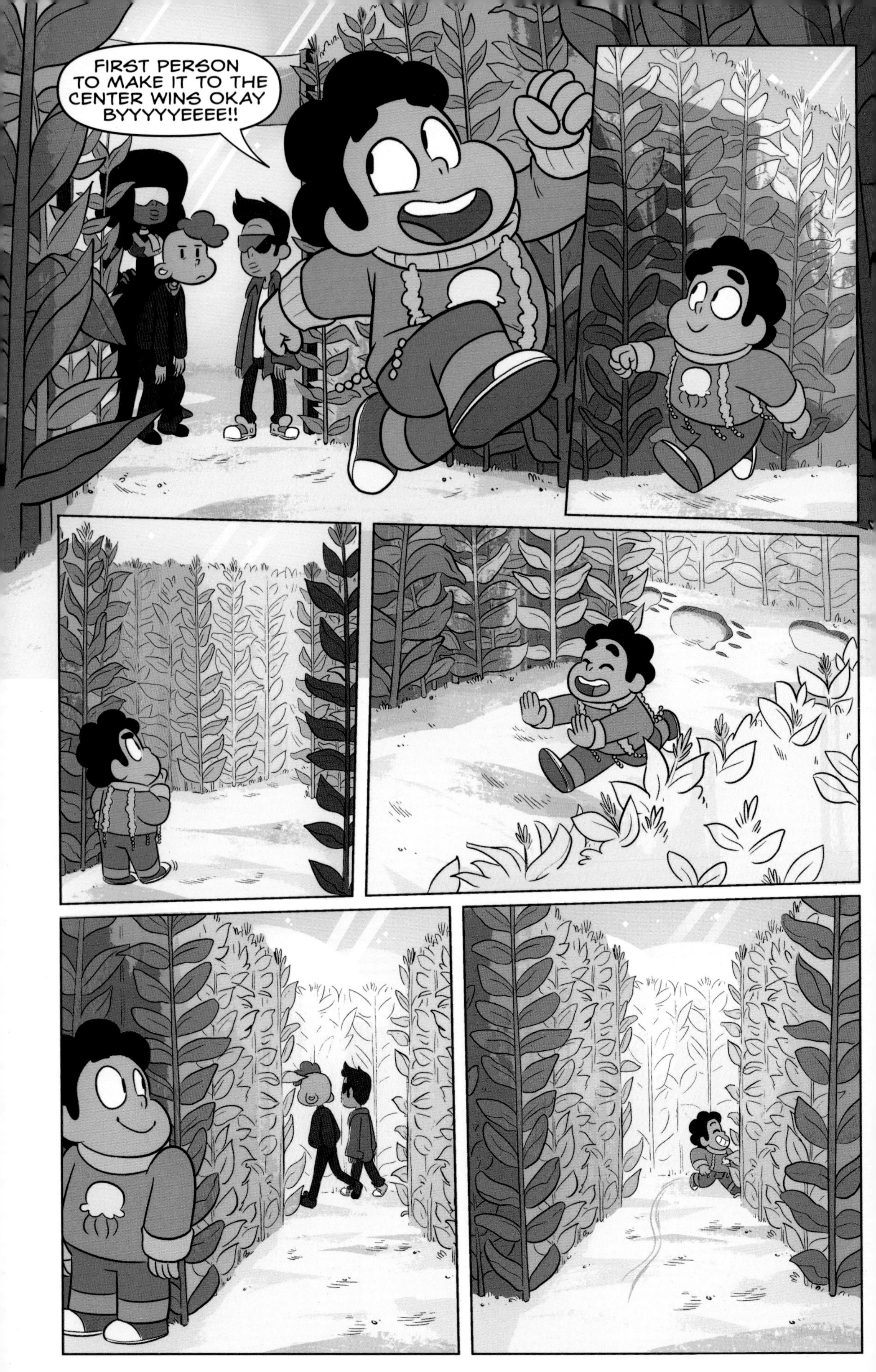
FIRST PERSON TO MAKE IT TO THE CENTER WINS OKAY BYYYYYEEEE!!

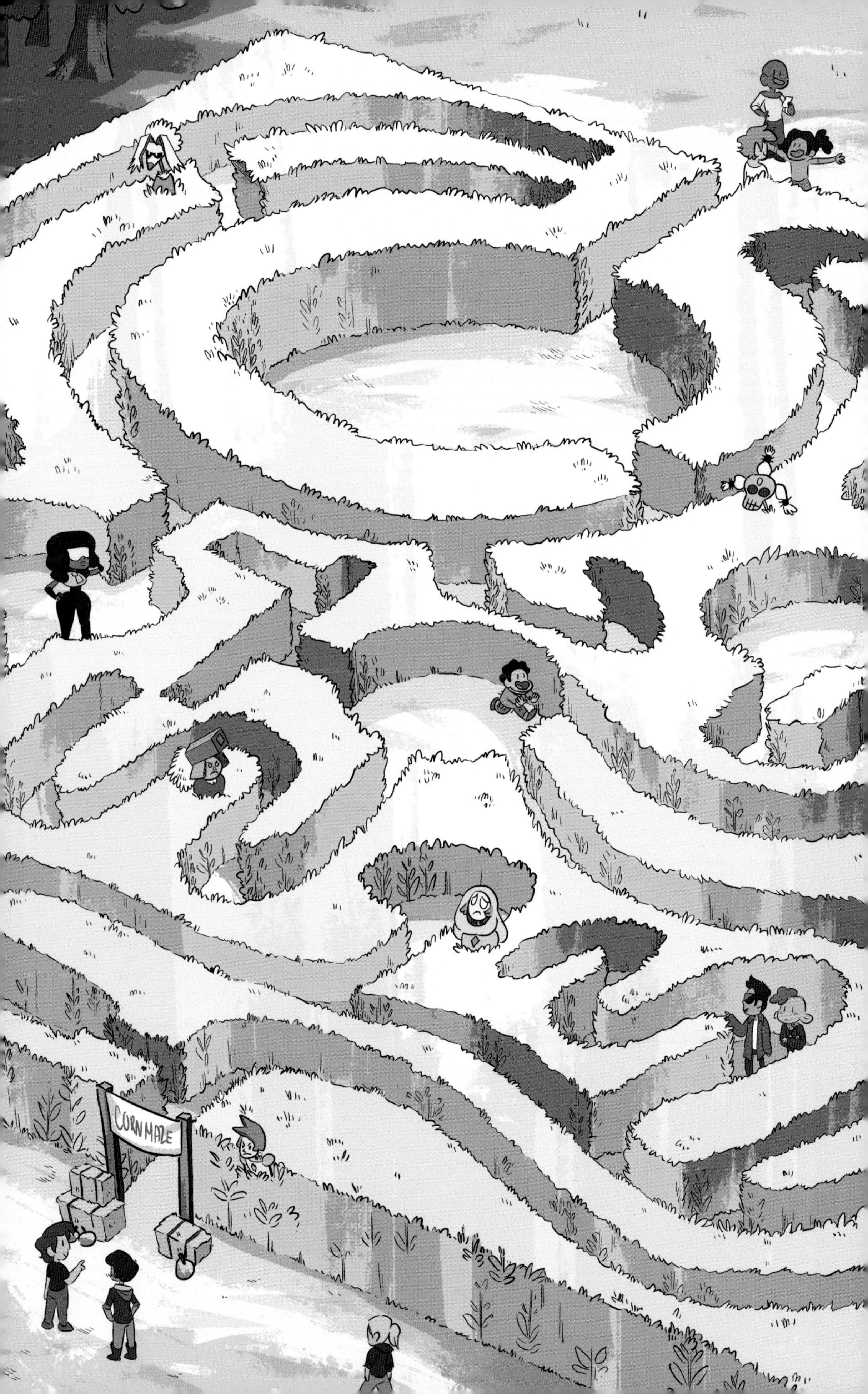
CORN MAZE

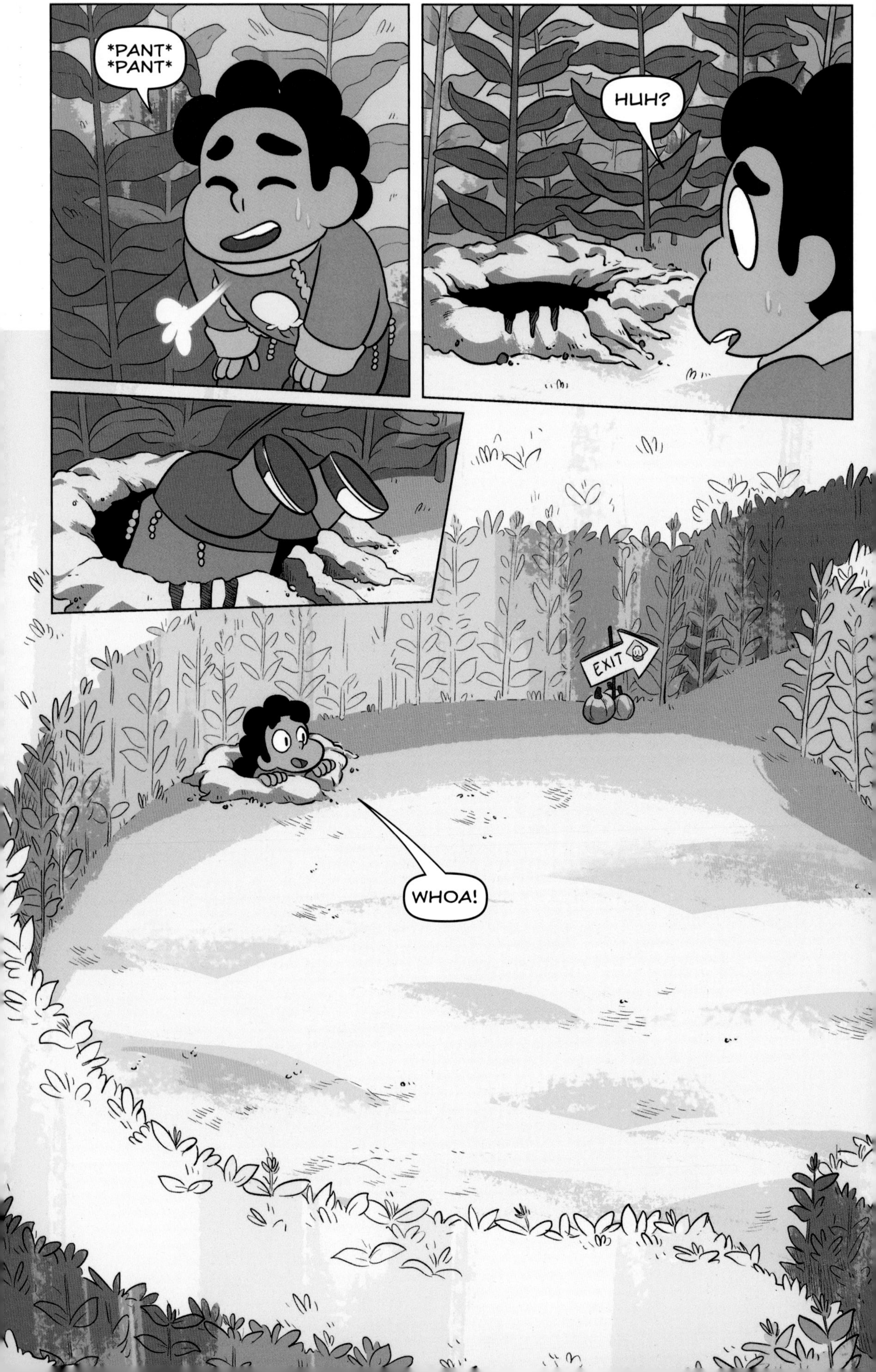
*PANT*
*PANT*
HUH?
EXIT
WHOA!

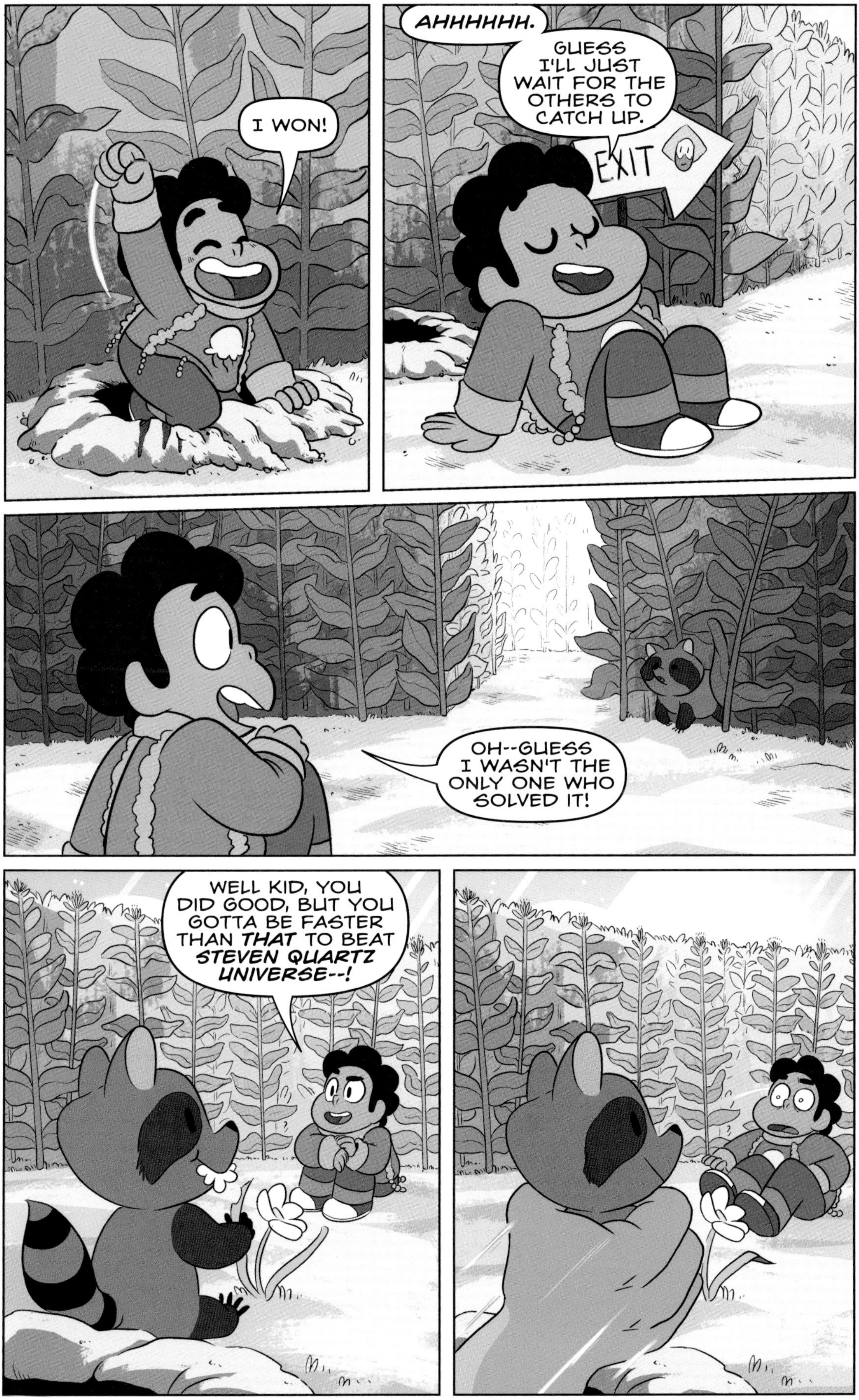
I WON!
AHHHHHH.
GUESS I'LL JUST WAIT FOR THE OTHERS TO CATCH UP.
EXIT
OH--GUESS I WASN'T THE ONLY ONE WHO SOLVED IT!
WELL KID, YOU DID GOOD, BUT YOU GOTTA BE FASTER THAN *THAT* TO BEAT *STEVEN QUARTZ UNIVERSE--!*

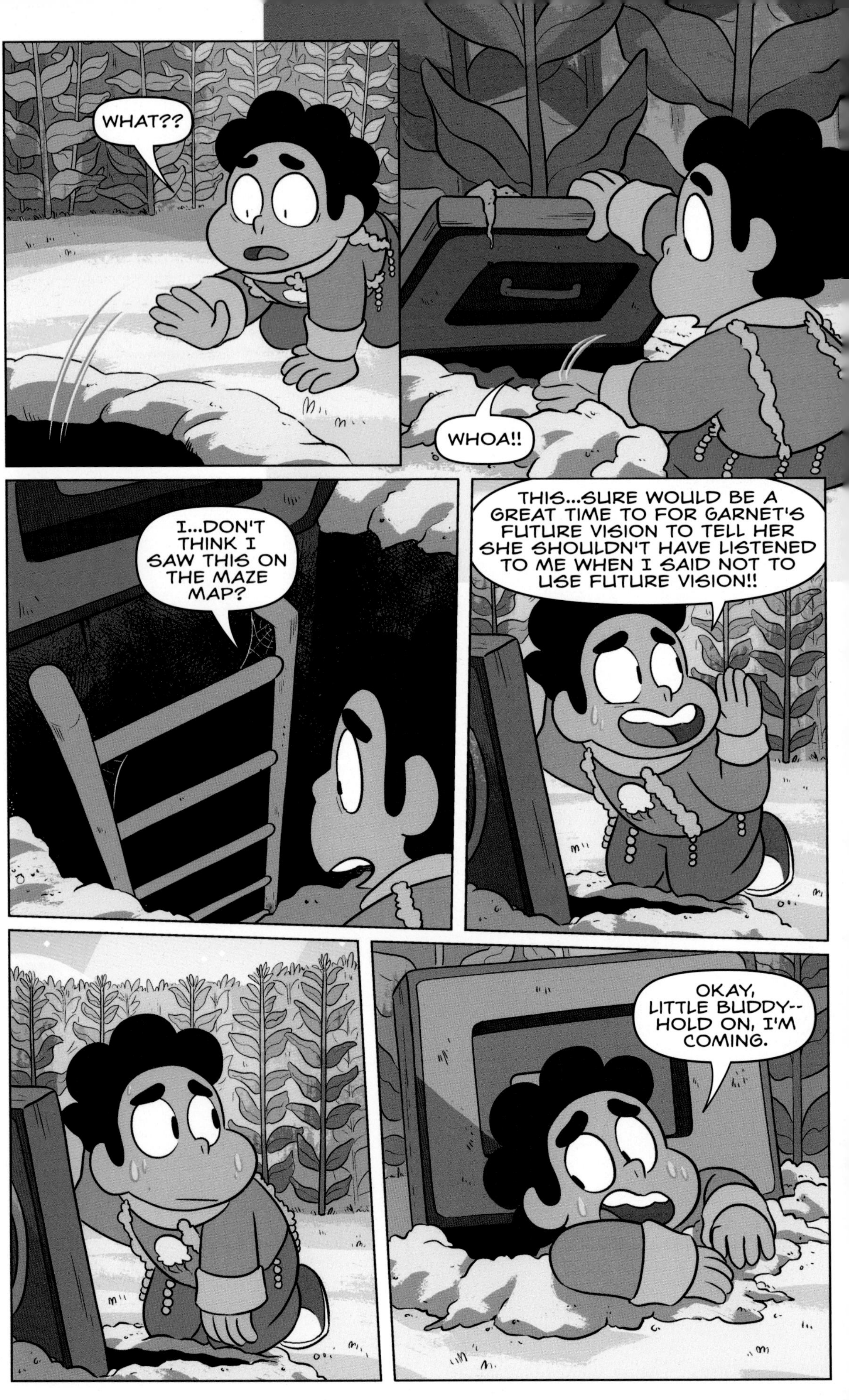
WHAT??
WHOA!!
I...DON'T THINK I SAW THIS ON THE MAZE MAP?
THIS...SURE WOULD BE A GREAT TIME TO FOR GARNET'S FUTURE VISION TO TELL HER SHE SHOULDN'T HAVE LISTENED TO ME WHEN I SAID NOT TO USE FUTURE VISION!!
OKAY, LITTLE BUDDY-- HOLD ON, I'M COMING.

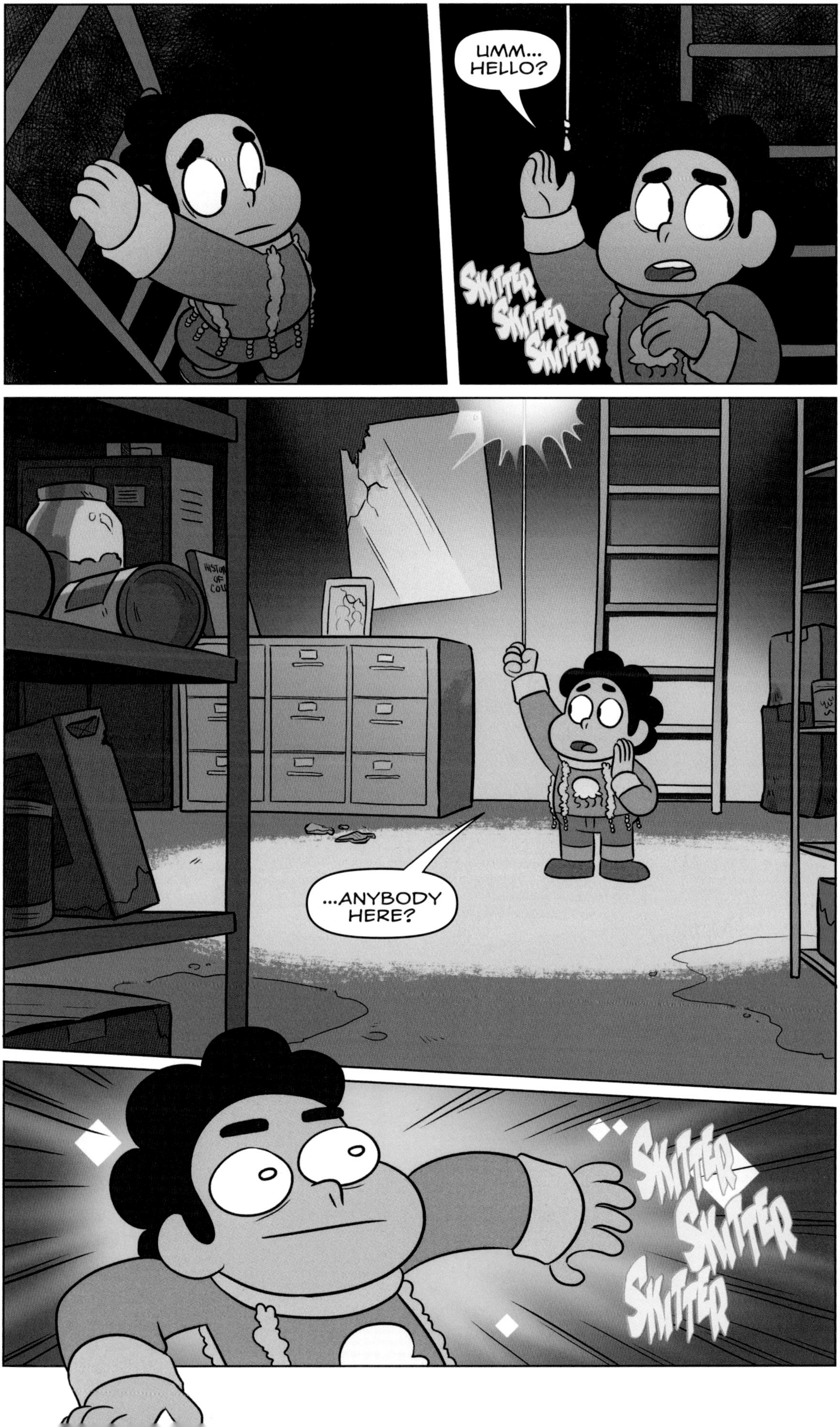
UMM... HELLO?
SKITTER SKITTER SKITTER
...ANYBODY HERE?
SKITTER SKITTER SKITTER

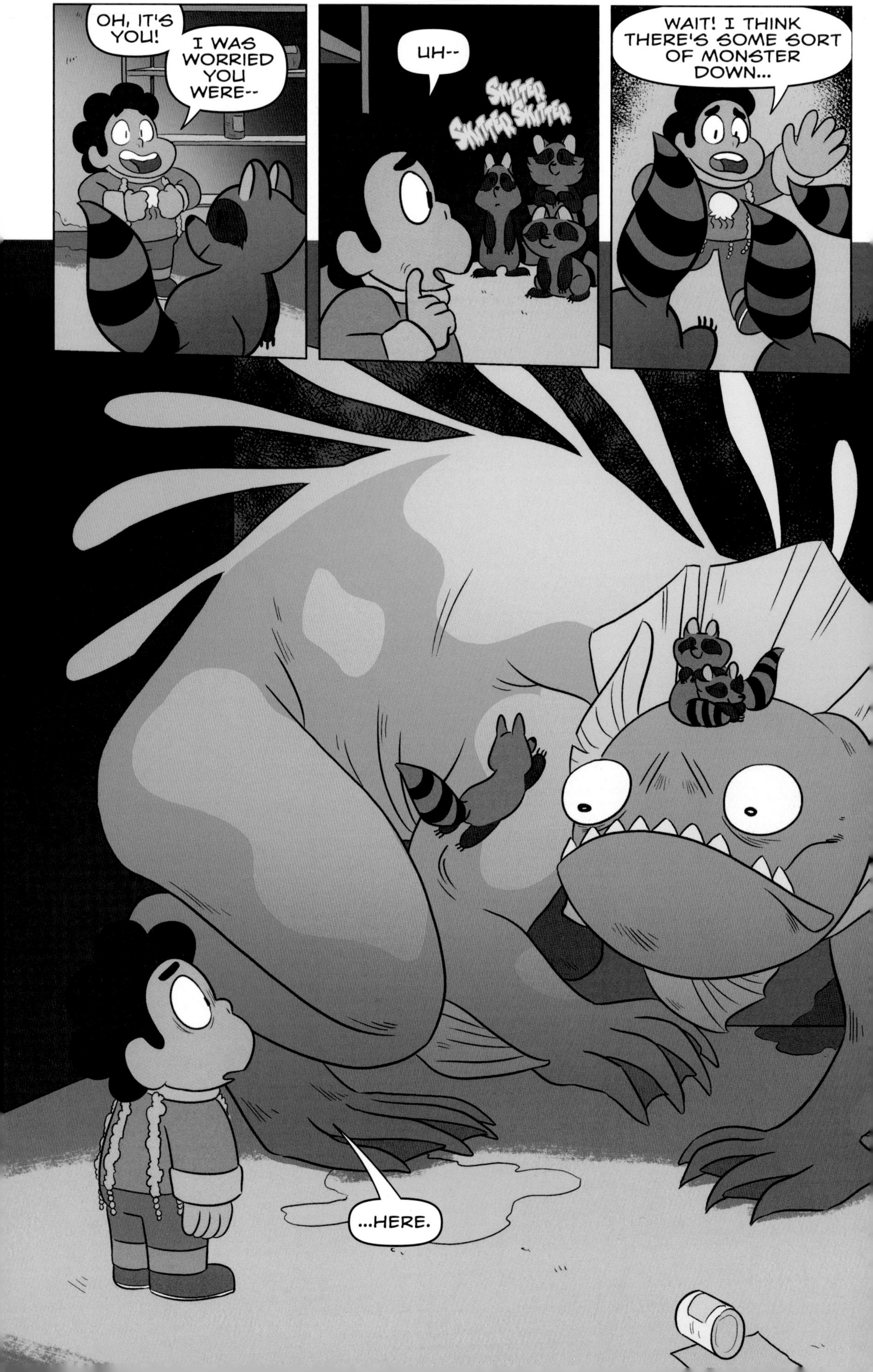
OH, IT'S YOU!
I WAS WORRIED YOU WERE--
UH--
SKITTER SKITTER SKITTER
WAIT! I THINK THERE'S SOME SORT OF MONSTER DOWN...
...HERE.

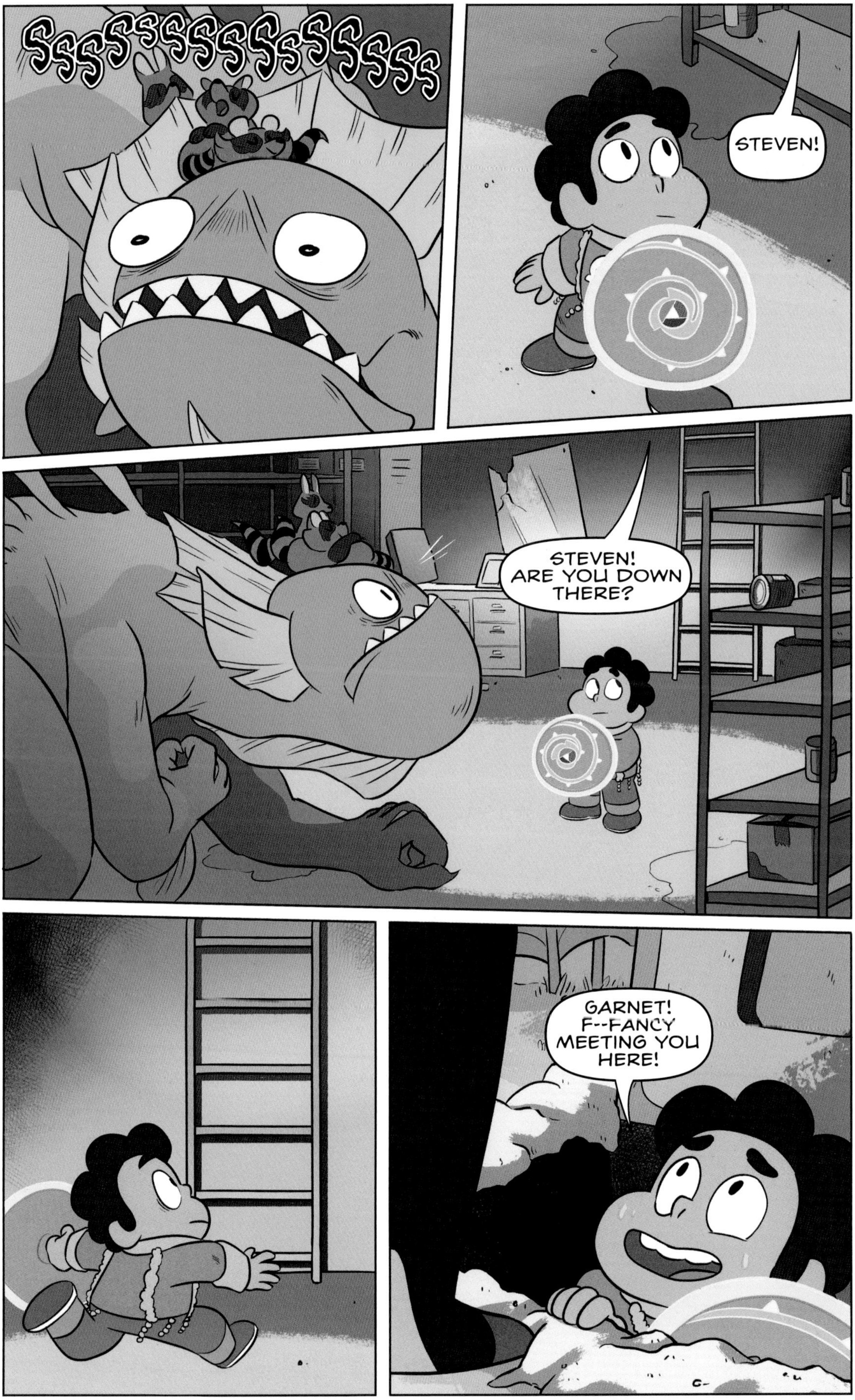
SSSSSSSSSSSSSSSS
STEVEN!
STEVEN! ARE YOU DOWN THERE?
GARNET! F--FANCY MEETING YOU HERE!

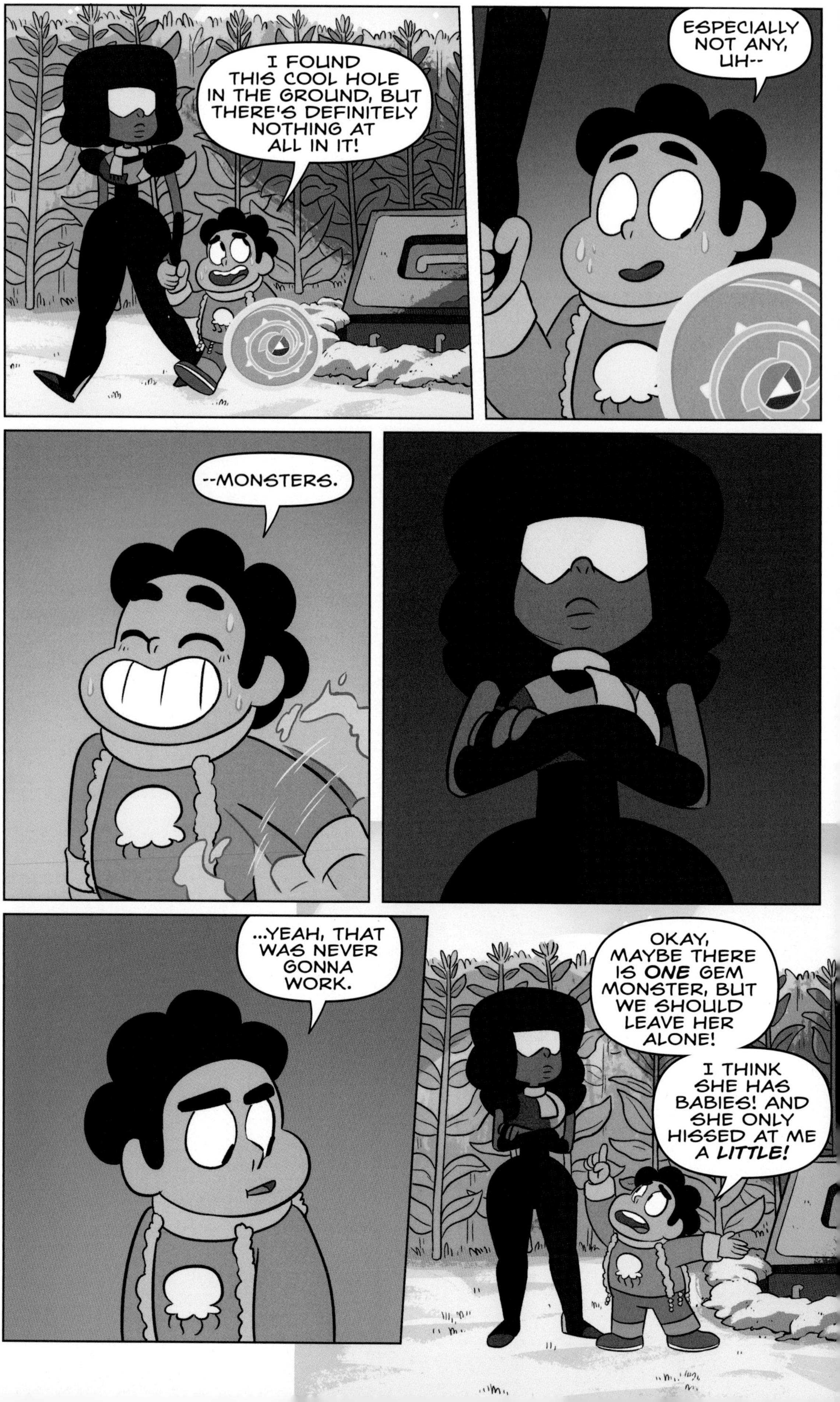
I FOUND THIS COOL HOLE IN THE GROUND, BUT THERE'S DEFINITELY NOTHING AT ALL IN IT!
ESPECIALLY NOT ANY, UH--
--MONSTERS.
...YEAH, THAT WAS NEVER GONNA WORK.
OKAY, MAYBE THERE IS *ONE* GEM MONSTER, BUT WE SHOULD LEAVE HER ALONE!
I THINK SHE HAS BABIES! AND SHE ONLY HISSED AT ME A *LITTLE!*

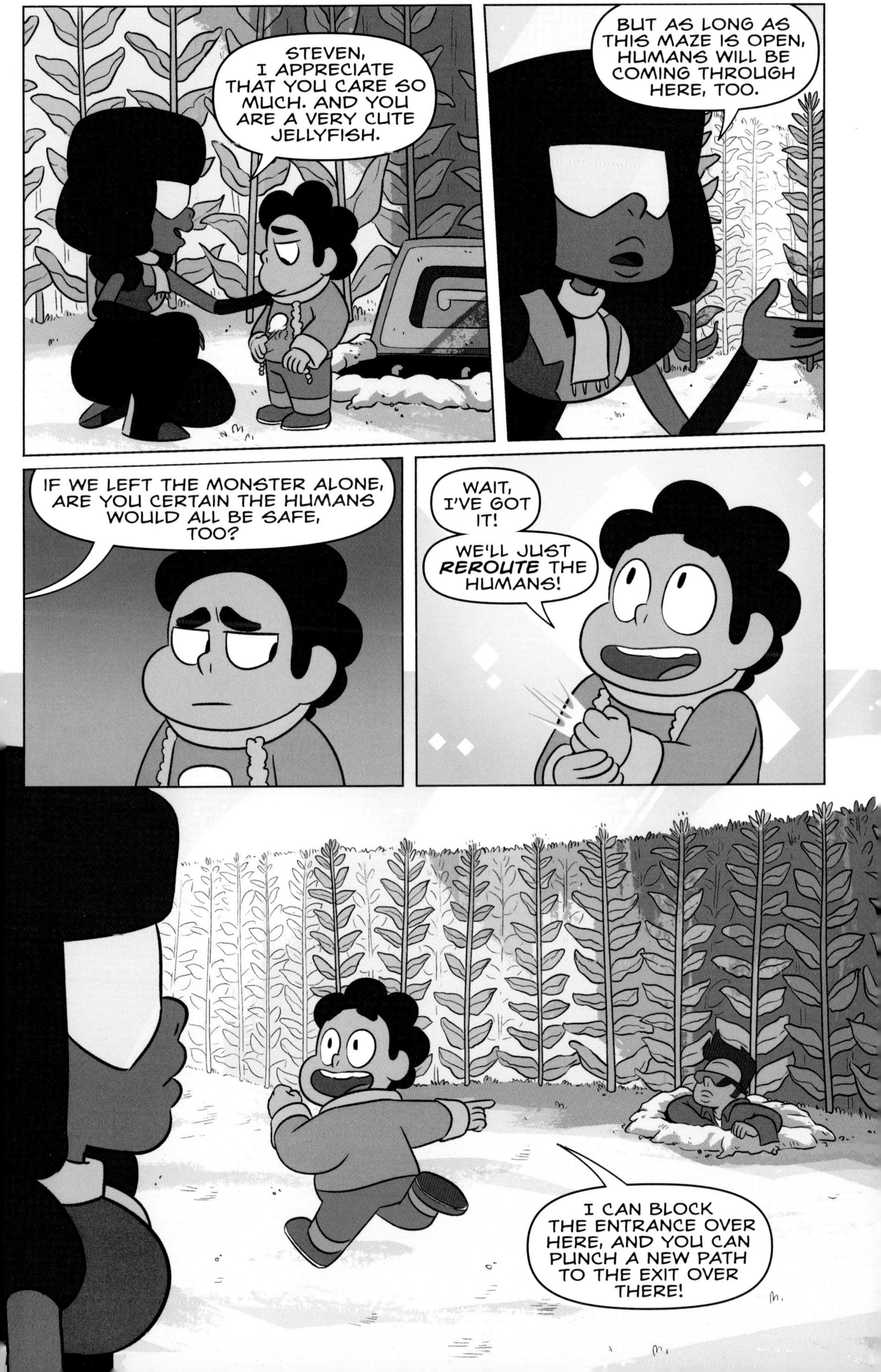
STEVEN, I APPRECIATE THAT YOU CARE SO MUCH. AND YOU ARE A VERY CUTE JELLYFISH.
BUT AS LONG AS THIS MAZE IS OPEN, HUMANS WILL BE COMING THROUGH HERE, TOO.
IF WE LEFT THE MONSTER ALONE, ARE YOU CERTAIN THE HUMANS WOULD ALL BE SAFE, TOO?
WAIT, I'VE GOT IT!
WE'LL JUST *REROUTE* THE HUMANS!
I CAN BLOCK THE ENTRANCE OVER HERE, AND YOU CAN PUNCH A NEW PATH TO THE EXIT OVER THERE!

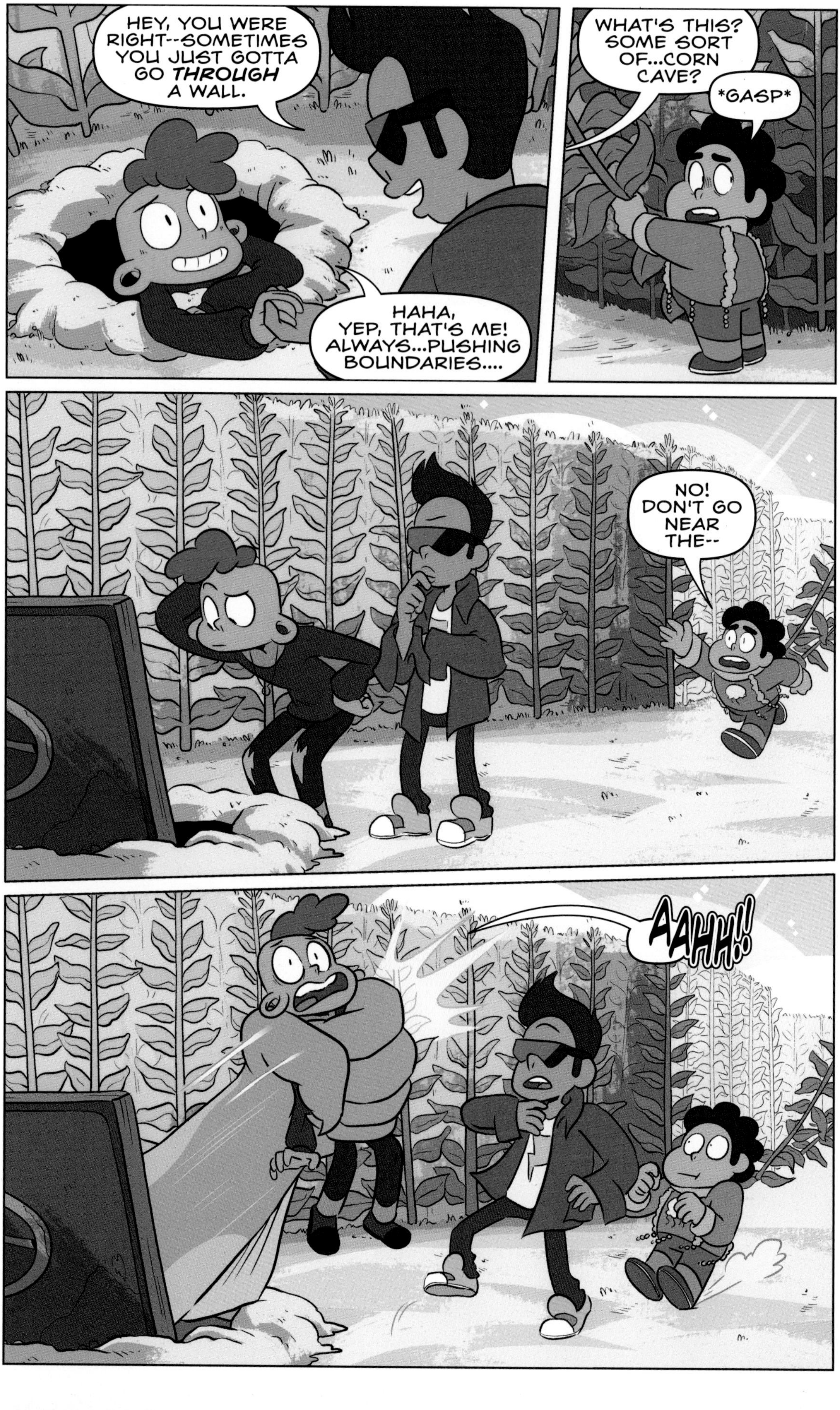

HEY, YOU WERE RIGHT--SOMETIMES YOU JUST GOTTA GO *THROUGH* A WALL.
HAHA, YEP, THAT'S ME! ALWAYS...PUSHING BOUNDARIES....
WHAT'S THIS? SOME SORT OF...CORN CAVE?
*GASP*
NO! DON'T GO NEAR THE--
AAHH!!

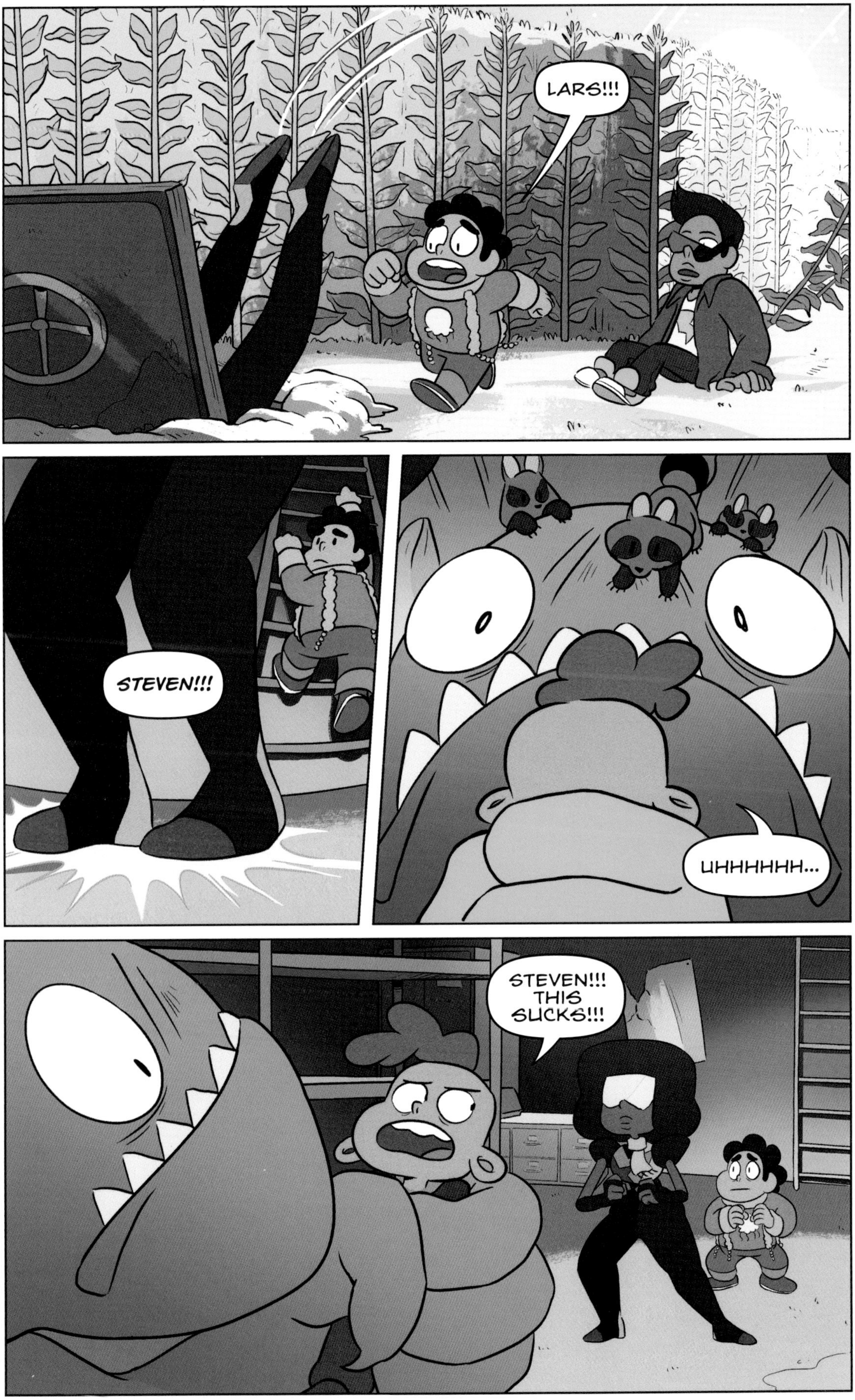
LARS!!!
STEVEN!!!
UHHHHHH...
STEVEN!!! THIS SUCKS!!!

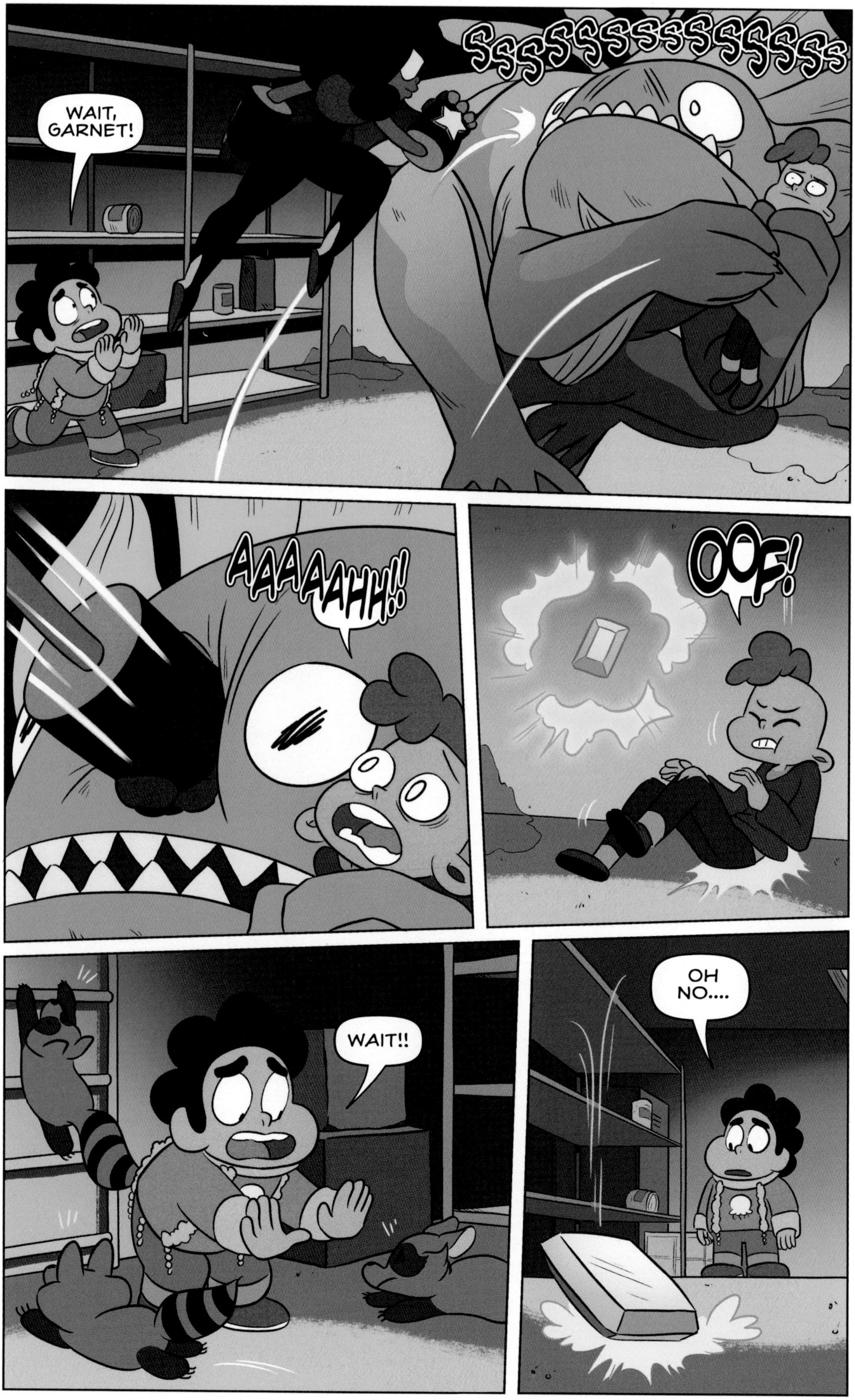
SSSSSSSSSSSSSSSs
WAIT, GARNET!
AAAAAHH!!
OOF!
WAIT!!
OH NO....

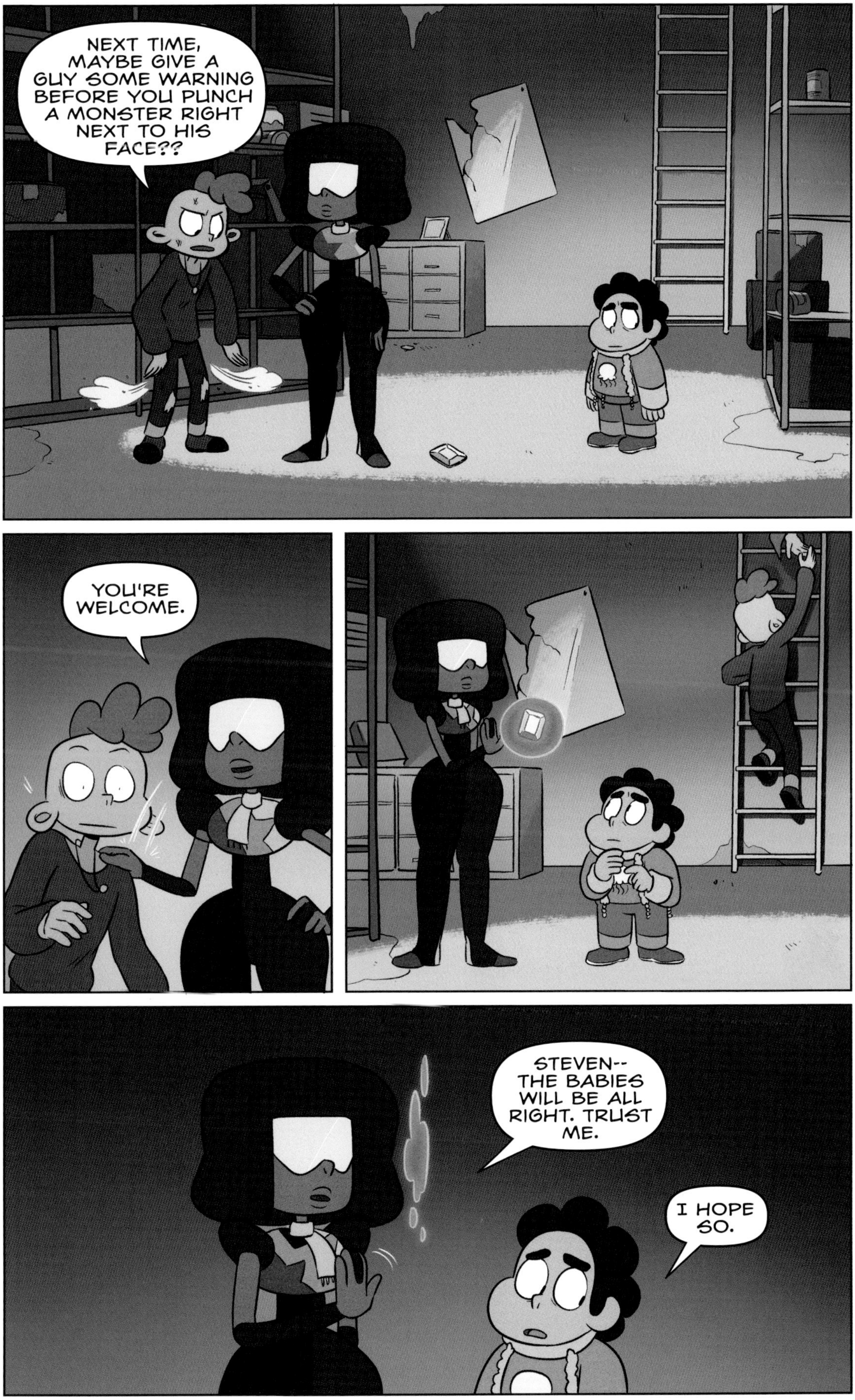
NEXT TIME, MAYBE GIVE A GUY SOME WARNING BEFORE YOU PUNCH A MONSTER RIGHT NEXT TO HIS FACE??
YOU'RE WELCOME.
STEVEN-- THE BABIES WILL BE ALL RIGHT. TRUST ME.
I HOPE SO.

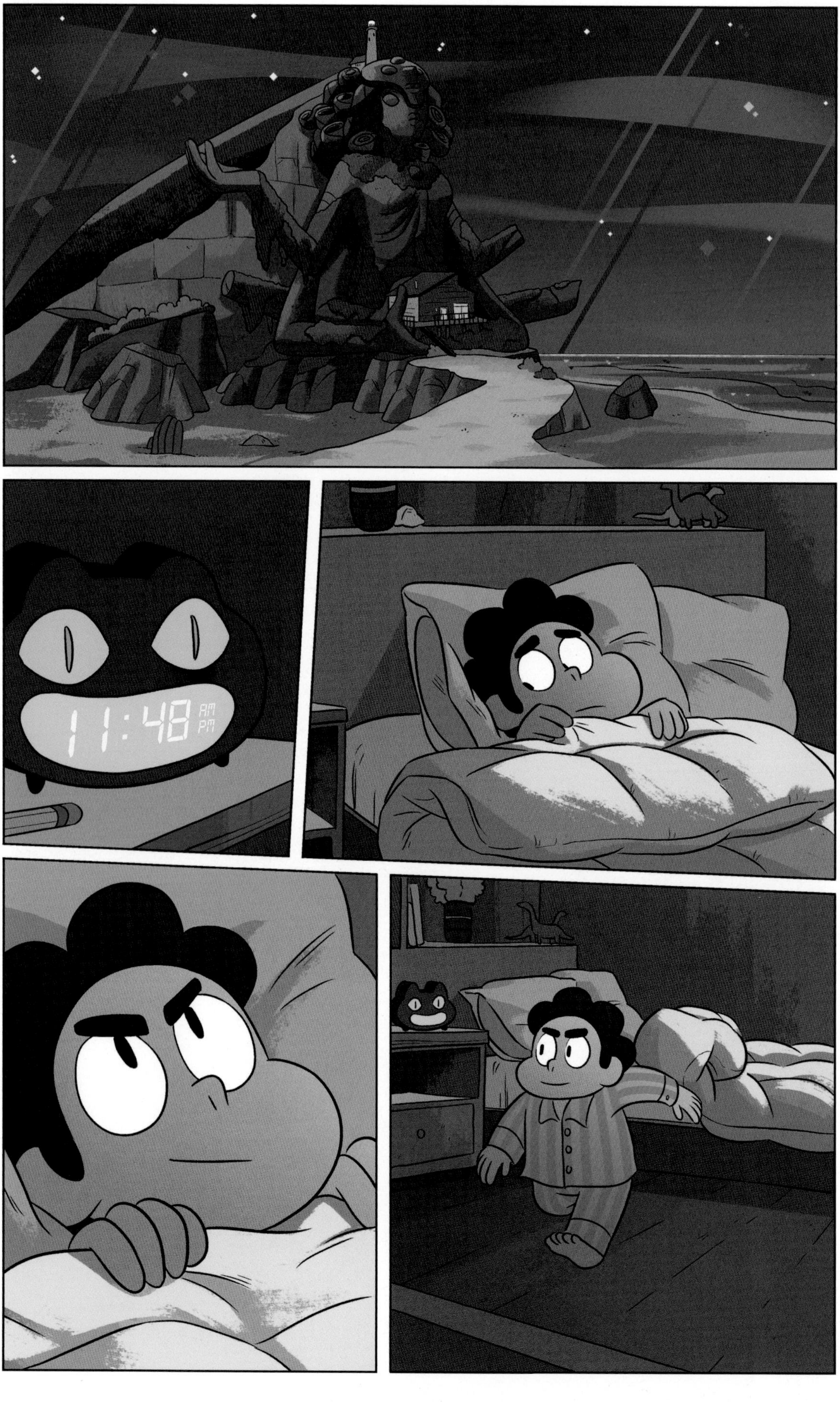
11:48
AM
PM

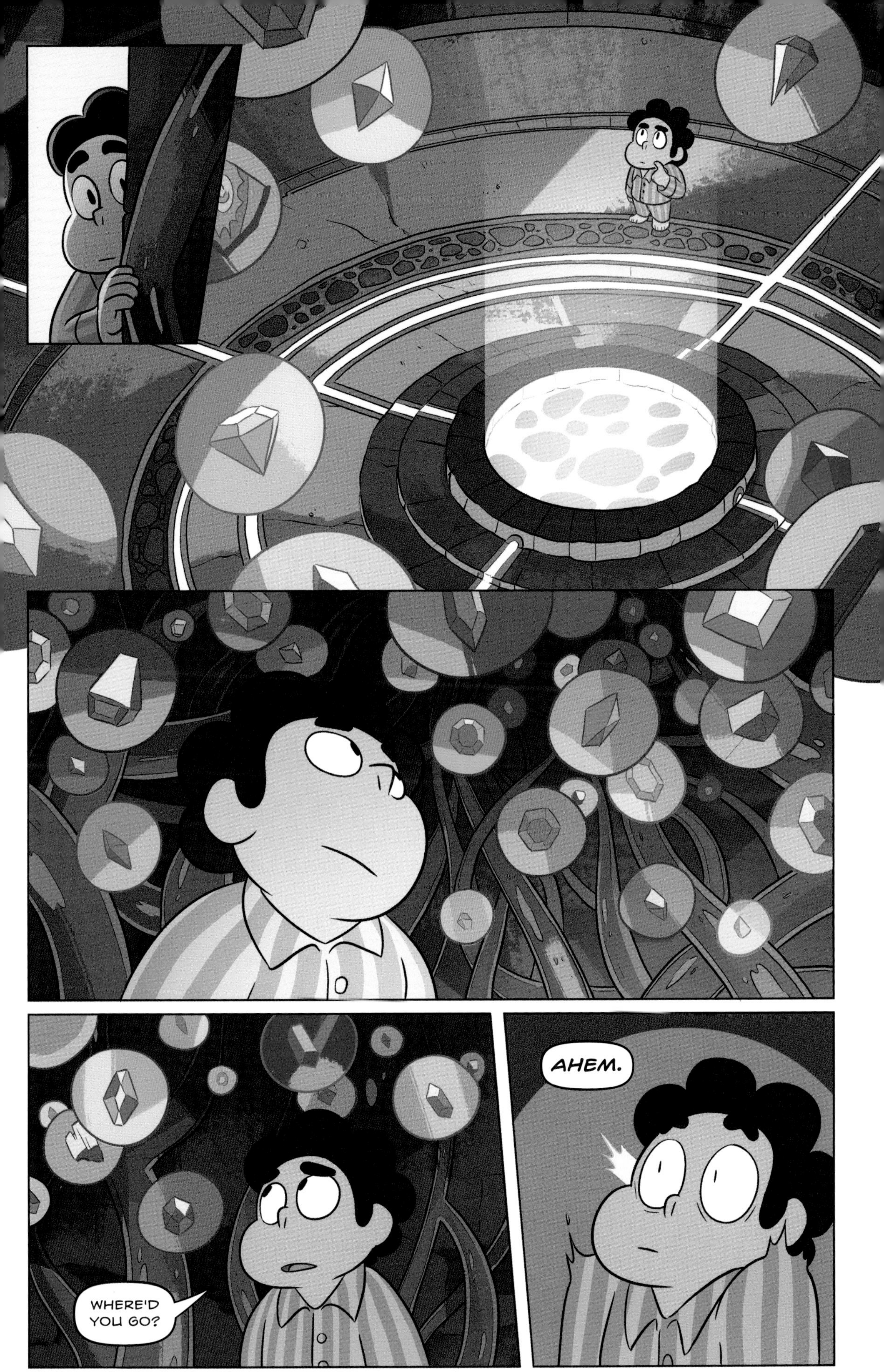
WHERE'D YOU GO?
AHEM.

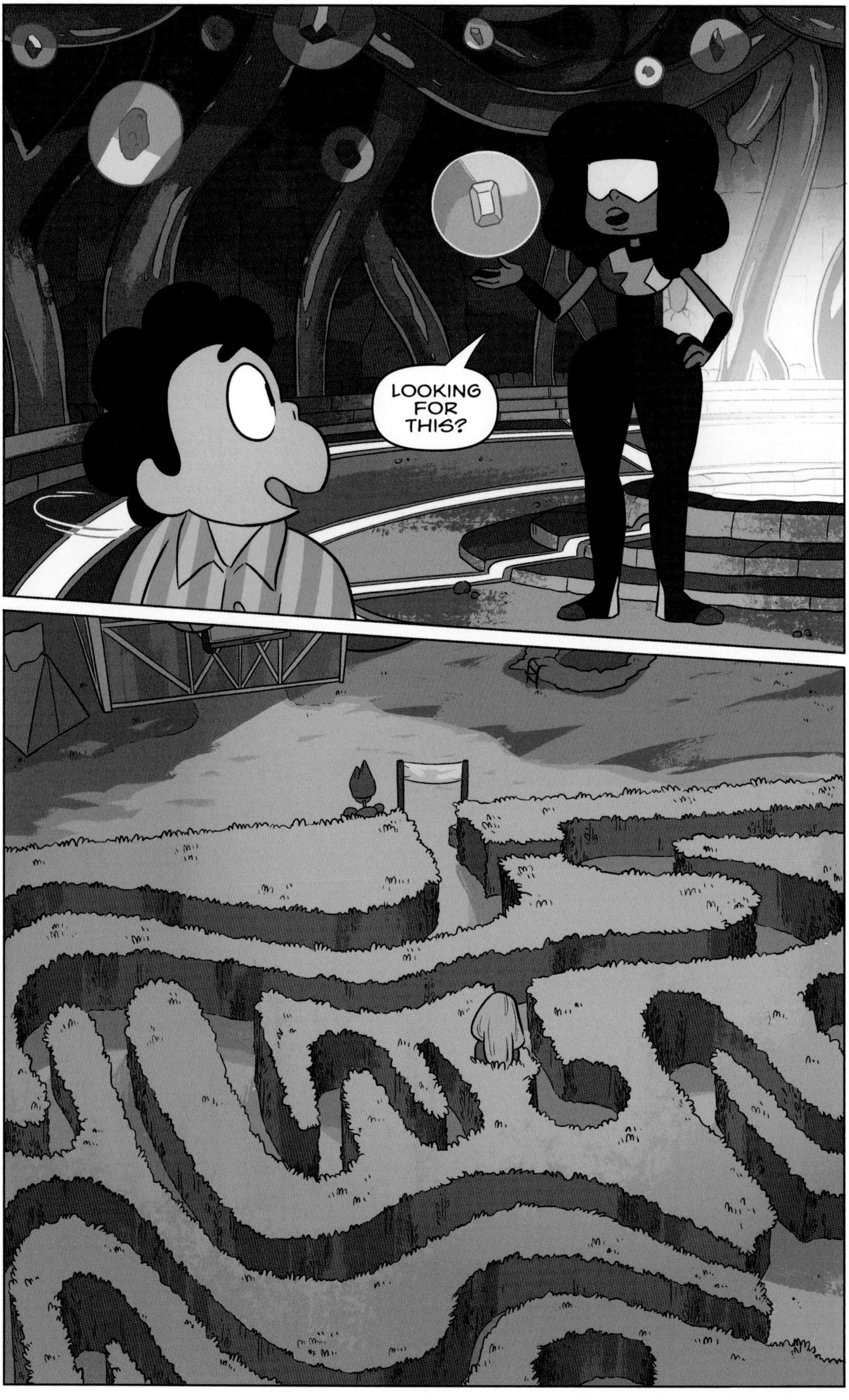
LOOKING FOR THIS?

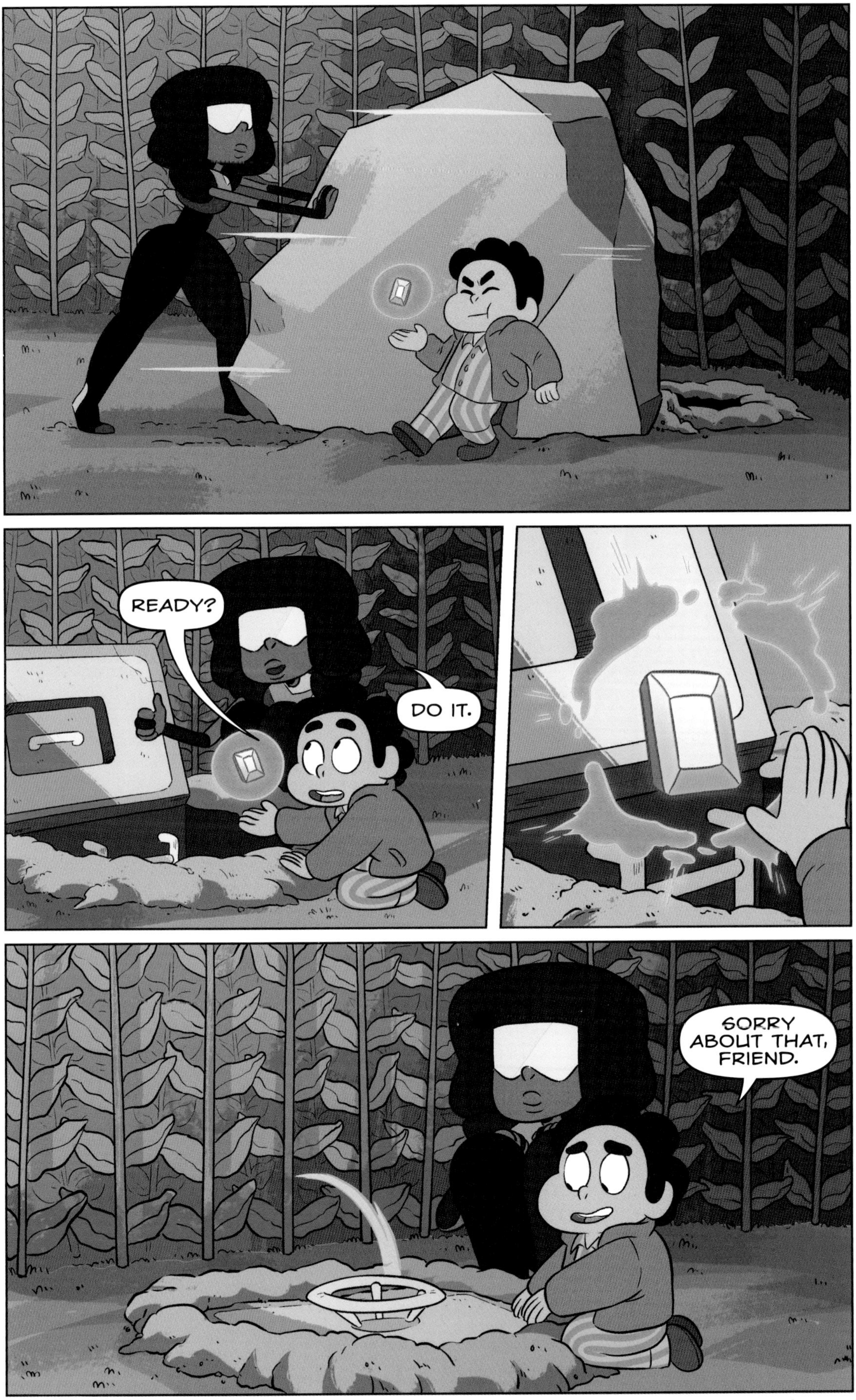
READY?
DO IT.
SORRY ABOUT THAT, FRIEND.

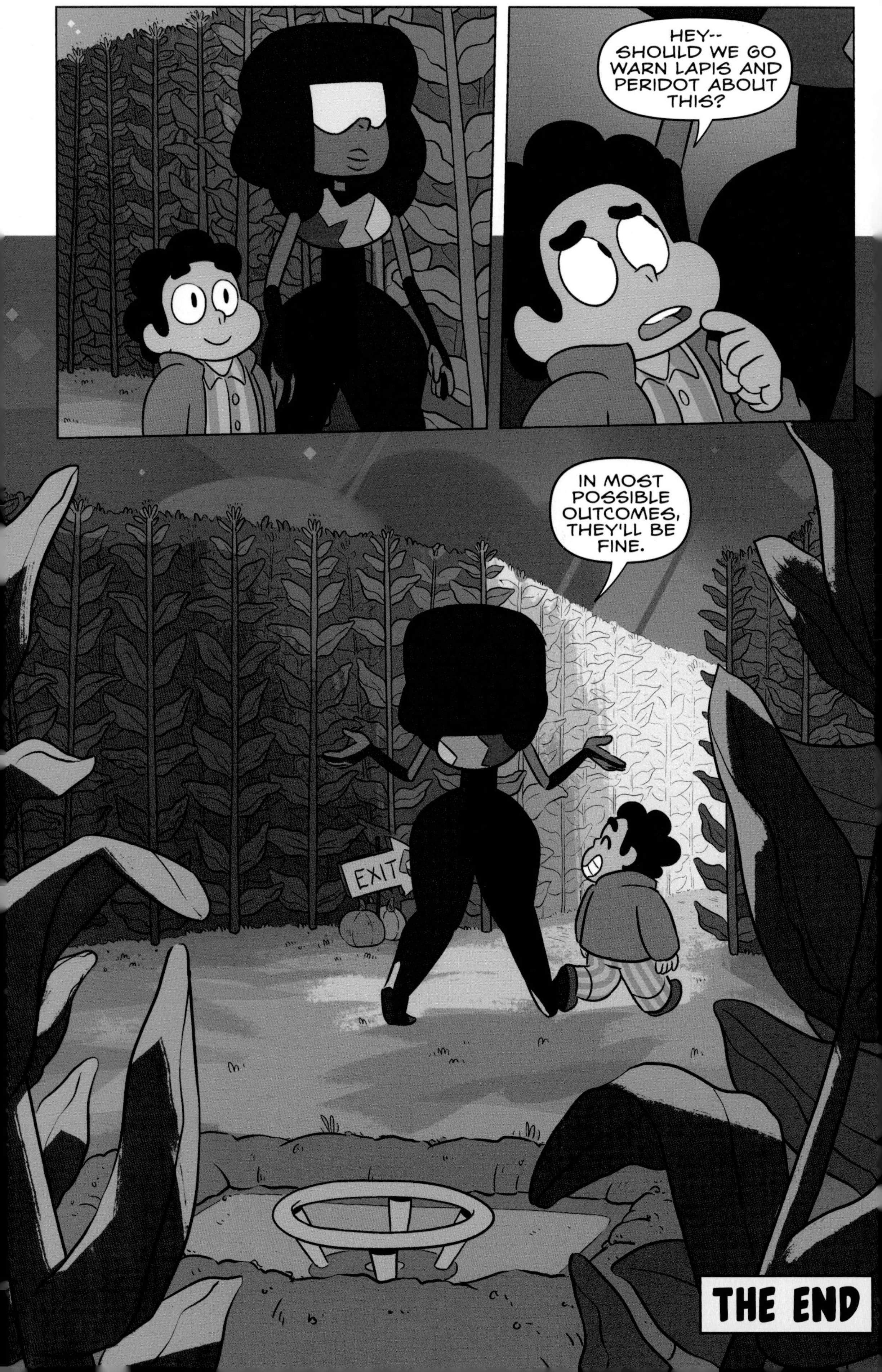
HEY-- SHOULD WE GO WARN LAPIS AND PERIDOT ABOUT THIS?
IN MOST POSSIBLE OUTCOMES, THEY'LL BE FINE.
EXIT
THE END

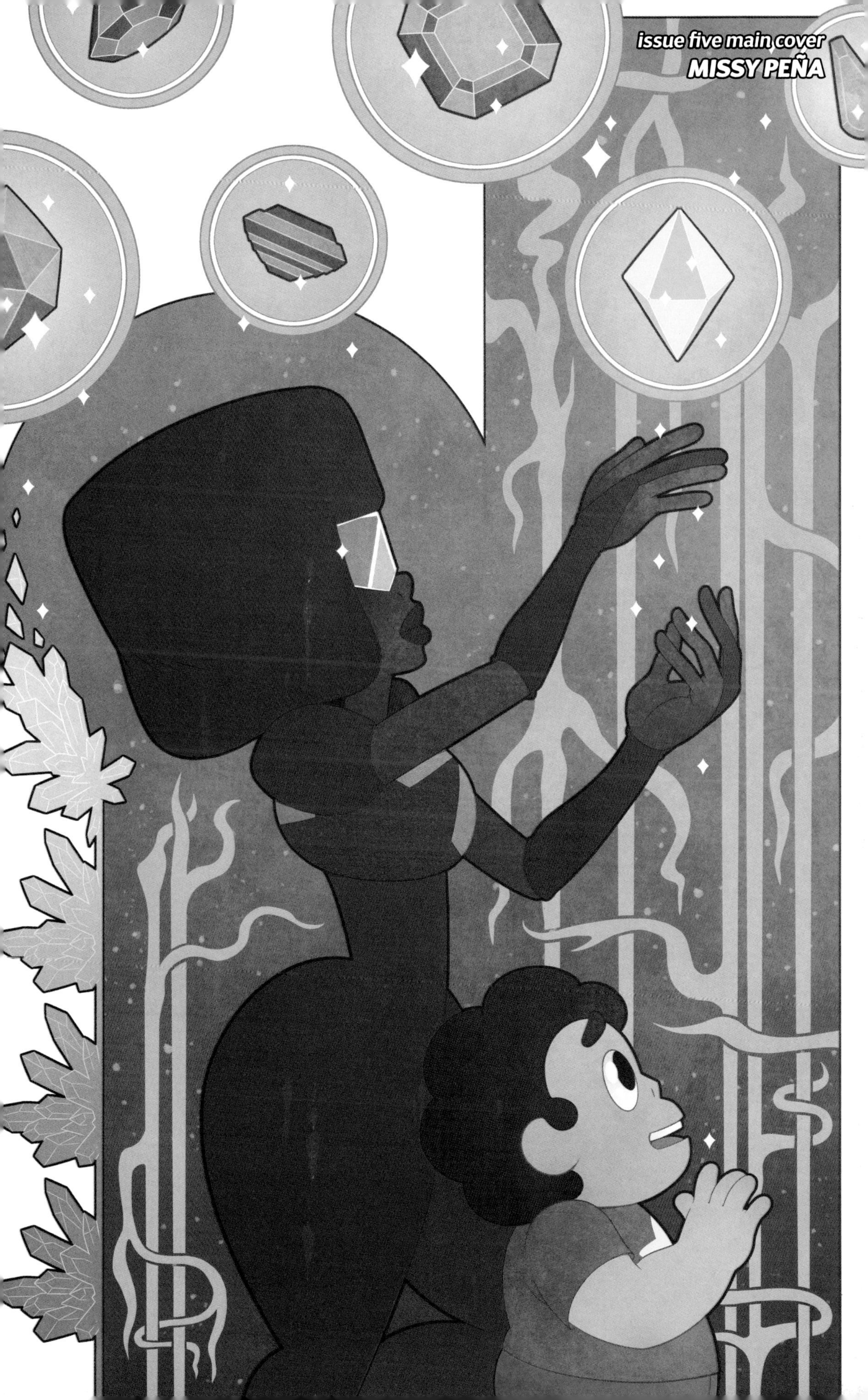
issue five main cover
MISSY PEÑA

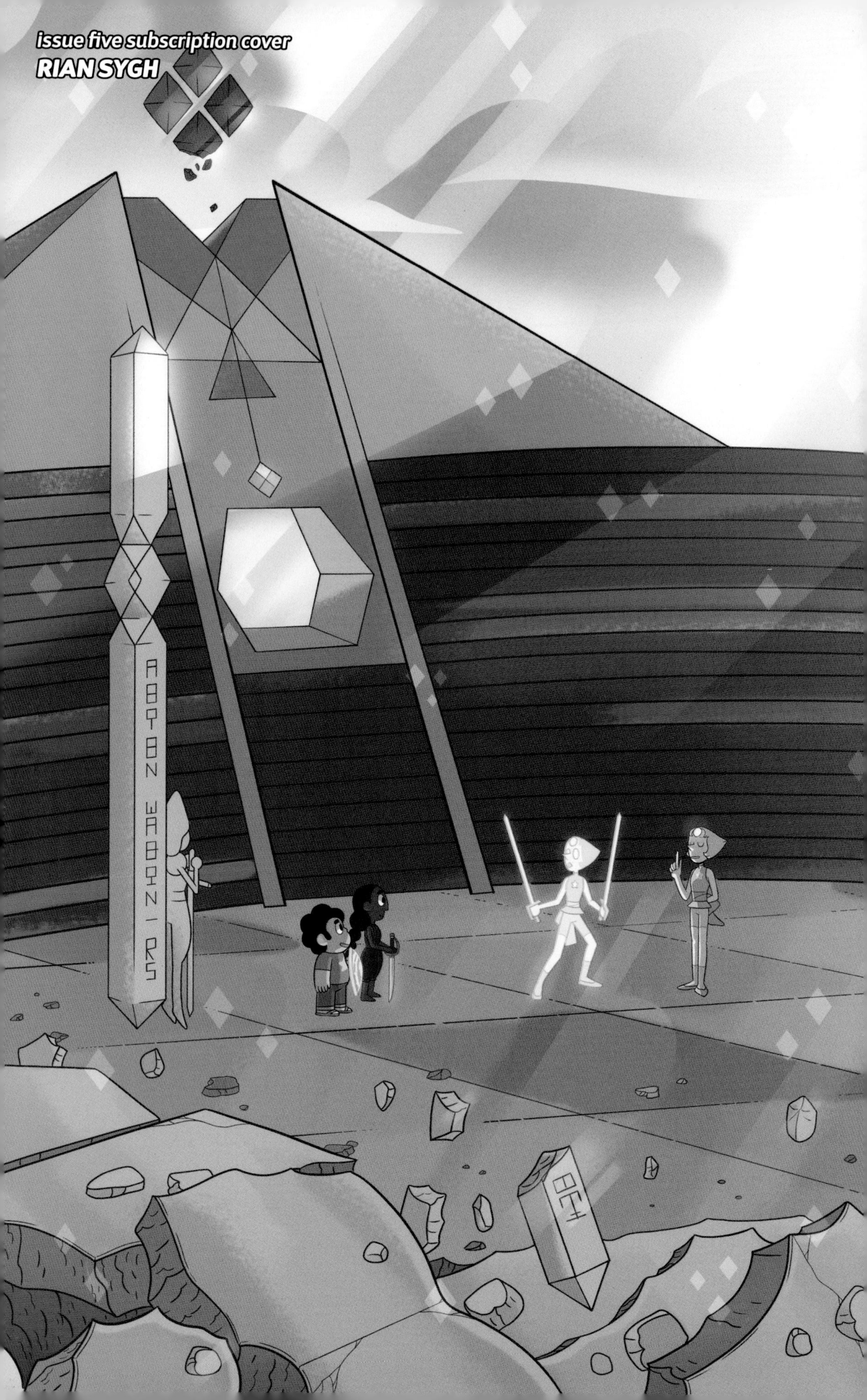

issue five subscription cover
**RIAN SYGH**

*issue five variant cover*
**SARA TALMADGE**

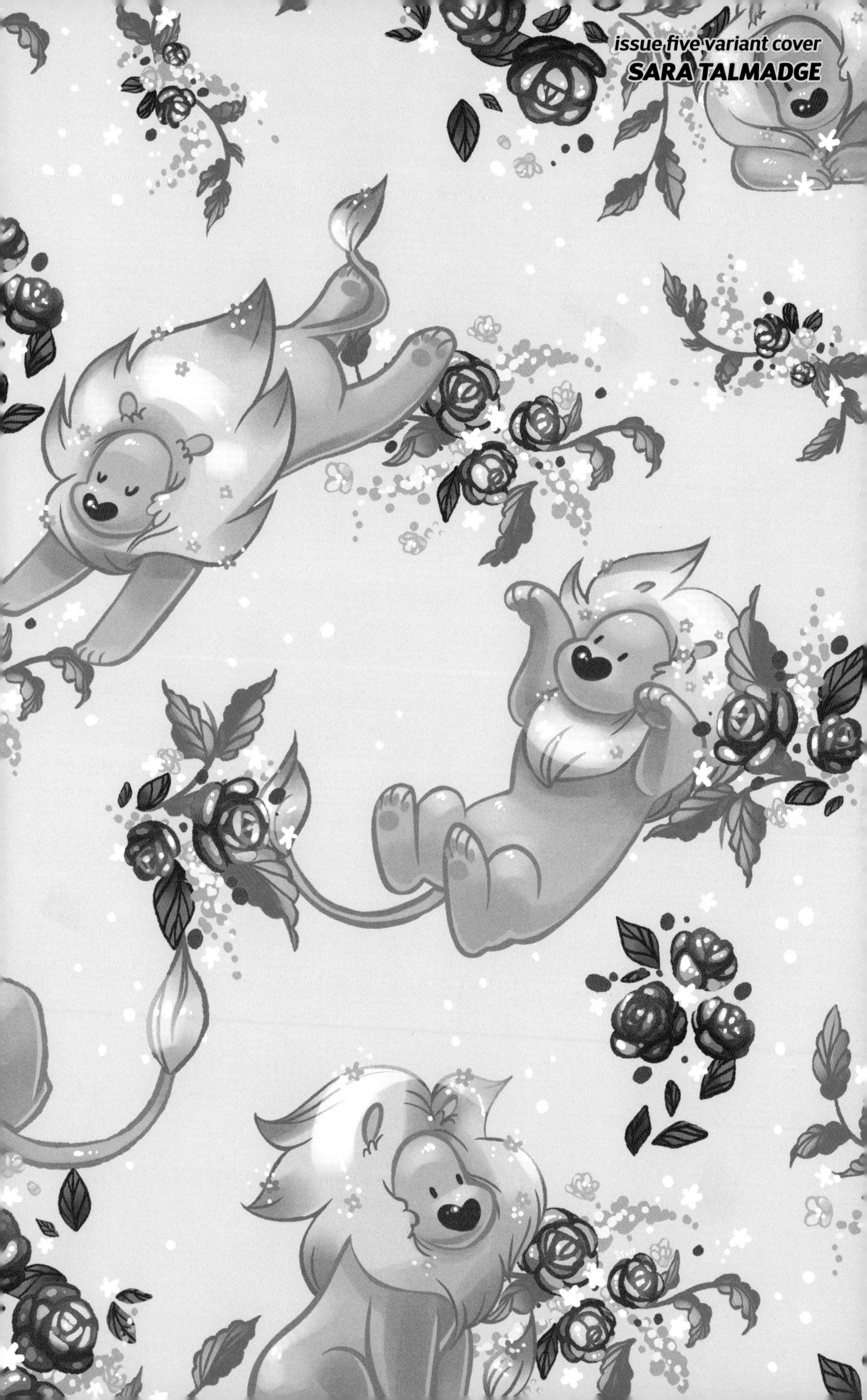

*issue five san diego comic-con exclusive cover*

**PAULINA GANUCHEAU**

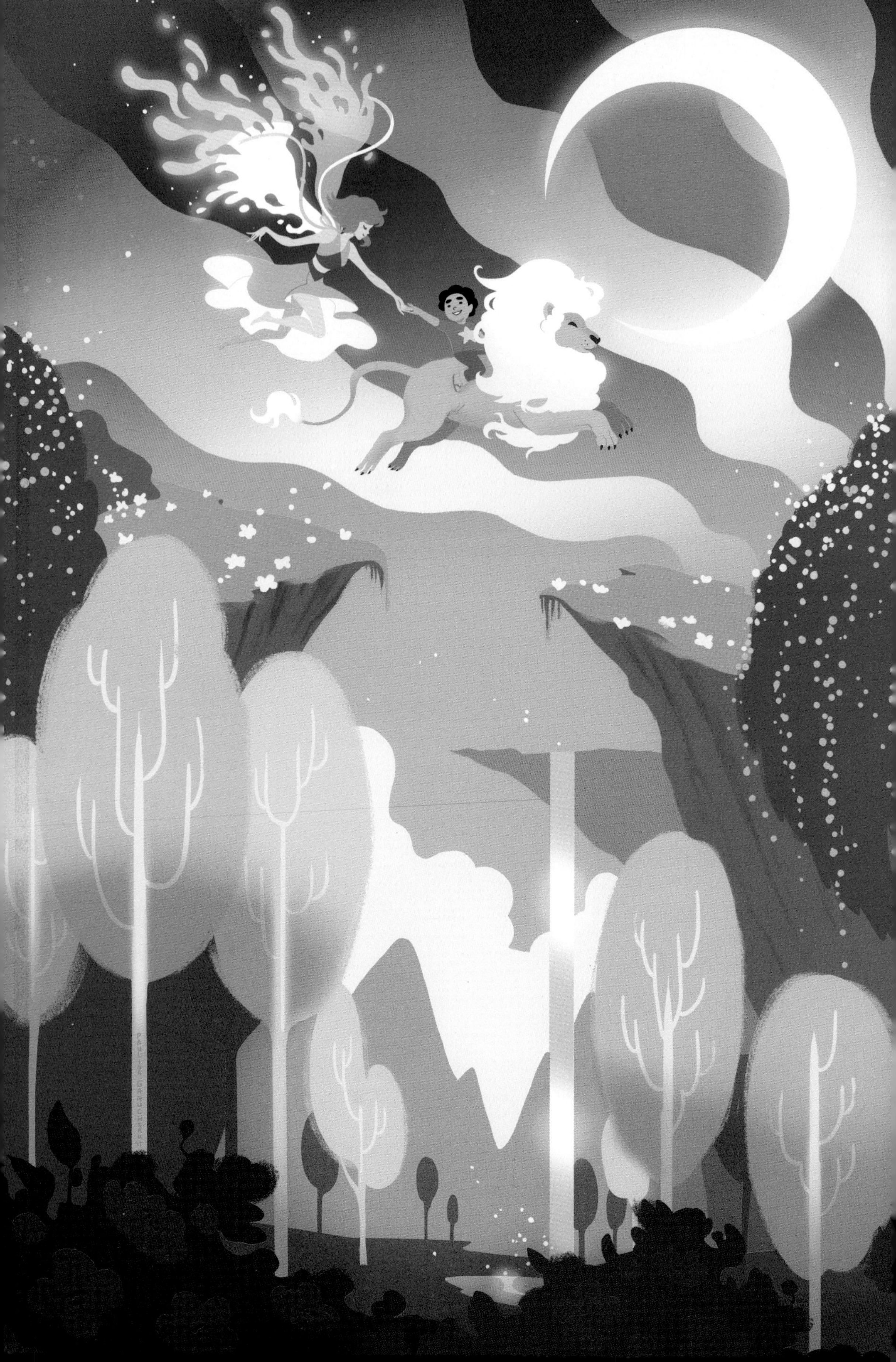

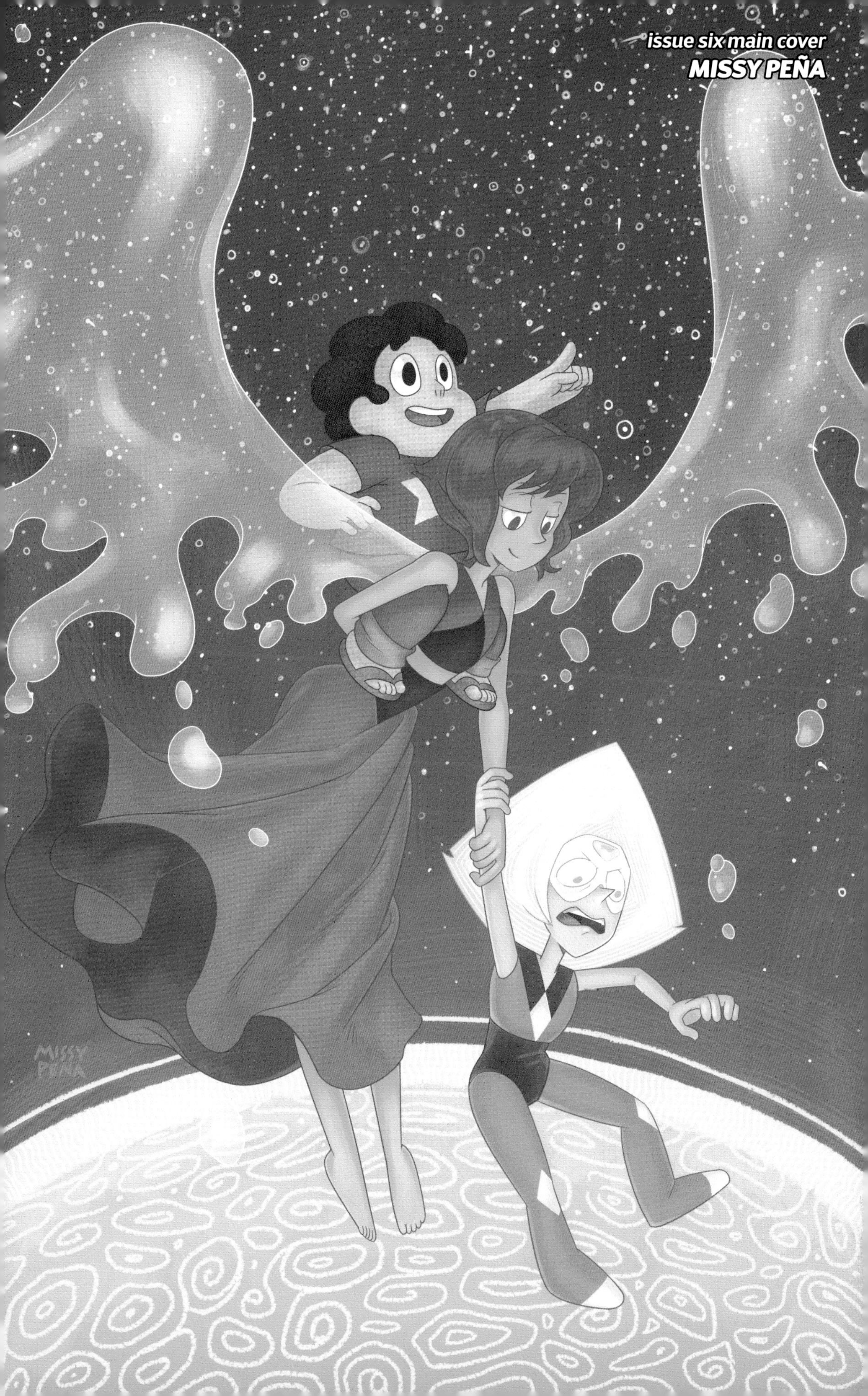
MISSY PEÑA

issue six main cover
**MISSY PEÑA**

issue six subscription cover

**JOSCELINE FENTON**

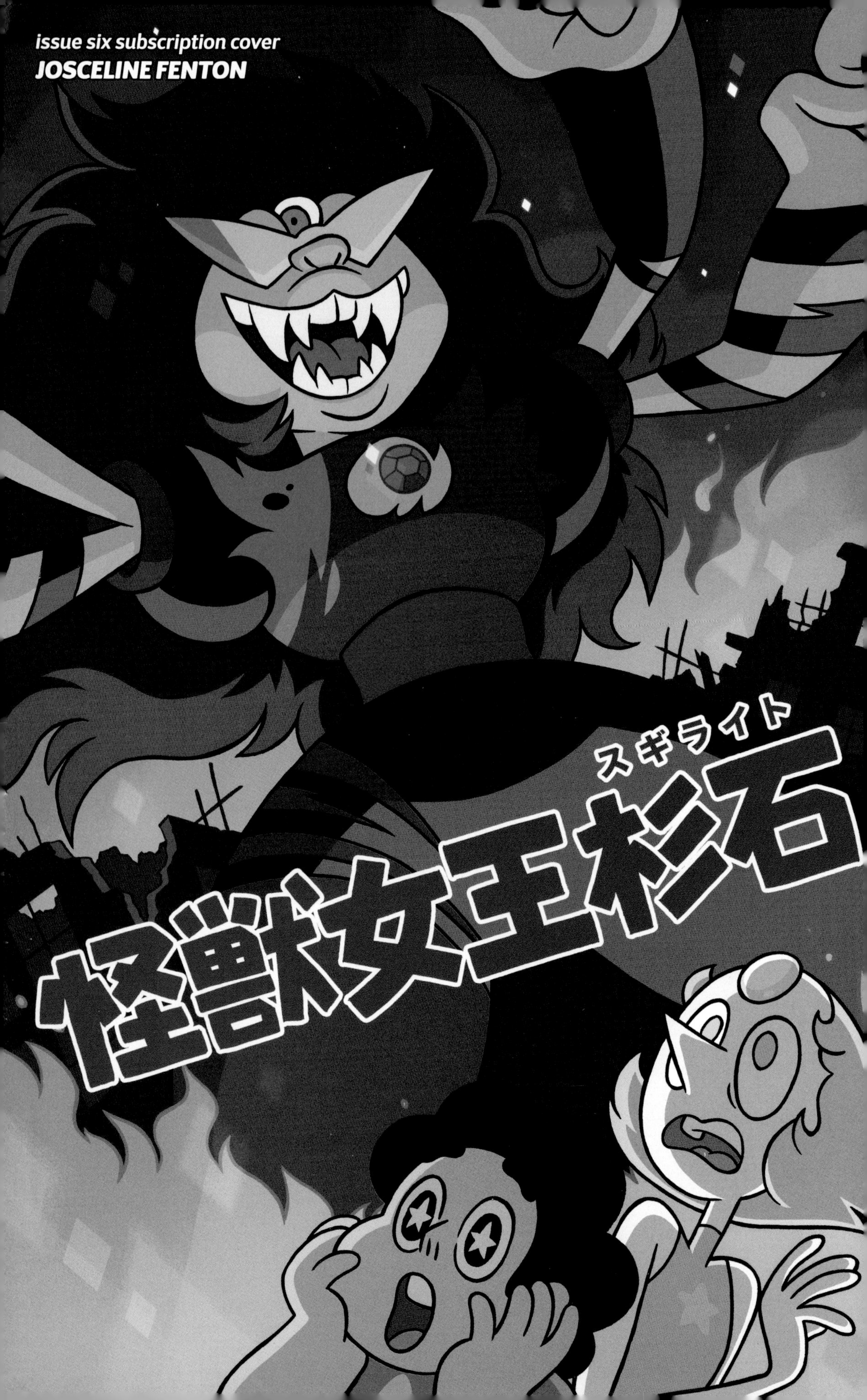
スギライト
怪獣女王杉石

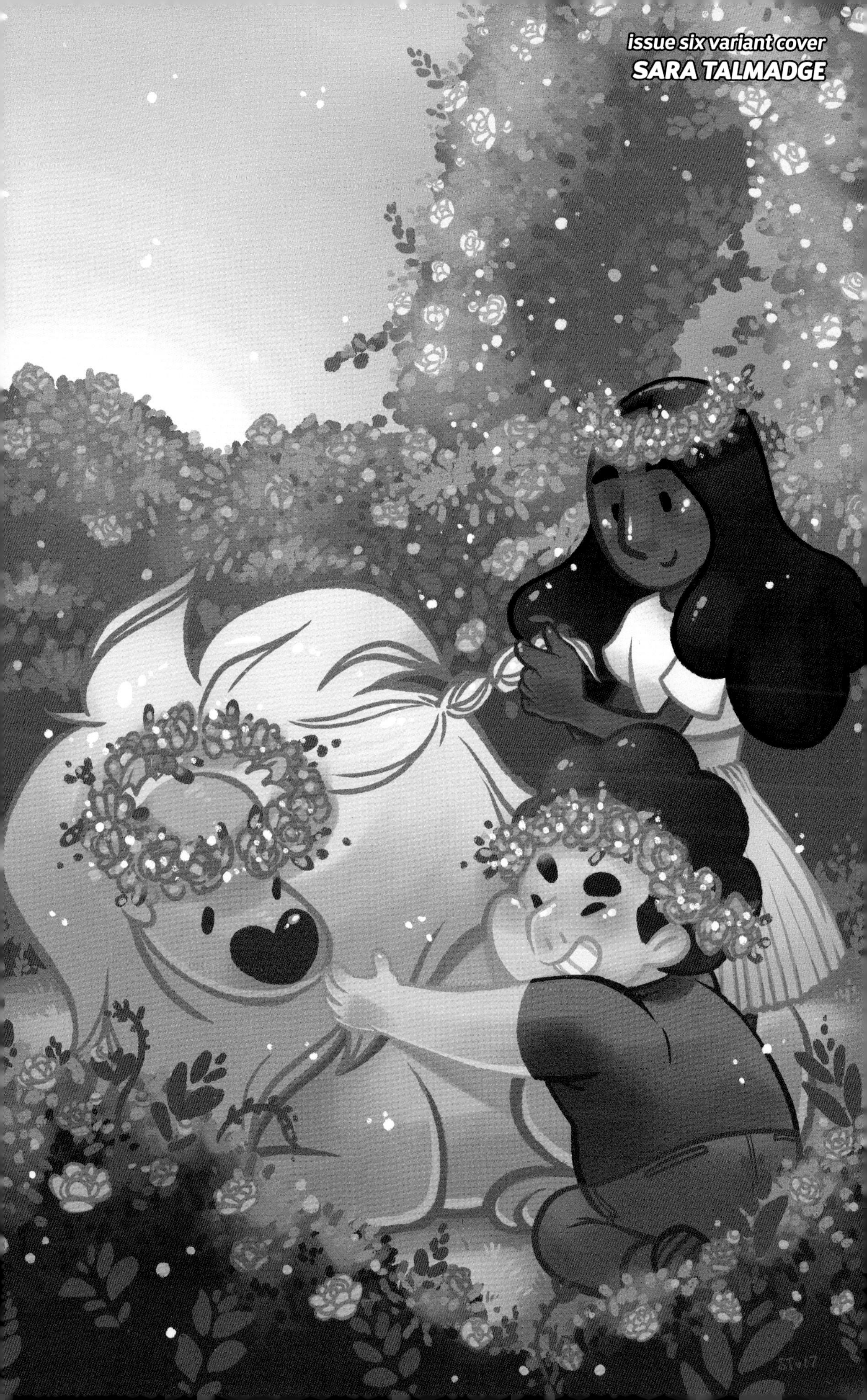

issue six variant cover
**SARA TALMADGE**

*issue seven main cover*
**MISSY PEÑA**

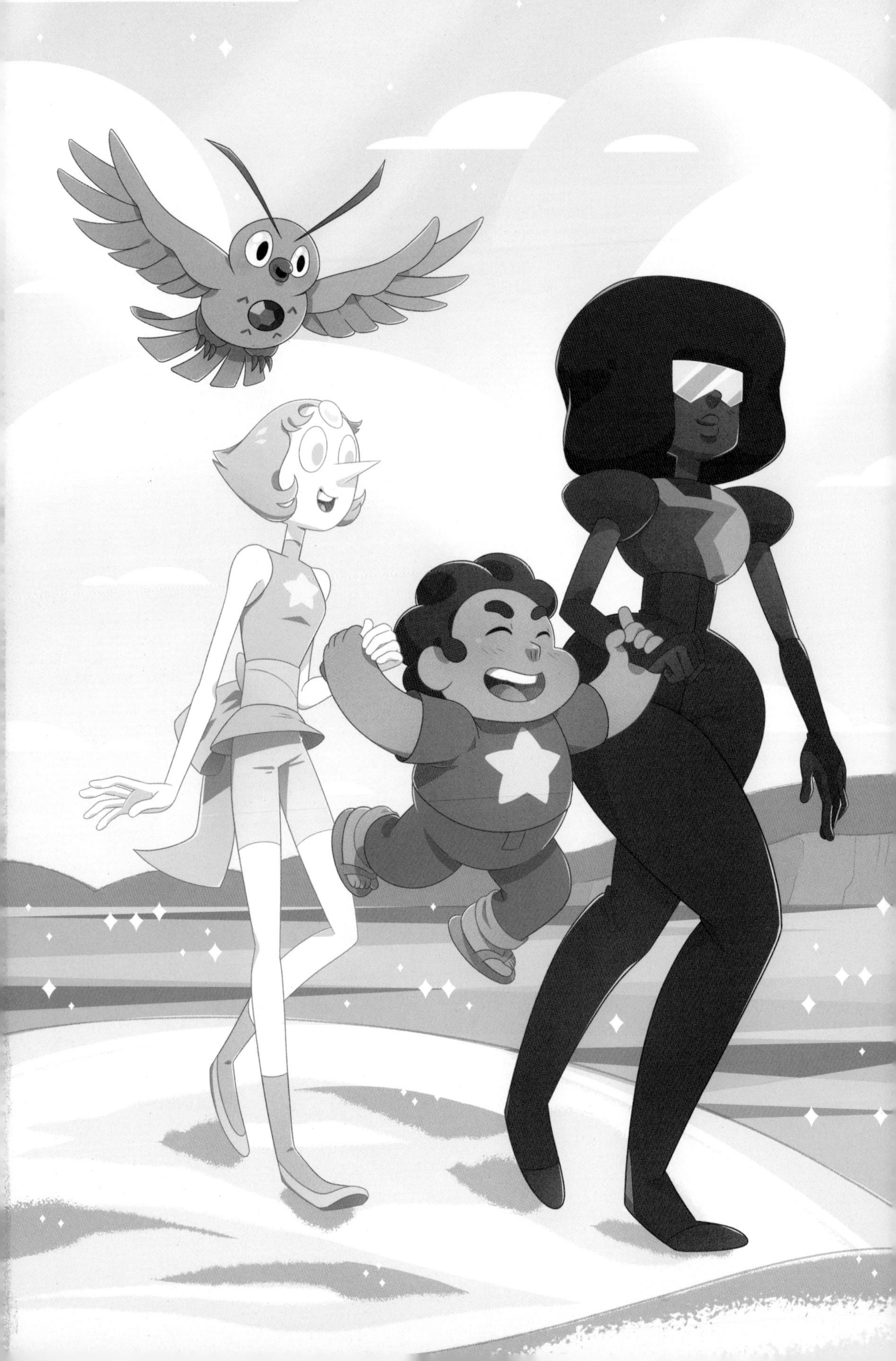

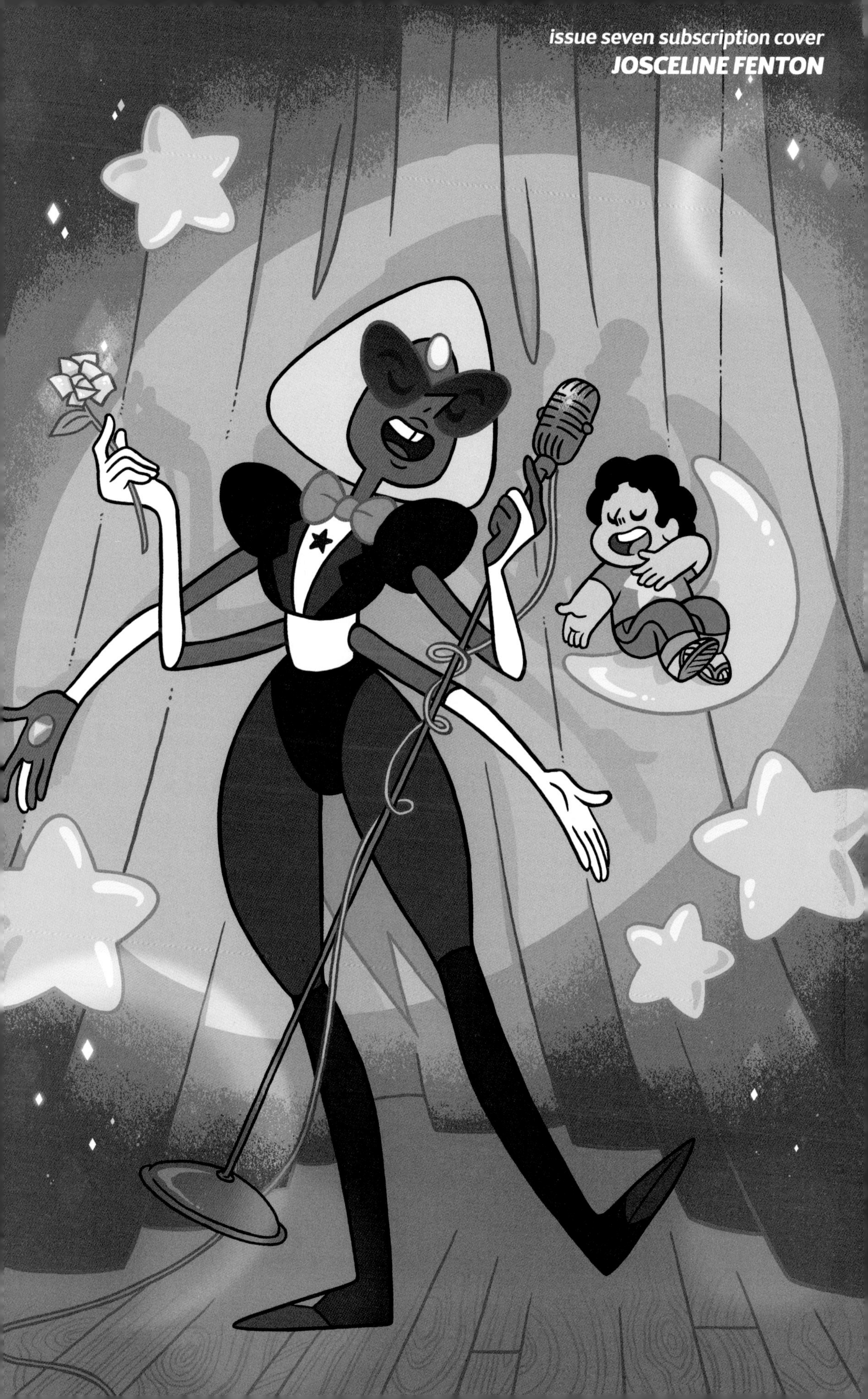

issue seven subscription cover
**JOSCELINE FENTON**

issue seven variant cover
**SARA TALMADGE**

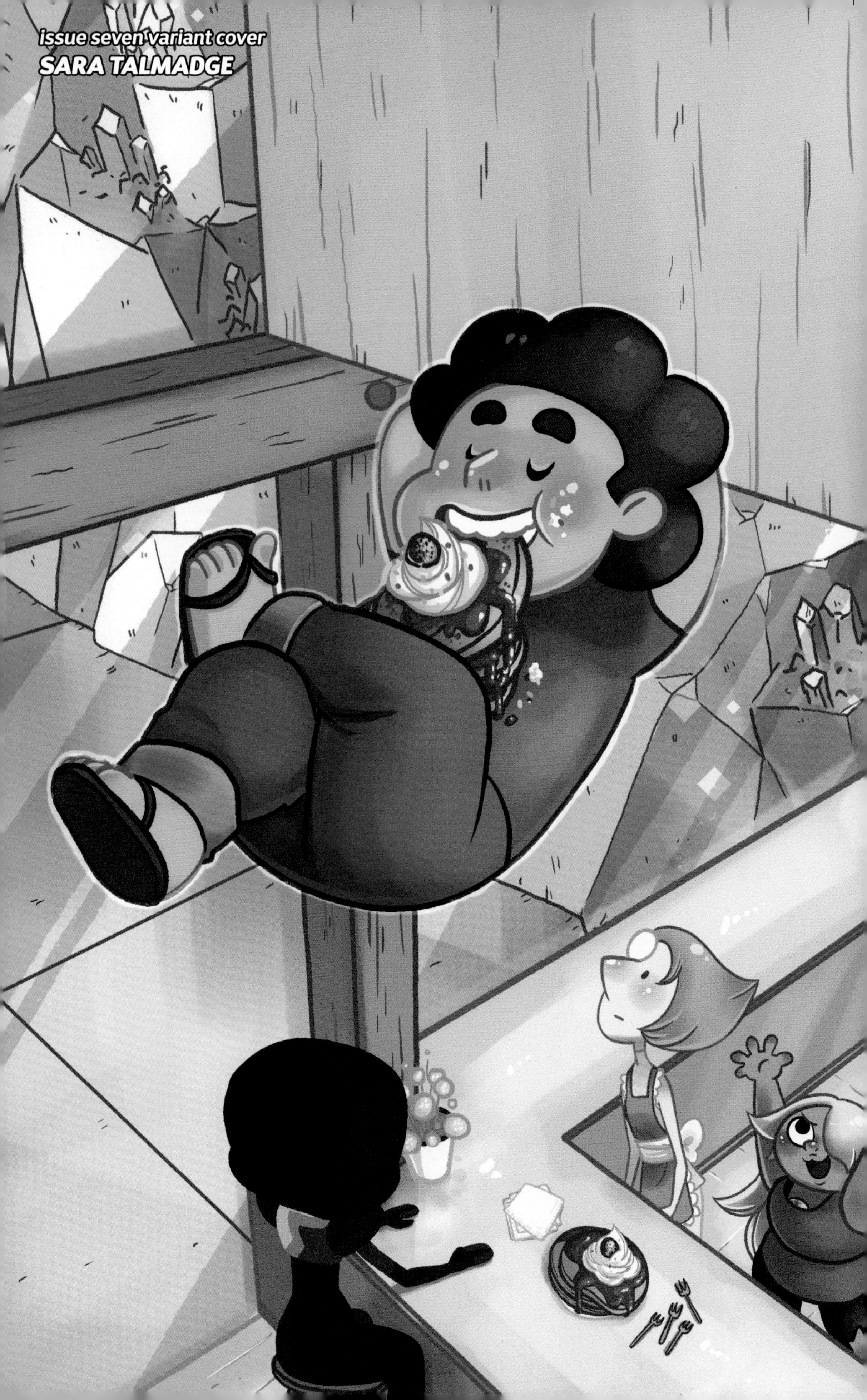

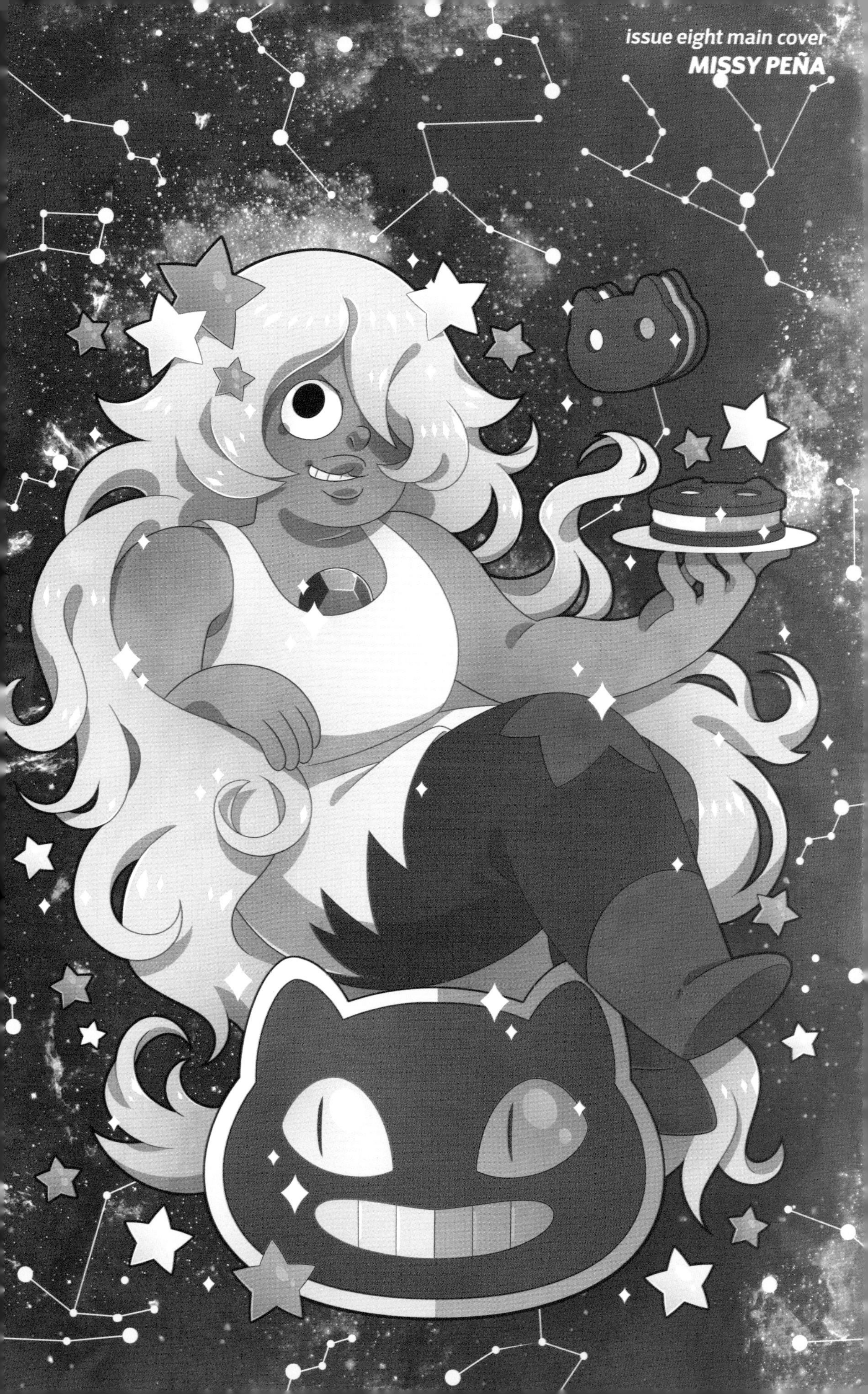

issue eight main cover
**MISSY PEÑA**

issue eight subscription cover
**PAULINA GANUCHEAU**

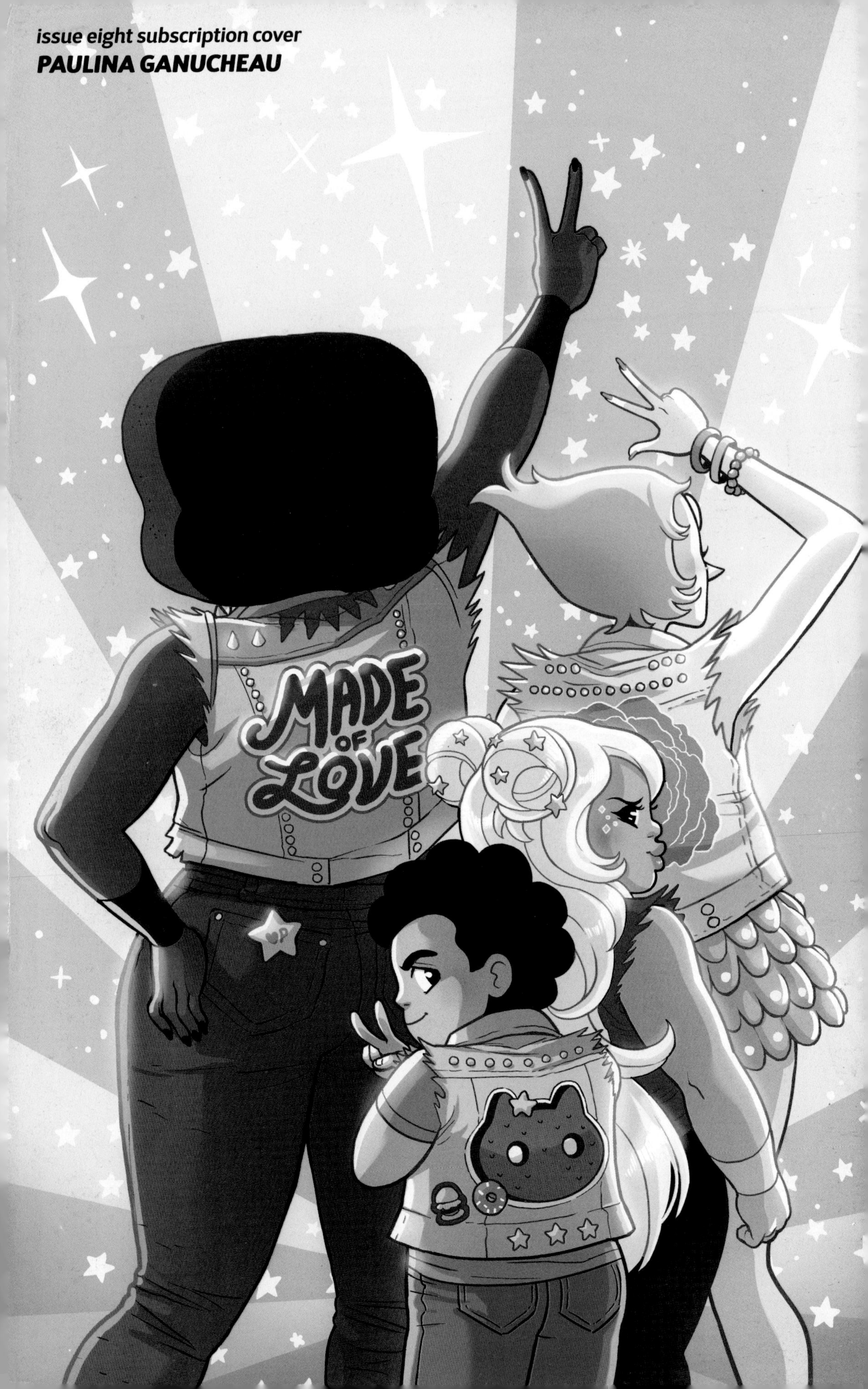
MADE OF LOVE

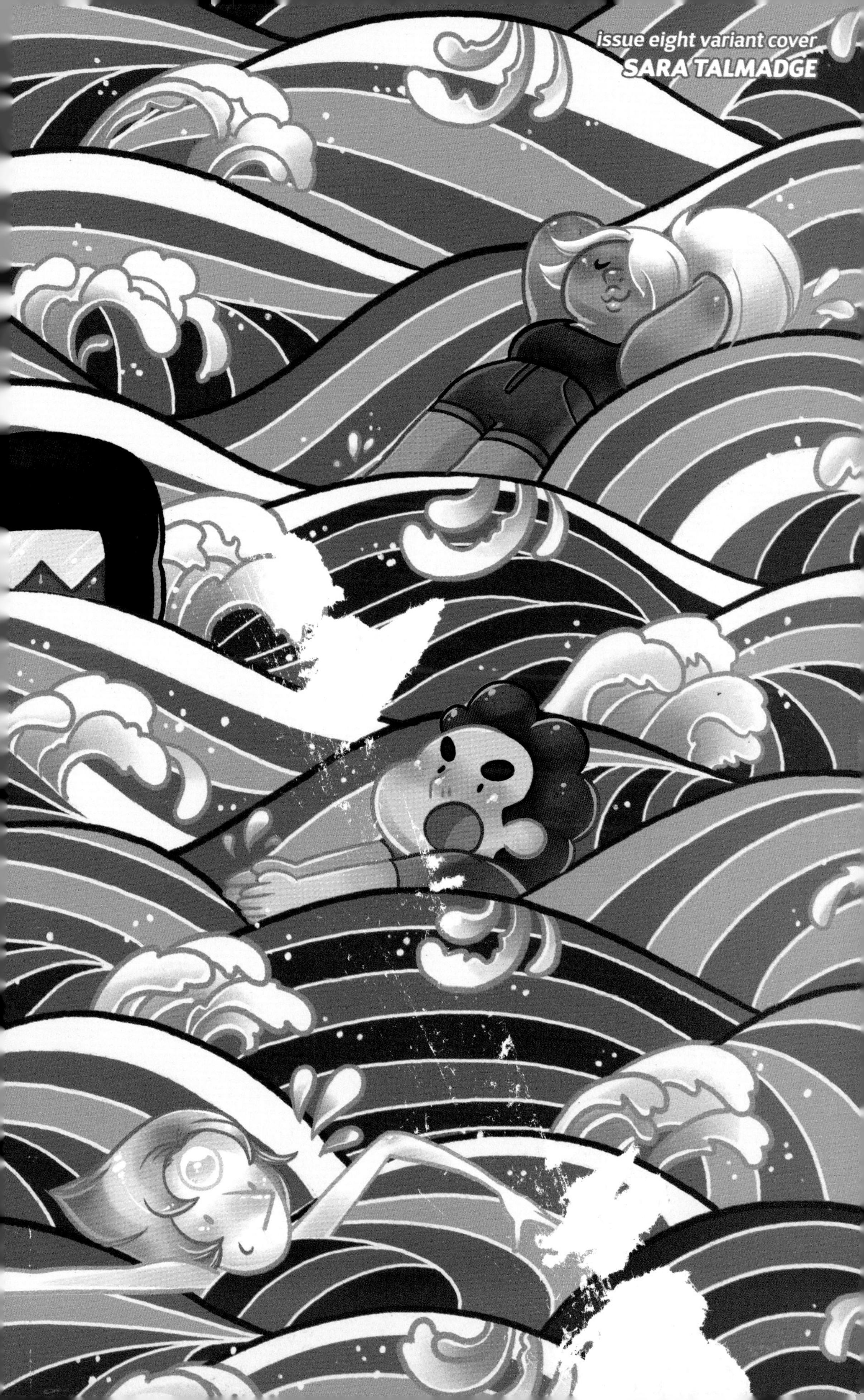

issue eight variant cover
**SARA TALMADGE**

DISCOVER
# EXPLOSIVE NEW WORLDS

ADVENTURE TIME

sam sykes · selina espiritu · sarah stern
BRAVE CHEF BRIANNA

KELLY THOMPSON BRIANNE DROUHARD M. VICTORIA ROBADO
MEGA PRINCESS

THE NOT-SO SECRET SOCIETY
DALEY · CRAFTS · CLARK · BRUNI

OVER THE GARDEN WALL

STEVEN UNIVERSE
VOLUME ONE

kaboom!™

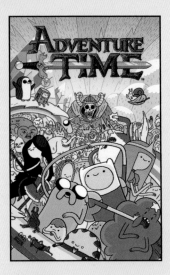

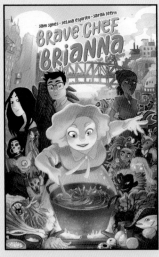

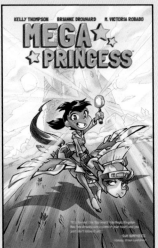

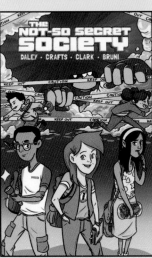

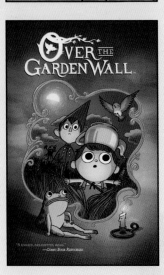

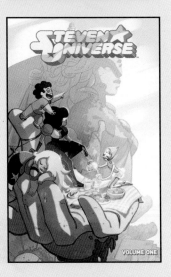

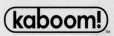

**AVAILABLE AT YOUR LOCAL COMICS SHOP AND BOOKSTORE**

To find a comics shop in your area, call 1-888-266-4226

WWW.**BOOM-STUDIOS**.COM

**Adventure Time**
*Pendleton Ward and Others*
**Volume 1**
ISBN: 978-1-60886-280-1 | $14.99 US
**Volume 2**
ISBN: 978-1-60886-323-5 | $14.99 US
**Adventure Time: Islands**
ISBN: 978-1-60886-972-5 | $9.99 US

**The Amazing World of Gumball**
*Ben Bocquelet and Others*
**Volume 1**
ISBN: 978-1-60886-488-1 | $14.99 US
**Volume 2**
ISBN: 978-1-60886-793-6 | $14.99 US

**Brave Chef Brianna**
*Sam Sykes, Selina Espiritu*
ISBN: 978-1-68415-050-2 | $14.99 US

**Mega Princess**
*Kelly Thompson, Brianne Drouhard*
ISBN: 978-1-68415-007-6 | $14.99 US

**The Not-So Secret Society**
*Matthew Daley, Arlene Daley, Wook Jin Clark*
ISBN: 978-1-60886-997-8 | $9.99 US

**Over the Garden Wall**
*Patrick McHale, Jim Campbell and Others*
**Volume 1**
ISBN: 978-1-60886-940-4 | $14.99 US
**Volume 2**
ISBN: 978-1-68415-006-9 | $14.99 US

**Steven Universe**
*Rebecca Sugar and Others*
**Volume 1**
ISBN: 978-1-60886-706-6 | $14.99 US
**Volume 2**
ISBN: 978-1-60886-796-7 | $14.99 US

**Steven Universe & The Crystal Gems**
ISBN: 978-1-60886-921-3 | $14.99 US

**Steven Universe: Too Cool for School**
ISBN: 978-1-60886-771-4 | $14.99 US